GRIMMS' FAIRY TALES

BY
JACOB AND WILHELM GRIMM

I0563454

ABOUT GRIM

German writers and cultural analysts Jacob and Wilhelm Grimm are well known for compiling a collection of folktales.January 4, 1785 saw the birth of Jacob, and February 24, 1786 saw the birth of Wilhelm. They were born into a family of eight in the small German town of Hanau, in the Hesse region.

Both brothers attended the University of Marburg, where they developed an interest in folklore and the history of the German language. Inspired by their studies, they began collecting and publishing traditional German folk tales, aiming to preserve the rich oral traditions of their homeland. Their first collection, "Children's and Household Tales," was published in 1812 and has since become one of the most famous collections of folk tales in the world.

The Grimms' tales include well-known stories such as "Cinderella," "Hansel and Gretel," "Snow White," and "Rapunzel." These stories, originally intended for adults, were later adapted for children, becoming beloved classics around the globe.

Aside from their work in folklore, the Brothers Grimm were also pioneering linguists. They made significant contributions to the field of philology, including the formulation of Grimm's Law, which explains the sound shifts in the Germanic languages. Their work laid the groundwork for modern linguistic studies.

Jacob and Wilhelm endured financial and political hardships throughout their lives, but they never wavered in their commitment to their mission. They relocated to

Göttingen, where they both took academic positions and carried on with their studies. Later in life, they embarked on an ambitious project called the "German Dictionary," which sought to provide readers a thorough mastery of the German language.

Jacob Grimm passed away on September 20, 1863, and Wilhelm followed on December 16, 1859. Their legacy lives on through their timeless stories and significant contributions to the study of language and folklore. The Brothers Grimm remain celebrated figures in literary history, known for their profound impact on both literature and linguistics.

SUMMARY

This book is a magical collection of timeless stories that transport readers to a world of enchantment, bravery, and wonder. This beloved anthology features some of the most famous fairy tales ever told, including "Cinderella," "Hansel and Gretel," "Snow White," and "Rapunzel." Each tale is filled with captivating characters, from cunning witches and talking animals to daring heroes and beautiful princesses.

The stories, originally gathered from German folklore, are rich with moral lessons, thrilling adventures, and unforgettable endings. Whether it's the cleverness of a young girl who escapes a wolf in "Little Red Riding Hood" or the determination of a prince who awakens a sleeping princess in "Briar Rose," each tale captures the imagination and teaches timeless values of courage, kindness, and perseverance.

"Grimms' Fairy Tales" is a treasure mine of cultural legacy that inspires future generations of readers and preserves the oral traditions of the past. It is more than just a collection of stories. For everyone who enjoys the charm of fairy tales, The Brothers Grimm's book is a must-read because of their vivid storytelling and fantastical realms. This book never fails to enchant and inspire.

CHARACTERS LIST

Cinderella - A lovely and loving young girl who, with the aid of her fairy godmother, triumphs over hardship.

Evil Stepmother (Cinderella) - Cinderella's cruel and jealous stepmother who treats her harshly.

Stepsisters (Cinderella) - Two vain and selfish sisters who make Cinderella's life miserable.

Prince (Cinderella) - A charming prince who falls in love with Cinderella and searches for her with a glass slipper.

Hansel and Gretel - Siblings who outsmart a wicked witch after being abandoned in the forest.

Witch (Hansel and Gretel) - A cunning witch who lives in a gingerbread house and lures children to eat them.

Father and Stepmother (Hansel and Gretel) - Hansel and Gretel's poor parents who abandon them in the forest.

Snow White - A beautiful princess with skin as white as snow, who is loved by everyone except her jealous stepmother.

Evil Queen (Snow White) - Snow White's vain and wicked stepmother who envies her beauty and plots to kill her.

Seven Dwarfs (Snow White) - A group of kind and hardworking dwarfs who protect Snow White and take her in.

Rapunzel - A girl with long, golden hair who is imprisoned in a tower by a sorceress.

Sorceress (Rapunzel) - A powerful and possessive woman who locks Rapunzel in a tower.

Prince (Rapunzel) - A brave prince who discovers Rapunzel and helps her escape from the tower.

Little Red Riding Hood - A young girl who encounters a cunning wolf on her way to visit her grandmother.

Wolf (Little Red Riding Hood) - A sly wolf who disguises himself as Little Red Riding Hood's grandmother to trick her.

Grandmother (Little Red Riding Hood) - Little Red Riding Hood's kind grandmother who is saved by a woodsman.

Briar Rose (Sleeping Beauty) - A princess cursed to sleep for a hundred years until awakened by a prince's kiss.

Wicked Fairy (Sleeping Beauty) - A malevolent fairy who curses Briar Rose to die on her sixteenth birthday.

Good Fairies (Sleeping Beauty) - Benevolent fairies who soften the curse and protect Briar Rose.

Prince (Sleeping Beauty) - A courageous prince who breaks the curse by kissing Briar Rose.

Rumpelstiltskin - A mysterious and magical dwarf who helps a miller's daughter spin straw into gold in exchange for her firstborn child.

Miller's Daughter (Rumpelstiltskin) - A young woman who makes a desperate deal with Rumpelstiltskin to save her life.

King (Rumpelstiltskin) - A king who demands the miller's daughter to spin straw into gold.

These characters, with their unique stories and adventures, form the heart of the enchanting world created by the Brothers Grimm, leaving a lasting impact on readers of all ages.

Contents

THE FROG-KING, OR IRON HENRY

IN OLD times when wishing still helped one, there lived a king whose daughters were all beautiful, but the youngest was so beautiful that the sun itself, which has seen so much, was astonished whenever it shone in her face. Close by the King's castle lay a great dark forest, and under an old lime-tree in the forest was a well, and when the day was very warm, the King's child went out into the forest and sat down by the side of the cool fountain, and when she was dull she took a golden ball, and threw it up on high and caught it, and this ball was her favorite plaything.

Now it so happened that on one occasion the princess's golden ball did not fall into the little hand which she was holding up for it, but on to the ground beyond, and rolled straight into the water. The King's daughter followed it with her eyes, but it vanished, and the well was deep, so deep that the bottom could not be seen. On this she began to cry, and cried louder and louder, and could not be comforted. And as she thus lamented some one said to her, "What ails thee, King's daughter? Thou weepest so that even a stone would show pity." She looked round to the side from whence the voice came, and saw a frog stretching forth its thick, ugly head from the water. "Ah! old water-splasher, is it thou?" said she; "I am weeping for my golden ball, which has fallen into the well."

"Be quiet, and do not weep," answered the frog, "I can help thee, but what wilt thou give me if I bring thy plaything up again?" "Whatever thou wilt have, dear frog," said she -- "My clothes, my pearls and jewels, and even the golden crown which I am wearing."

The frog answered, "I do not care for thy clothes, thy pearls and jewels, or thy golden crown, but if thou wilt love me and let me be thy companion and play-fellow, and sit by thee at thy little table, and eat off thy little golden plate, and drink out of thy little cup, and sleep in thy little bed -- if thou wilt promise me this I will go down below, and bring thee thy golden ball up again."

"Oh yes," said she, "I promise thee all thou wishest, if thou wilt but bring me my ball back again." She, however, thought, "How the silly frog does talk! He lives in the water with the other frogs, and croaks, and can be no companion to any human being!"

But the frog when he had received this promise, put his head into the water and sank down, and in a short while came swimmming up again with the ball in his mouth, and threw it on the grass. The King's daughter was delighted to see her pretty plaything once more, and picked it up, and ran away with it. "Wait, wait," said the frog. "Take me with thee. I can't run as thou canst." But what did it avail him to scream his croak, croak, after her, as loudly as he could? She did not listen to it, but ran home and soon forgot the poor frog, who was forced to go back into his well again.

The next day when she had seated herself at table with the King and all the courtiers, and was eating from her little golden plate, something came creeping splish splash, splish splash, up the marble staircase, and when it had got to the top, it knocked at the door and cried, "Princess, youngest princess, open the door for me." She ran to see who was outside, but when she opened the door, there sat the frog in front of it. Then she slammed the door to, in great haste, sat down to dinner again, and was quite frightened. The King saw plainly that her heart was beating violently, and said, "My child, what art thou so afraid of? Is there perchance a giant outside who wants to carry thee away?" "Ah, no," replied she. "It is no giant but a disgusting frog."

"What does a frog want with thee?" "Ah, dear father, yesterday as I was in the forest sitting by the well, playing, my golden ball fell into the water. And because I cried so, the frog brought it out again for me, and because he so insisted, I promised him he should be my companion, but I never thought he would be able to come out of his water! And now he is outside there, and wants to come in to me."

In the meantime it knocked a second time, and cried,

"Princess! youngest princess!
Open the door for me!
Dost thou not know what thou saidst to me
Yesterday by the cool waters of the fountain?
Princess, youngest princess!
Open the door for me!"

Then said the King, "That which thou hast promised must thou perform. Go and let him in." She went and opened the door, and the frog hopped in and followed her, step by step, to her chair. There he sat and cried, "Lift me up beside thee." She delayed, until at last the King commanded her to do it. When the frog was once on the chair he wanted to be on the table, and when he was on the table he said, "Now, push thy little golden plate nearer to me that we may eat together." She did this, but it was easy to see that she did not do it willingly. The frog enjoyed what he ate, but almost every mouthful she took choked her. At length he said, "I have eaten and am satisfied; now I am tired, carry me into thy little room and make thy little silken bed ready, and we will both lie down and go to sleep."

The King's daughter began to cry, for she was afraid of the cold frog which she did not like to touch, and which was now to sleep in her pretty, clean little bed. But the King grew angry and said, "He who helped thee when thou wert in trouble ought not afterwards to be despised by thee." So she took hold of the frog with two fingers, carried him upstairs, and put him in a corner. But when she was in bed he crept to her and said, "I am tired, I want to sleep as well as thou, lift me up or I will tell thy father." Then she was terribly angry, and took him up and threw him with all her might against the wall. "Now, thou wilt be quiet, odious frog," said she. But when he fell down he was no frog but a King's son with beautiful kind eyes. He by her father's will was now her dear companion and husband. Then he told her how he had been bewitched by a wicked witch, and how no one could have delivered him from the well but herself, and that to-morrow they would go together into his kingdom. Then they went to sleep, and next morning when the sun awoke them, a carriage came driving up with eight white horses, which had white ostrich feathers on their heads, and were harnessed with golden chains, and behind stood the young King's servant Faithful Henry. Faithful Henry had been so unhappy when his master was changed into a frog, that he had caused three iron bands to be laid round his heart, lest it should burst with grief and sadness. The carriage was to conduct the young King into his Kingdom. Faithful Henry helped them both in, and placed himself behind again, and was full of joy because of this deliverance. And when they had driven a part of the way the King's son heard a cracking behind him as if something had broken. So he turned round and cried, "Henry, the carriage is breaking."

"No, master, it is not the carriage. It is a band from my heart, which was put there in my great pain when you were a frog and imprisoned in the well." Again and once again while they were on their way something cracked, and each time the King's son thought the carriage was breaking; but it was only the bands which were springing from the heart of faithful Henry because his master was set free and was happy.

The Wolf And The Seven Little Kids

THERE was once upon a time an old goat who had seven little kids, and loved them with all the love of a mother for her children. One day she wanted to go into the forest and fetch some food. So she called all seven to her and said, "Dear children, I have to go into the forest, be on your guard against the wolf; if he come in, he will devour you all -- skin, hair, and all. The wretch often disguises himself, but you will know him at once by his rough voice and his black feet." The kids said, "Dear mother, we will take good care of ourselves; you may go away without any anxiety." Then the old one bleated, and went on her way with an easy mind.

It was not long before some one knocked at the house-door and called, "Open the door, dear children; your mother is here, and has brought something back with her for each of you." But the little kids knew that it was the wolf, by the rough voice; "We will not open the door," cried they, "thou art not our mother. She has a soft, pleasant voice, but thy voice is rough; thou art the wolf!" Then the wolf went away to a shopkeeper and bought himself a great lump of chalk, ate this and made his voice soft with it. The he came back, knocked at the door of the house, and cried, "Open the door, dear children, your mother is here and has brought something back with her for each of you." But the wolf had laid his black paws against the window, and the children saw them and cried,

"We will not open the door, our mother has not black feet like thee; thou art the wolf." Then the wolf ran to a baker and said, "I have hurt my feet, rub some dough over them for me." And when the baker had rubbed his feet over, he ran to the miller and said, "Strew some white meal over my feet for me." The miller thought to himself, "The wolf wants to deceive someone," and refused; but the wolf said, "If thou wilt not do it, I will devour thee." Then the miller was afraid, and made his paws white for him. Truly men are like that.

So now the wretch went for the third time to the house-door, knocked at it and said, "Open the door for me, children, your dear little mother has come home, and has brought every one of you something back from the forest with her."

The little kids cried, "First show us thy paws that we may know if thou art our dear little mother."

Then he put his paws in through the window, and when the kids saw that they were white, they believed that all he said was true, and opened the door. But who should come in but the wolf! They were terrified and wanted to hide themselves. One sprang under the table, the second into the bed, the third into the stove, the fourth into the kitchen, the fifth into the cupboard, the sixth under the washing-bowl, and the seventh into the clock-case. But the wolf found them all, and used no great ceremony; one after the other he swallowed them down his throat. The youngest, who was in the clock-case, was the only one he did not find. When the wolf had satisfied his appetite he took himself off, laid himself down under a tree in the green meadow outside, and began to sleep. Soon afterwards the old goat came home again from the forest. Ah! What a sight she saw there! The house-door stood wide open. The table, chairs, and benches were thrown down, the washing-bowl lay broken to pieces, and the quilts and pillows were pulled off the bed. She sought her children, but they were nowhere to be found. She called them one after another by name, but no one answered. At last, when she came to the youngest, a soft voice cried, "Dear mother, I am in the clock-case." She took the kid out, and it told her that the wolf had come and had eaten all the others. Then you may imagine how she wept over her poor children.

At length in her grief she went out, and the youngest kid ran with her. When they came to the meadow, there lay the wolf by the tree and snored so loud that the branches shook. She looked at him on every side and saw that something was moving and struggling in his gorged belly. "Ah, heavens," said she, "is it possible that my poor children whom he has swallowed down for his supper, can be still alive?" Then the kid had to run home and fetch scissors, and a needle and thread, and the goat cut open the monster's stomach, and hardly had she make one cut, than one little kid thrust its head out, and when she cut farther, all six sprang out one after another, and were all still alive, and had suffered no injury whatever, for in his greediness the monster had swallowed them down whole. What rejoicing there was! They embraced their dear mother, and jumped like a sailor at his wedding. The mother, however, said, "Now go and look for some big stones, and we will fill the wicked beast's stomach with them while he is still asleep." Then the seven kids dragged the stones thither with all speed, and put as many of them into his stomach as they could get in; and the mother sewed him up again in the greatest haste, so that he was not aware of anything and never once stirred.

When the wolf at length had had his sleep out, he got on his legs, and as the stones in his stomach made him very thirsty, he wanted to go to a well to drink. But when he began to walk and move about, the stones in his stomach knocked against each other and rattled. Then cried he,

"What rumbles and tumbles
Against my poor bones?
I thought 't was six kids,
But it's naught but big stones."

And when he got to the well and stooped over the water and was just about to drink, the heavy stones made him fall in, and there was no help, but he had to drown miserably. When the seven kids saw that, they came running to the spot and cried aloud, "The wolf is dead! The wolf is dead!" and danced for joy round about the well with their mother.

RAPUNZEL

THERE were once a man and a woman who had long in vain wished for a child. At length the woman hoped that God was about to grant her desire. These people had a little window at the back of their house from which a splendid garden could be seen, which was full of the most beautiful flowers and herbs. It was, however, surrounded by a high wall, and no one dared to go into it because it belonged to an enchantress, who had great power and was dreaded by all the world. One day the woman was standing by this window and looking down into the garden, when she saw a bed which was planted with the most beautiful rampion (rapunzel), and it looked so fresh and green that she longed for it, and had the greatest desire to eat some. This desire increased every day, and as she knew that she could not get any of it, she quite pined away, and looked pale and miserable. Then her husband was alarmed, and asked, "What aileth thee, dear wife?" "Ah," she replied, "if I can't get some of the rampion, which is in the garden behind our house, to eat, I shall die." The man, who loved her, thought, "Sooner than let thy wife die, bring her some of the rampion thyself, let it cost thee what it will." In the twilight of the evening, he clambered down over the wall into the garden of the enchantress, hastily clutched a handful of rampion, and took it to his wife. She at once made herself a salad of it, and ate it with much relish. She, however, liked it so much -- so very much, that the next day she longed for it three times as much as before. If he was to have any rest, her husband must once more descend into the garden. In the gloom of evening, therefore, he let himself down again; but when he had clambered down the wall he was terribly afraid, for he saw the enchantress standing before him. "How canst thou dare," said she with angry look, "to descend into my garden and steal my rampion like a thief? Thou shalt suffer for it!" "Ah," answered he, "let mercy take the place of justice, I only made up my mind to do it out of necessity. My wife saw your rampion from the window, and felt such a longing for it that she would have died if she had not got some to eat." Then the enchantress allowed her anger to be softened, and said to him, "If the case be as thou sayest, I will allow thee to take away with thee as much rampion as thou wilt, only I make one condition, thou must give me the child which thy wife will bring into the world; it shall be well treated, and I will care for it like a mother." The man in his terror consented to everything, and when the woman was brought to bed, the enchantress appeared at once, gave the child the name of Rapunzel, and took it away with her.

Rapunzel grew into the most beautiful child beneath the sun. When she was twelve years old, the enchantress shut her into a tower, which lay in a forest, and had neither stairs nor door, but quite at the top was a little window. When the enchantress wanted to go in, she placed herself beneath it and cried,

"Rapunzel, Rapunzel,
Let down thy hair to me."

Rapunzel had magnificent long hair, fine as spun gold, and when she heard the voice of the enchantress she unfastened her braided tresses, wound them round one of the hooks of the window above, and then the hair fell twenty ells down, and the enchantress climbed up by it.

After a year or two, it came to pass that the King's son rode through the forest and went by the tower. Then he heard a song, which was so charming that he stood still and listened. This was Rapunzel, who in her solitude passed her time in letting her sweet voice resound. The King's son wanted to climb up to her, and looked for the door of the tower, but none was to be found. He rode home, but the singing had so deeply touched his heart, that every day he went out into the forest and listened to it. Once when he was thus standing behind a tree, he saw that an enchantress came there, and he heard how she cried,

"Rapunzel, Rapunzel,
Let down thy hair."

Then Rapunzel let down the braids of her hair, and the enchantress climbed up to her. "If that is the ladder by which one mounts, I will for once try my fortune," said he, and the next day when it began to grow dark, he went to the tower and cried,

"Rapunzel, Rapunzel,
Let down thy hair."

Immediately the hair fell down and the King's son climbed up.
At first Rapunzel was terribly frightened when a man such as her eyes had never yet beheld, came to her; but the King's son began to talk to her quite like a friend, and told her that his heart had been so stirred that it had let him have no rest, and he had been forced to see her. Then

Rapunzel lost her fear, and when he asked her if she would take him for her husband, and she saw that he was young and handsome, she thought, "He will love me more than old Dame Gothel does;" and she said yes, and laid her hand in his. She said, "I will willingly go away with thee, but I do not know how to get down. Bring with thee a skein of silk every time that thou comest, and I will weave a ladder with it, and when that is ready I will descend, and thou wilt take me on thy horse." They agreed that until that time he should come to her every evening, for the old woman came by day. The enchantress remarked nothing of this, until once Rapunzel said to her, "Tell me, Dame Gothel, how it happens that you are so much heavier for me to draw up than the young King's son -- he is with me in a moment." "Ah! thou wicked child," cried the enchantress "What do I hear thee say! I thought I had separated thee from all the world, and yet thou hast deceived me. In her anger she clutched Rapunzel's beautiful tresses, wrapped them twice round her left hand, seized a pair of scissors with the right, and snip, snap, they were cut off, and the lovely braids lay on the ground. And she was so pitiless that she took poor Rapunzel into a desert where she had to live in great grief and misery.

On the same day, however, that she cast out Rapunzel, the enchantress in the evening fastened the braids of hair which she had cut off, to the hook of the window, and when the King's son came and cried,

"Rapunzel, Rapunzel,
Let down thy hair,"

she let the hair down. The King's son ascended, but he did not find his dearest Rapunzel above, but the enchantress, who gazed at him with wicked and venomous looks. "Aha!" she cried mockingly, "Thou wouldst fetch thy dearest, but the beautiful bird sits no longer singing in the nest; the cat has got it, and will scratch out thy eyes as well. Rapunzel is lost to thee; thou wilt never see her more." The King's son was beside himself with pain, and in his despair he leapt down from the tower. He escaped with his life, but the thorns into which he fell, pierced his eyes. Then he wandered quite blind about the forest, ate nothing but roots and berries, and did nothing but lament and weep over the loss of his dearest wife. Thus he roamed about in misery for some years, and at length came to the desert where Rapunzel, with the twins to which she had given birth, a boy and a girl, lived in wretchedness. He heard a voice, and it seemed so familiar to him that he went towards it, and when he approached, Rapunzel knew him and fell on his neck and wept. Two of her tears wetted his eyes and they grew clear again, and he could see with them as before. He led her to his kingdom where he was joyfully received, and they lived for a long time afterwards, happy and contented.

Little Brother And Little Sister

LITTLE brother took his little sister by the hand and said, "Since our mother died we have had no happiness; our step-mother beats us every day, and if we come near her she kicks us away with her foot. Our meals are the hard crusts of bread that are left over; and the little dog under the table is better off, for she often throws it a nice bit. May Heaven pity us. If our mother only knew! Come, we will go forth together into the wide world."

They walked the whole day over meadows, fields, and stony places; and when it rained the little sister said, "Heaven and our hearts are weeping together." In the evening they came to a large forest, and they were so weary with sorrow and hunger and the long walk, that they lay down in a hollow tree and fell asleep.

The next day when they awoke, the sun was already high in the sky, and shone down hot into the tree. Then the brother said, "Sister, I am thirsty; if I knew of a little brook I would go and just take a drink; I think I hear one running." The brother got up and took the little sister by the hand, and they set off to find the brook.

But the wicked step-mother was a witch, and had seen how the two children had gone away, and had crept after them privily, as witches do creep, and had bewitched all the brooks in the forest.

Now when they found a little brook leaping brightly over the stones, the brother was going to drink out of it, but the sister heard how it said as it ran, "Who drinks of me will be a tiger; who drinks of me will be a tiger." Then the sister cried, "Pray, dear brother, do not drink, or you will become a wild beast, and tear me to pieces." The brother did not drink, although he was so thirsty, but said, "I will wait for the next spring."

When they came to the next brook the sister heard this also say, "Who drinks of me will be a wolf; who drinks of me will be a wolf." Then the sister cried out, "Pray, dear brother, do not drink, or you will become a wolf, and devour me." The brother did not drink, and said, "I will wait until we come to the next spring, but then I must drink, say what you like; for my thirst is too great."

And when they came to the third brook the sister heard how it said as it ran, "Who drinks of me will be a roebuck; who drinks of me will be a roebuck." The sister said, "Oh, I pray you, dear brother, do not drink, or you will become a roebuck, and run away from me." But the brother had knelt down at once by the brook, and had bent down and drunk some of the water, and as soon as the first drops touched his lips he lay there a young roebuck.

And now the sister wept over her poor bewitched brother, and the little roe wept also, and sat sorrowfully near to her. But at last the girl said, "Be quiet, dear little roe, I will never, never leave you."

Then she untied her golden garter and put it round the roebuck's neck, and she plucked rushes and wove them into a soft cord. With this she tied the little beast and led it on, and she walked deeper and deeper into the forest.

And when they had gone a very long way they came at last to a little house, and the girl looked in; and as it was empty, she thought, "We can stay here and live." Then she sought for leaves and moss to make a soft bed for the roe; and every morning she went out and gathered roots and berries and nuts for herself, and brought tender grass for the roe, who ate out of her hand, and was content and played round about her. In the evening, when the sister was tired, and had said her prayer, she laid her head upon the roebuck's back: that was her pillow, and she slept softly on it. And if only the brother had had his human form it would have been a delightful life.

For some time they were alone like this in the wilderness. But it happened that the King of the country held a great hunt in the forest. Then the blasts of the horns, the barking of dogs, and the merry shouts of the huntsmen rang through the trees, and the roebuck heard all, and was only too anxious to be there. "Oh," said he, to his sister, "let me be off to the hunt, I cannot bear it any longer;" and he begged so much that at last she agreed. "But," said she to him, "come back to me in the evening; I must shut my door for fear of the rough huntsmen, so knock and say, 'My little sister, let me in!' that I may know you; and if you do not say that, I shall not open the door." Then the young roebuck sprang away; so happy was he and so merry in the open air.

The King and the huntsmen saw the pretty creature, and started after him, but they could not catch him, and when they thought that they surely had him, away he sprang through the bushes and could not be seen. When it was dark he ran to the cottage, knocked, and said, "My little sister, let me in." Then the door was opened for him, and he jumped in, and rested himself the whole night through upon his soft bed.

The next day the hunt went on afresh, and when the roebuck again heard the bugle-horn, and the ho! ho! of the huntsmen, he had no peace, but said, "Sister, let me out, I must be off." His sister opened the door for him, and said, "But you must be here again in the evening and say your pass-word."

When the King and his huntsmen again saw the young roebuck with the golden collar, they all chased him, but he was too quick and nimble for them.

This went on for the whole day, but at last by the evening the huntsmen had surrounded him, and one of them wounded him a little in the foot, so that he limped and ran slowly.

Then a hunter crept after him to the cottage and heard how he said, "My little sister, let me in," and saw that the door was opened for him, and was shut again at once. The huntsman took notice of it all, and went to the King and told him what he had seen and heard. Then the King said, "To-morrow we will hunt once more."

The little sister, however, was dreadfully frightened when she saw that her fawn was hurt. She washed the blood off him, laid herbs on the wound, and said, "Go to your bed, dear roe, that you may get well again." But the wound was so slight that the roebuck, next morning, did not feel it any more. And when he again heard the sport outside, he said, "I cannot bear it, I must be there; they shall not find it so easy to catch me."

The sister cried, and said, "This time they will kill you, and here am I alone in the forest and forsaken by all the world. I will not let you out." "Then you will have me die of grief," answered the roe; "when I hear the bugle-horns I feel as if I must jump out of my skin." Then the sister could not do otherwise, but opened the door for him with a heavy heart, and the roebuck, full of health and joy, bounded into the forest.

When the King saw him, he said to his huntsmen, "Now chase him all day long till night-fall, but take care that no one does him any harm."

As soon as the sun had set, the King said to the huntsman,

"Now come and show me the cottage in the wood;" and when he was at the door, he knocked and called out, "Dear little sister, let me in."

Then the door opened, and the King walked in, and there stood a maiden more lovely than any he had ever seen. The maiden was frightened when she saw, not her little roe, but a man come in who wore a golden crown upon his head.

But the King looked kindly at her, stretched out his hand, and said, "Will you go with me to my palace and be my dear wife?"

"Yes, indeed," answered the maiden, "but the little roe must go with me, I cannot leave him." The King said, "It shall stay with you as long as you live, and shall want nothing." Just then he came running in, and the sister again tied him with the cord of rushes, took it in her own hand, and went away with the King from the cottage.

The King took the lovely maiden upon his horse and carried her to his palace, where the wedding was held with great pomp. She was now the Queen, and they lived for a long time happily together; the roebuck was tended and cherished, and ran about in the palace-garden.

But the wicked step-mother, because of whom the children had gone out into the world, thought all the time that the sister had been torn to pieces by the wild beasts in the wood, and that the brother had been shot for a roebuck by the huntsmen. Now when she heard that they were so happy, and so well off, envy and hatred rose in her heart and left her no peace, and she thought of nothing but how she could bring them again to misfortune. Her own daughter, who was ugly as night, and had only one eye, grumbled at her and said, "A Queen! that ought to have been my luck." "Only be quiet," answered the old woman, and comforted her by saying, "when the time comes I shall be ready."

As time went on, the Queen had a pretty little boy, and it happened that the King was out hunting; so the old witch took the form of the chamber-maid, went into the room where the Queen lay, and said to her, "Come, the bath is ready; it will do you good, and give you fresh strength; make haste before it gets cold."

The daughter also was close by; so they carried the weakly Queen into the bath-room, and put her into the bath; then they shut the door and ran away. But in the bath-room they had made a fire of such deadly heat that the beautiful young Queen was soon suffocated.

When this was done the old woman took her daughter, put a nightcap on her head, and laid her in bed in place of the Queen. She gave her too the shape and the look of the Queen, only she could not make good the lost eye. But in order that the King might not see it, she was to lie on the side on which she had no eye.

In the evening when he came home and heard that he had a son he was heartily glad, and was going to the bed of his dear wife to see how she was. But the old woman quickly called out, "For your life leave the curtains closed; the Queen ought not to see the light yet, and must have rest." The King went away, and did not find out that a false Queen was lying in the bed.

But at midnight, when all slept, the nurse, who was sitting in the nursery by the cradle, and who was the only person awake, saw the door open and the true Queen walk in. She took the child out of the cradle, laid it on her arm, and suckled it. Then she shook up its pillow, laid the child down again, and covered it with the little quilt. And she did not forget the roebuck, but went into the corner where it lay, and stroked its back. Then she went quite silently out of the door again. The next morning the nurse asked the guards whether anyone had come into the palace during the night, but they answered, "No, we have seen no one."

She came thus many nights and never spoke a word: the nurse always saw her, but she did not dare to tell anyone about it.

When some time had passed in this manner, the Queen began to speak in the night, and said --

"How fares my child, how fares my roe?
Twice shall I come, then never more."

The nurse did not answer, but when the Queen had gone again, went to the King and told him all. The King said, "Ah, heavens! what is this? To-morrow night I will watch by the child." In the evening he went into the nursery, and at midnight the Queen again appeared and said --

"How fares my child, how fares my roe?
Once will I come, then never more."

And she nursed the child as she was wont to do before she disappeared. The King dared not speak to her, but on the next night he watched again. Then she said --

"How fares my child, how fares my roe?
This time I come, then never more."

Then the King could not restrain himself; he sprang towards her, and said, "You can be none other than my dear wife." She answered, "Yes, I am your dear wife," and at the same moment she received life again, and by God's grace became fresh, rosy, and full of health.

Then she told the King the evil deed which the wicked witch and her daughter had been guilty of towards her. The King ordered both to be led before the judge, and judgment was delivered against them. The daughter was taken into the forest where she was torn to pieces by wild beasts, but the witch was cast into the fire and miserably burnt. And as soon as she was burnt the roebuck changed his shape, and received his human form again, so the sister and brother lived happily together all their lives.

The Star-Money

THERE was once on a time a little girl whose father and mother were dead, and she was so poor that she no longer had any little room to live in, or bed to sleep in, and at last she had nothing else but the clothes she was wearing and a little bit of bread in her hand which some charitable soul had given her.

She was, however, good and pious. And as she was thus forsaken by all the world, she went forth into the open country, trusting in the good God. Then a poor man met her, who said, "Ah, give me something to eat, I am so hungry!" She reached him the whole of her piece of bread, and said, "May God bless it to thy use," and went onwards.

Then came a child who moaned and said, "My head is so cold, give me something to cover it with." So she took off her hood and gave it to him; and when she had walked a little farther, she met another child who had no jacket and was frozen with cold.

Then she gave it her own; and a little farther on one begged for a frock, and she gave away that also. At length she got into a forest and it had already become dark, and there came yet another child, and asked for a little shirt, and the good little girl thought to herself, "It is a dark night and no one sees thee, thou canst very well give thy little shirt away," and took it off, and gave away that also. And as she so stood, and had not one single thing left, suddenly some stars from heaven fell down, and they were nothing else but hard smooth pieces of money, and although she had just given her little shirt away, she had a new one which was of the very finest linen. Then she gathered together the money into this, and was rich all the days of her life.

The Fisherman And His Wife

THERE was once on a time a Fisherman who lived with his wife in a miserable hovel close by the sea, and every day he went out fishing. And once as he was sitting with his rod, looking at the clear water, his line suddenly went down, far down below, and when he drew it up again he brought out a large Flounder. Then the Flounder said to him, "Hark, you Fisherman, I pray you, let me live, I am no Flounder really, but an enchanted prince. What good will it do you to kill me? I should not be good to eat, put me in the water again, and let me go." "Come," said the Fisherman, "there is no need for so many words about it -- a fish that can talk I should certainly let go, anyhow," with that he put him back again into the clear water, and the Flounder went to the bottom, leaving a long streak of blood behind him. Then the Fisherman got up and went home to his wife in the hovel.

"Husband," said the woman, "have you caught nothing to-day?" "No," said the man, "I did catch a Flounder, who said he was an enchanted prince, so I let him go again." "Did you not wish for anything first?" said the woman. "No," said the man; "what should I wish for?" "Ah," said the woman, "it is surely hard to have to live always in this dirty hovel; you might have wished for a small cottage for us. Go back and call him. Tell him we want to have a small cottage, he will certainly give us that." "Ah," said the man, "why should I go there again?" "Why," said the woman, "you did catch him, and you let him go again; he is sure to do it. Go at once." The man still did not quite like to go, but did not like to oppose his wife, and went to the sea.

When he got there the sea was all green and yellow, and no longer so smooth; so he stood still and said,

"Flounder, flounder in the sea,
Come, I pray thee, here to me;
For my wife, good Ilsabil,
Wills not as I'd have her will."

Then the Flounder came swimming to him and said, "Well what does she want, then?" "Ah," said the man, "I did catch you, and my wife says I really ought to have wished for something. She does not like to live in a wretched hovel any longer. She would like to have a cottage." "Go, then," said the Flounder, "she has it already."

When the man went home, his wife was no longer in the hovel, but instead of it there stood a small cottage, and she was sitting on a bench before the door. Then she took him by the hand and said to him, "Just come inside, look, now isn't this a great deal better?" So they went in, and there was a small porch, and a pretty little parlor and bedroom, and a kitchen and pantry, with the best of furniture, and fitted up with the most beautiful things made of tin and brass, whatsoever was wanted. And behind the cottage there was a small yard, with hens and ducks, and a little garden with flowers and fruit. "Look," said the wife, "is not that nice!" "Yes," said the husband, "and so we must always think it, -- now we will live quite contented." "We will think about that," said the wife. With that they ate something and went to bed.

Everything went well for a week or a fortnight, and then the woman said, "Hark you, husband, this cottage is far too small for us, and the garden and yard are little; the Flounder might just as well have given us a larger house. I should like to live in a great stone castle; go to the Flounder, and tell him to give us a castle." "Ah, wife," said the man, "the cottage is quite good enough; why should we live in a castle?" "What!" said the woman; "just go there, the Flounder can always do that." "No, wife," said the man, "the Flounder has just given us the cottage, I do not like to go back so soon, it might make him angry." "Go," said the woman, "he can do it quite easily, and will be glad to do it; just you go to him."

The man's heart grew heavy, and he would not go. He said to himself, "It is not right," and yet he went. And when he came to the sea the water was quite purple and dark-blue, and grey and thick, and no longer so green and yellow, but it was still quiet. And he stood there and said --

"Flounder, flounder in the sea,
Come, I pray thee, here to me;
For my wife, good Ilsabil,
Wills not as I'd have her will."

"Well, what does she want, then?" said the Flounder. "Alas," said the man, half scared, "she wants to live in a great stone castle." "Go to it, then, she is standing before the door," said the Flounder.

Then the man went away, intending to go home, but when he got there, he found a great stone palace, and his wife was just standing on the steps going in, and she took him by the hand and said, "Come in." So he went in with her, and in the castle was a great hall paved with marble, and many servants, who flung wide the doors; And the walls were all bright with beautiful hangings, and in the rooms were chairs and tables of pure gold, and crystal chandeliers hung from the ceiling, and all the rooms and bed-rooms had carpets, and food and wine of the very best were standing on all the tables, so that they nearly broke down beneath it. Behind the house, too, there was a great court-yard, with stables for horses and cows, and the very best of carriages; there was a magnificent large garden, too, with the most beautiful flowers and fruit-trees, and a park quite half a mile long, in which were stags, deer, and hares, and everything that could be desired. "Come," said the woman, "isn't that beautiful?" "Yes, indeed," said the man, "now let it be; and we will live in this beautiful castle and be content." "We will consider about that," said the woman, "and sleep upon it;" thereupon they went to bed.

Next morning the wife awoke first, and it was just daybreak, and from her bed she saw the beautiful country lying before her. Her husband was still stretching himself, so she poked him in the side with her elbow, and said, "Get up, husband, and just peep out of the window. Look you, couldn't we be the King over all that land? Go to the Flounder, we will be the King." "Ah, wife," said the man, "why should we be King? I do not want to be King." "Well," said the wife, "if you won't be King, I will; go to the Flounder, for I will be King." "Ah, wife," said the man, "why do you want to be King? I do not like to say that to him." "Why not?" said the woman; "go to him this instant; I must be King!" So the man went, and was quite unhappy because his wife wished to be King. "It is not right; it is not right," thought he. He did not wish to go, but yet he went.

And when he came to the sea, it was quite dark-grey, and the water heaved up from below, and smelt putrid. Then he went and stood by it, and said,

"Flounder, flounder in the sea,
Come, I pray thee, here to me;
For my wife, good Ilsabil,
Wills not as I'd have her will"

"Well, what does she want, then?" said the Flounder. "Alas," said the man, "she wants to be King." "Go to her; she is King already."

So the man went, and when he came to the palace, the castle had become much larger, and had a great tower and magnificent ornaments, and the sentinel was standing before the door, and there were numbers of soldiers with kettle-drums and trumpets. And when he went inside the house, everything was of real marble and gold, with velvet covers and great golden tassels. Then the doors of the hall were opened, and there was the court in all its splendour, and his wife was sitting on a high throne of gold and diamonds, with a great crown of gold on her head, and a sceptre of pure gold and jewels in her hand, and on both sides of her stood her maids-in-waiting in a row, each of them always one head shorter than the last.

Then he went and stood before her, and said, "Ah, wife, and now you are King." "Yes," said the woman, "now I am King." So he stood and looked at her, and when he had looked at her thus for some time, he said, "And now that you are King, let all else be, now we will wish for nothing more." "Nay, husband," said the woman, quite anxiously, "I find time pass very heavily, I can bear it no longer; go to the Flounder -- I am King, but I must be Emperor, too." "Alas, wife, why do you wish to be Emperor?" "Husband," said she, "go to the Flounder. I will be Emperor." "Alas, wife," said the man, "he cannot make you Emperor; I may not say that to the fish. There is only one Emperor in the land. An Emperor the Flounder cannot make you! I assure you he cannot."

"What!" said the woman, "I am the King, and you are nothing but my husband; will you go this moment? go at once! If he can make a King he can make an emperor. I will be Emperor; go instantly." So he was forced to go. As the man went, however, he was troubled in mind, and thought to himself, "It will not end well; it will not end well! Emperor is too shameless! The Flounder will at last be tired out."

With that he reached the sea, and the sea was quite black and thick, and began to boil up from below, so that it threw up bubbles, and such a sharp wind blew over it that it curdled, and the man was afraid. Then he went and stood by it, and said,

"Flounder, flounder in the sea,
Come, I pray thee, here to me;
For my wife, good Ilsabil,
Wills not as I'd have her will."

"Well, what does she want, then?" said the Flounder. "Alas, Flounder," said he, "my wife wants to be

Emperor." "Go to her," said the Flounder; "she is Emperor already."

So the man went, and when he got there the whole palace was made of polished marble with alabaster figures and golden ornaments, and soldiers were marching before the door blowing trumpets, and beating cymbals and drums; and in the house, barons, and counts, and dukes were going about as servants. Then they opened the doors to him, which were of pure gold. And when he entered, there sat his wife on a throne, which was made of one piece of gold, and was quite two miles high; and she wore a great golden crown that was three yards high, and set with diamonds and carbuncles, and in one hand she had the sceptre, and in the other the imperial orb; and on both sides of her stood the yeomen of the guard in two rows, each being smaller than the one before him, from the biggest giant, who was two miles high, to the very smallest dwarf, just as big as my little finger. And before it stood a number of princes and dukes.

Then the man went and stood among them, and said, "Wife, are you Emperor now?" "Yes," said she, "now I am Emperor."

Then he stood and looked at her well, and when he had looked at her thus for some time, he said, "Ah, wife, be content, now that you are Emperor." "Husband," said she, "why are you standing there? Now, I am Emperor, but I will be Pope too; go to the Flounder." "Alas, wife," said the man, "what will you not wish for? You cannot be Pope. There is but one in Christendom. He cannot make you Pope." "Husband," said she, "I will be Pope; go immediately, I must be Pope this very day." "No, wife," said the man, "I do not like to say that to him; that would not do, it is too much; the Flounder can't make you Pope." "Husband," said she, "what nonsense! If he can make an emperor he can make a pope. Go to him directly. I am Emperor, and you are nothing but my husband; will you go at once?"

Then he was afraid and went; but he was quite faint, and shivered and shook, and his knees and legs trembled. And a high wind blew over the land, and the clouds flew, and towards evening all grew dark, and the leaves fell from the trees, and the water rose and roared as if it were boiling, and splashed upon the shore. And in the distance he saw ships which were firing guns in their sore need, pitching and tossing on the waves. And yet in the midst of the sky there was still a small bit of blue, though on every side it was as red as in a heavy storm. So, full of despair, he went and stood in much fear and said,

"Flounder, flounder in the sea,
Come, I pray thee, here to me;"
For my wife, good Ilsabil,
Wills not as I'd have her will.

"Well, what does she want, then?" said the Flounder. "Alas," said the man, "she wants to be Pope." "Go to her then," said the Flounder; "she is Pope already."

So he went, and when he got there, he saw what seemed to be a large church surrounded by palaces. He pushed his way through the crowd. Inside, however, everything was lighted up with thousands and thousands of candles, and his wife was clad in gold, and she was sitting on a much higher throne, and had three great golden crowns on, and round about her there was much ecclesiastical splendour;

and on both sides of her was a row of candles the largest of which was as tall as the very tallest tower, down to the very smallest kitchen candle, and all the emperors and kings were on their knees before her, kissing her shoe. "Wife," said the man, and looked attentively at her, "are you now Pope?" "Yes," said she, "I am Pope." So he stood and looked at her, and it was just as if he was looking at the bright sun. When he had stood looking at her thus for a short time, he said, "Ah, wife, if you are Pope, do let well alone!" But she looked as stiff as a post, and did not move or show any signs of life. Then said he, "Wife, now that you are Pope, be satisfied, you cannot become anything greater now." "I will consider about that," said the woman. Thereupon they both went to bed, but she was not satisfied, and greediness let her have no sleep, for she was continually thinking what there was left for her to be.

The man slept well and soundly, for he had run about a great deal during the day; but the woman could not fall asleep at all, and flung herself from one side to the other the whole night through, thinking always what more was left for her to be, but unable to call to mind anything else. At length the sun began to rise, and when the woman saw the red of dawn, she sat up in bed and looked at it. And when, through the window, she saw the sun thus rising, she said, "Cannot I, too, order the sun and moon to rise?" "Husband," she said, poking him in the ribs with her elbows, "wake up! go to the Flounder, for I wish to be even as God is." The man was still half asleep, but he was so horrified that he fell out of bed. He thought he must have heard amiss, and rubbed his eyes, and said, "Alas, wife, what are you saying?" "Husband," said she, "if I can't order the sun and moon to rise, and have to look on and see the sun and moon rising, I can't bear it. I shall not know what it is to have another happy hour, unless I can make them rise myself." Then she looked at him so terribly that a shudder ran over him, and said, "Go at once; I wish to be like unto God." "Alas, wife," said the man, falling on his knees before her, "the Flounder cannot do that; he can make an emperor and a pope; I beseech you, go on as you are, and be Pope." Then she fell into a rage, and her hair flew wildly about her head, and she cried, "I will not endure this, I'll not bear it any longer; wilt thou go?" Then he put on his trousers and ran away like a madman. But outside a great storm was raging, and blowing so hard that he could scarcely keep his feet; houses and trees toppled over, the mountains trembled, rocks rolled into the sea, the sky was pitch black, and it thundered and lightened, and the sea came in with black waves as high as church-towers and mountains, and all with crests of white foam at the top. Then he cried, but could not hear his own words,

"Flounder, flounder in the sea,
Come, I pray thee, here to me;
For my wife, good Ilsabil,
Wills not as I'd have her will."

"Well, what does she want, then?" said the Flounder. "Alas," said he, "she wants to be like unto God." "Go to her, and you will find her back again in the dirty hovel." And there they are living still at this very time.

THE WHITE SNAKE

A LONG time ago there lived a king who was famed for his wisdom through all the land. Nothing was hidden from him, and it seemed as if news of the most secret things was brought to him through the air. But he had a strange custom; every day after dinner, when the table was cleared, and no one else was present, a trusty servant had to bring him one more dish. It was covered, however, and even the servant did not know what was in it, neither did anyone know, for the King never took off the cover to eat of it until he was quite alone.

This had gone on for a long time, when one day the servant, who took away the dish, was overcome with such curiosity that he could not help carrying the dish into his room. When he had carefully locked the door, he lifted up the cover, and saw a white snake lying on the dish. But when he saw it he could not deny himself the pleasure of tasting it, so he cut off a little bit and put it into his mouth. No sooner had it touched his tongue than he heard a strange whispering of little voices outside his window. He went and listened, and then noticed that it was the sparrows who were chattering together, and telling one another of all kinds of things which they had seen in the fields and woods. Eating the snake had given him power of understanding the language of animals.

Now it so happened that on this very day the Queen lost her most beautiful ring, and suspicion of having stolen it fell upon this trusty servant, who was allowed to go everywhere. The King ordered the man to be brought before him, and threatened with angry words that unless he could before the morrow point out the thief, he himself should be looked upon as guilty and executed. In vain he declared his innocence; he was dismissed with no better answer.

In his trouble and fear he went down into the courtyard and took thought how to help himself out of his trouble. Now some ducks were sitting together quietly by a brook and taking their rest; and, whilst they were making their feathers smooth with their bills, they were having a confidential conversation together. The servant stood by and listened. They were telling one another of all the places where they had been waddling about all the morning, and what good food they had found, and one said in a pitiful tone, "Something lies heavy on my stomach; as I was eating in haste I swallowed a ring which lay under the Queen's window." The servant at once seized her by the neck, carried her to the kitchen, and said to the cook, "Here is a fine duck; pray, kill her." "Yes," said the cook, and weighed her in his hand; "she has spared no trouble to fatten herself, and has been waiting to be roasted long enough." So he cut off her head, and as she was being dressed for the spit, the Queen's ring was found inside her.

The servant could now easily prove his innocence; and the King, to make amends for the wrong, allowed him to ask a favor, and promised him the best place in the court that he could wish for. The servant refused everything, and only asked for a horse and some money for traveling, as he had a mind to see the world and go about a little.

When his request was granted he set out on his way, and one day came to a pond, where he saw three fishes caught in the reeds and gasping for water. Now, though it is said that fishes are dumb, he heard them lamenting that they must perish so miserably, and, as he had a kind heart, he got off his horse and put the three prisoners back into the water. They quivered with delight, put out their heads, and cried to him, "We will remember you and repay you for saving us!"

He rode on, and after a while it seemed to him that he heard a voice in the sand at his feet. He listened, and heard an ant-king complain, "Why cannot folks, with their clumsy beasts, keep off our bodies? That stupid horse, with his heavy hoofs, has been treading down my people without mercy!" So he turned on to a side path and the ant-king cried out to him, 'We will remember you -- one good turn deserves another!"

The path led him into a wood, and here he saw two old ravens standing by their nest, and throwing out their young ones. "Out with you, you idle, good-for-nothing creatures!" cried they; "we cannot find food for you any longer; you are big enough, and can provide for yourselves." But the poor young ravens lay upon the ground, flapping their wings, and crying, "Oh, what helpless chicks we are! We must shift for ourselves, and yet we cannot fly! What can we do, but lie here and starve?" So the good young fellow alighted and killed his horse with his sword, and gave it to them for food. Then they came hopping up to it, satisfied their hunger, and cried, "We will remember you -- one good turn deserves another!"

And now he had to use his own legs, and when he had walked a long way, he came to a large city. There was a great noise and crowd in the streets, and a man rode up on horseback, crying aloud, "The King's daughter wants a husband; but whoever sues for her hand must perform a hard task, and if he does not succeed he will forfeit his life." Many had already made the attempt, but in vain; nevertheless when the youth saw the King's daughter he was so overcome by her great beauty that he forgot all danger, went before the King, and declared himself a suitor.

So he was led out to the sea, and a gold ring was thrown into it, in his sight; then the King ordered him to fetch this ring up from the bottom of the sea, and added, "If you come up again without it you will be thrown in again and again until you perish amid the waves." All the people grieved for the handsome youth; then they went away, leaving him alone by the sea.

He stood on the shore and considered what he should do, when suddenly he saw three fishes come swimming towards him, and they were the very fishes whose lives he had saved. The one in the middle held a mussel in its mouth, which it laid on the shore at the youth's feet, and when he had taken it up and opened it, there lay the gold ring in the shell. Full of joy he took it to the King, and expected that he would grant him the promised reward.

But when the proud princess perceived that he was not her equal in birth, she scorned him, and required him first to perform another task. She went down into the garden and strewed with her own hands ten sacks-full of millet-seed on the grass; then she said, "To-morrow morning before sunrise these must be picked up, and not a single grain be wanting."

The youth sat down in the garden and considered how it might be possible to perform this task, but he could think of nothing, and there he sat sorrowfully awaiting the break of day, when he should be led to death. But as soon as the first rays of the sun shone into the garden he saw all the ten sacks standing side by side, quite full, and not a single grain was missing. The ant-king had come in the night with thousands and thousands of ants, and the grateful creatures had by great industry picked up all the millet-seed and gathered them into the sacks.

Presently the King's daughter herself came down into the garden, and was amazed to see that the young man had done the task she had given him. But she could not yet conquer her proud heart, and said, "Although he has performed both the tasks, he shall not be my husband until he has brought me an apple from the Tree of Life."

The youth did not know where the Tree of Life stood, but he set out, and would have gone on for ever, as long as his legs would carry him, though he had no hope of finding it. After he had wandered through three kingdoms, he came one evening to a wood, and lay down under a tree to sleep. But he heard a rustling in the branches, and a golden apple fell into his hand. At the same time three ravens flew down to him, perched themselves upon his knee, and said, "We are the three young ravens whom you saved from starving; when we had grown big, and heard that you were seeking the Golden Apple, we flew over the sea to the end of the world, where the Tree of Life stands, and have brought you the apple." The youth, full of joy, set out homewards, and took the Golden Apple to the King's beautiful daughter, who had no more excuses left to make. They cut the Apple of Life in two and ate it together; and then her heart became full of love for him, and they lived in undisturbed happiness to a great age.

HANSEL AND GRETHEL

HARD by a great forest dwelt a poor wood-cutter with his wife and his two children. The boy was called Hansel and the girl Grethel. He had little to bite and to break, and once when great scarcity fell on the land, he could no longer procure daily bread. Now when he thought over this by night in his bed, and tossed about in his anxiety, he groaned and said to his wife, "What is to become of us? How are we to feed our poor children, when we no longer have anything even for ourselves?" "I'll tell you what, husband," answered the woman, "Early to-morrow morning we will take the children out into the forest to where it is the thickest, there we will light a fire for them, and give each of them one piece of bread more, and then we will go to our work and leave them alone. They will not find the way home again, and we shall be rid of them." "No, wife," said the man, "I will not do that; how can I bear to leave my children alone in the forest? -- the wild animals would soon come and tear them to pieces." "O, thou fool!" said she, "Then we must all four die of hunger, thou mayest as well plane the planks for our coffins," and she left him no peace until he consented. "But I feel very sorry for the poor children, all the same," said the man.

The two children had also not been able to sleep for hunger, and had heard what their step-mother had said to their father. Grethel wept bitter tears, and said to Hansel, "Now all is over with us." "Be quiet, Grethel," said Hansel, "do not distress thyself, I will soon find a way to help us." And when the old folks had fallen asleep, he got up, put on his little coat, opened the door below, and crept outside. The moon shone brightly, and the white pebbles which lay in front of the house glittered like real silver pennies. Hansel stooped and put as many of them in the little pocket of his coat as he could possibly get in. Then he went back and said to Grethel, "Be comforted, dear little sister, and sleep in peace, God will not forsake us," and he lay down again in his bed. When day dawned, but before the sun had risen, the woman came and awoke the two children, saying "Get up, you sluggards! we are going into the forest to fetch wood." She gave each a little piece of bread, and said, "There is something for your dinner, but do not eat it up before then, for you will get nothing else." Grethel took the bread under her apron, as Hansel had the stones in his pocket. Then they all set out together on the way to the forest. When they had walked a short time, Hansel stood still and peeped back at the house, and did so again and again. His father said, "Hansel, what art thou looking at there and staying behind for? Mind what thou art about, and do not forget how to use thy legs." "Ah, father," said Hansel, "I am looking at my little white cat, which is sitting up on the roof, and wants to say good-bye to me." The wife said, "Fool, that is not thy little cat, that is the morning sun which is shining on the chimneys." Hansel, however, had not been looking back at the cat, but had been constantly throwing one of the white pebble-stones out of his pocket on the road.

When they had reached the middle of the forest, the father said, "Now, children, pile up some wood, and I will light a fire that you may not be cold." Hansel and Grethel gathered brushwood together, as high as a little hill. The brushwood was lighted, and when the flames were burning very high, the woman said, "Now, children, lay yourselves down by the fire and rest, we will go into the forest and cut some wood. When we have done, we will come back and fetch you away."

Hansel and Grethel sat by the fire, and when noon came, each ate a little piece of bread, and as they heard the strokes of the wood-axe they believed that their father was near. It was not, however, the axe, it was a branch which he had fastened to a withered tree which the wind was blowing backwards and forwards. And as they had been sitting such a long time, their eyes shut with fatigue, and they fell fast asleep. When at last they awoke, it was already dark night. Grethel began to cry and said, "How are we to get out of the forest now?" But Hansel comforted her and said, "Just wait a little, until the moon has risen, and then we will soon find the way." And when the full moon had risen, Hansel took his little sister by the hand, and followed the pebbles which shone like newly-coined silver pieces, and showed them the way.

They walked the whole night long, and by break of day came once more to their father's house. They knocked at the door, and when the woman opened it and saw that it was Hansel and Grethel, she said, "You naughty children, why have you slept so long in the forest? -- we thought you were never coming back at all!" The father, however, rejoiced, for it had cut him to the heart to leave them behind alone.

Not long afterwards, there was once more great scarcity in all parts, and the children heard their mother saying at night to their father, "Everything is eaten again, we have one half loaf left, and after that there is an end. The children must go, we will take them farther into the wood, so that they will not find their way out again; there is no other means of saving ourselves!" The man's heart was heavy, and he thought "it would be better for thee to share the last mouthful with thy children." The woman, however, would listen to nothing that he had to say, but scolded and reproached him. He who says A must say B, likewise, and as he had yielded the first time, he had to do so a second time also.

The children were, however, still awake and had heard the conversation. When the old folks were asleep, Hansel again got up, and wanted to go out and pick up pebbles as he had done before, but the woman had locked the door, and Hansel could not get out. Nevertheless he comforted his little sister, and said, "Do not cry, Grethel, go to sleep quietly, the good God will help us."

Early in the morning came the woman, and took the children out of their beds. Their bit of bread was given to them, but it was still smaller than the time before. On the way into the forest Hansel crumbled his in his pocket, and often stood still and threw a morsel on the ground. "Hansel, why dost thou stop and look round?" said the father, "go on." "I am looking back at my little pigeon which is sitting on the roof, and wants to say good-bye to me," answered Hansel. "Simpleton!" said the woman, "that is not thy little pigeon, that is the morning sun that is shining on the chimney." Hansel, however, little by little, threw all the crumbs on the path.

The woman led the children still deeper into the forest, where they had never in their lives been before. Then a great fire was again made, and the mother said, "Just sit there, you children, and when you are tired you may sleep a little; we are going into the forest to cut wood, and in the evening when we are done, we will come and fetch you away." When it was noon, Grethel shared her piece of bread with Hansel, who had scattered his by the way. Then they fell asleep and evening came and went, but no one came to the poor children. They did not awake until it was dark night, and Hansel comforted his little sister and said, "Just wait, Grethel, until the moon rises, and then we shall see the crumbs of bread which I have strewn about, they will show us our way home again." When the moon came they set out, but they found no crumbs, for the many thousands of birds which fly about in the woods and fields had picked them all up. Hansel said to Grethel, "We shall soon find the way," but they did not find it. They walked the whole night and all the next day too from morning till evening, but they did not get out of the forest, and were very hungry, for they had nothing to eat but two or three berries, which grew on the ground. And as they were so weary that their legs would carry them no longer, they lay down beneath a tree and fell asleep.

It was now three mornings since they had left their father's house. They began to walk again, but they always got deeper into the forest, and if help did not come soon, they must die of hunger and weariness. When it was mid-day, they saw a beautiful snow-white bird sitting on a bough, which sang so delightfully that they stood still and listened to it. And when it had finished its song, it spread its wings and flew away before them, and they followed it until they reached a little house, on the roof of which it alighted; and when they came quite up to little house they saw that it was built of bread and covered with cakes, but that the windows were of clear sugar. "We will set to work on that," said Hansel, "and have a good meal. I will eat a bit of the roof, and thou, Grethel, canst eat some of the window, it will taste sweet." Hansel reached up above, and broke off a little of the roof to try how it tasted, and Grethel leant against the window and nibbled at the panes. Then a soft voice cried from the room,

"Nibble, nibble, gnaw,
Who is nibbling at my little house?"

The children answered,

"The wind, the wind,
The heaven-born wind,"

and went on eating without disturbing themselves. Hansel, who thought the roof tasted very nice, tore down a great piece of it, and Grethel pushed out the whole of one round window-pane, sat down, and enjoyed herself with it. Suddenly the door opened, and a very, very old woman, who supported herself on crutches, came creeping out. Hansel and Grethel were so terribly frightened that they let fall what they had in their hands. The old woman, however, nodded her head, and said, "Oh, you dear children, who has brought you here? Do come in, and stay with me. No harm shall happen to you." She took them both by the hand, and led them into her little house. Then good food was set before them, milk and pancakes, with sugar, apples, and nuts. Afterwards two pretty little beds were covered with clean white linen, and Hansel and Grethel lay down in them, and thought they were in heaven.

The old woman had only pretended to be so kind; she was in reality a wicked witch, who lay in wait for children, and had only built the little house of bread in order to entice them there. When a child fell into her power, she killed it, cooked and ate it, and that was a feast day with her. Witches have red eyes, and cannot see far, but they have a keen scent like the beasts, and are aware when human beings draw near. When Hansel and Grethel came into her neighborhood, she laughed maliciously, and said mockingly, "I have them, they shall not escape me again!" Early in the morning before the children were awake, she was already up, and when she saw both of them sleeping and looking so pretty, with their plump red cheeks, she muttered to herself, "That will be a dainty mouthful!" Then she seized Hansel with her shrivelled hand, carried him into a little stable, and shut him in with a grated door. He might scream as he liked, that was of no use. Then she went to Grethel, shook her till she awoke, and cried, "Get up, lazy thing, fetch some water, and cook something good for thy brother, he is in the stable outside, and is to be made fat. When he is fat, I will eat him." Grethel began to weep bitterly, but it was all in vain, she was forced to do what the wicked witch ordered her.

And now the best food was cooked for poor Hansel, but Grethel got nothing but crab-shells. Every morning the woman crept to the little stable, and cried, "Hansel, stretch out thy finger that I may feel if thou wilt soon be fat." Hansel, however, stretched out a little bone to her, and the old woman, who had dim eyes, could not see it, and thought it was Hansel's finger, and was astonished that there was no way of fattening him. When four weeks had gone by, and Hansel still continued thin, she was seized with impatience and would not wait any longer. "Hola, Grethel," she cried to the girl, "be active, and bring some water. Let Hansel be fat or lean, to-morrow I will kill him, and cook him." Ah, how the poor little sister did lament when she had to fetch the water, and how her tears did flow down over her cheeks! "Dear God, do help us," she cried. "If the wild beasts in the forest had but devoured us, we should at any rate have died together." "Just keep thy noise to thyself," said the old woman, "all that won't help thee at all."

Early in the morning, Grethel had to go out and hang up the cauldron with the water, and light the fire. "We will bake first," said the old woman, "I have already heated the oven, and kneaded the dough." She pushed poor Grethel out to the oven, from which flames of fire were already darting. "Creep in," said the witch, "and see if it is properly heated, so that we can shut the bread in." And when once Grethel was inside, she intended to shut the oven and let her bake in it, and then she would eat her, too. But Grethel saw what she had in her mind, and said, "I do not know how I am to do it; how do you get in?" "Silly goose," said the old woman, "The door is big enough; just look, I can get in myself!" and she crept up and thrust her head into the oven. Then Grethel gave her a push that drove her far into it, and shut the iron door, and fastened the bolt. Oh! then she began to howl quite horribly, but Grethel ran away, and the godless witch was miserably burnt to death.

Grethel, however, ran like lightning to Hansel, opened his little stable, and cried, "Hansel, we are saved! The old witch is dead!" Then Hansel sprang out like a bird from its cage when the door is opened for it. How they did rejoice and embrace each other, and dance about and kiss each other! And as they had no longer any need to fear her, they went into the witch's house, and in every corner there stood chests full of pearls and jewels. "These are far better than pebbles!" said Hansel, and thrust into his pockets whatever could be got in, and Grethel said, "I, too, will take something home with me," and filled her pinafore full. "But now we will go away." said Hansel, "that we may get out of the witch's forest."

When they had walked for two hours, they came to a great piece of water. "We cannot get over," said Hansel, "I see no foot-plank, and no bridge." "And no boat crosses either," answered Grethel, "but a white duck is swimming there; if I ask her, she will help us over." Then she cried,

"Little duck, little duck, dost thou see,
Hansel and Grethel are waiting for thee?
There's never a plank, or bridge in sight,
Take us across on thy back so white."

The duck came to them, and Hansel seated himself on its back, and told his sister to sit by him. "No," replied Grethel, "that will be too heavy for the little duck; she shall take us across, one after the other." The good little duck did so, and when they were once safely across and had walked for a short time, the forest seemed to be more and more familiar to them, and at length they saw from afar their father's house. Then they began to run, rushed into the parlour, and threw themselves into their father's arms. The man had not known one happy hour since he had left the children in the forest; the woman, however, was dead. Grethel emptied her pinafore until pearls and precious stones ran about the room, and Hansel threw one handful after another out of his pocket to add to them. Then all anxiety was at an end, and they lived together in perfect happiness. My tale is done, there runs a mouse, whosoever catches it, may make himself a big fur cap out of it.

THE SEVEN RAVENS

THERE was once a man who had seven sons, and still he had no daughter, however much he wished for one. At length his wife again gave him hope of a child, and when it came into the world it was a girl. The joy was great, but the child was sickly and small, and had to be privately baptized on account of its weakness. The father sent one of the boys in haste to the spring to fetch water for the baptism. The other six went with him, and as each of them wanted to be first to fill it, the jug fell into the well. There they stood and did not know what to do, and none of them dared to go home. As they still did not return, the father grew impatient, and said, "They have certainly forgotten it for some game, the wicked boys!" He became afraid that the girl would have to die without being baptized, and in his anger cried, "I wish the boys were all turned into ravens." Hardly was the word spoken before he heard a whirring of wings over his head in the air, looked up and saw seven coal-black ravens flying away. The parents could not recall the curse, and however sad they were at the loss of their seven sons, they still to some extent comforted themselves with their dear little daughter, who soon grew strong and every day became more beautiful. For a long time she did not know that she had had brothers, for her parents were careful not to mention them before her, but one day she accidentally heard some people saying of herself, "that the girl was certainly beautiful, but that in reality she was to blame for the misfortune which had befallen her seven brothers." Then she was much troubled, and went to her father and mother and asked if it was true that she had had brothers, and what had become of them? The parents now dared keep the secret no longer, but said that what had befallen her brothers was the will of Heaven, and that her birth had only been the innocent cause. But the maiden took it to heart daily, and thought she must deliver her brothers. She had no rest or peace until she set out secretly, and went forth into the wide world to trace out her brothers and set them free, let it cost what it might. She took nothing with her but a little ring belonging to her parents as a keepsake, a loaf of bread against hunger, a little pitcher of water against thirst, and a little chair as a provision against weariness.

And now she went continually onwards, far, far to the very end of the world. Then she came to the sun, but it was too hot and terrible, and devoured little children. Hastily she ran away, and ran to the moon, but it was far too cold, and also awful and malicious, and when it saw the child, it said, "I smell, I smell the flesh of men." On this she ran swiftly away, and came to the stars, which were kind and good to her, and each of them sat on its own particular little chair.

But the morning star arose, and gave her the drumstick of a chicken, and said, "If you thou hast not that drumstick thou canst not open the Glass mountain, and in the Glass mountain are thy brothers."

The maiden took the drumstick, wrapped it carefully in a cloth, and went onwards again until she came to the Glass mountain. The door was shut, and she thought she would take out the drumstick; but when she undid the cloth, it was empty, and she had lost the good star's present. What was she now to do? She wished to rescue her brothers, and had no key to the Glass mountain. The good sister took a knife, cut off one of her little fingers, put it in the door, and succeeded in opening it. When she had gone inside, a little dwarf came to meet her, who said, "My child, what are you looking for?" "I am looking for my brothers, the seven ravens," she replied. The dwarf said, "The lord ravens are not at home, but if you will wait here until they come, step in." Thereupon the little dwarf carried the ravens' dinner in, on seven little plates, and in seven little glasses, and the little sister ate a morsel from each plate, and from each little glass she took a sip, but in the last little glass she dropped the ring which she had brought away with her.

Suddenly she heard a whirring of wings and a rushing through the air, and then the little dwarf said, "Now the lord ravens are flying home." Then they came, and wanted to eat and drink, and looked for their little plates and glasses.

Then said one after the other, "Who has eaten something from my plate? Who has drunk out of my little glass? It was a human mouth." And when the seventh came to the bottom of the glass, the ring rolled against his mouth. Then he looked at it, and saw that it was a ring belonging to his father and mother, and said, "God grant that our sister may be here, and then we shall be free." When the maiden, who was standing behind the door watching, heard that wish, she came forth, and on this all the ravens were restored to their human form again. And they embraced and kissed each other, and went joyfully home.

ASHPUTTEL

The wife of a rich man fell sick; and when she felt that her end drew nigh, she called her only daughter to her bed-side, and said, 'Always be a good girl, and I will look down from heaven and watch over you.' Soon afterwards she shut her eyes and died, and was buried in the garden; and the little girl went every day to her grave and wept, and was always good and kind to all about her. And the snow fell and spread a beautiful white covering over the grave; but by the time the spring came, and the sun had melted it away again, her father had married another wife. This new wife had two daughters of her own, that she brought home with her; they were fair in face but foul at heart, and it was now a sorry time for the poor little girl. 'What does the good-for-nothing want in the parlour?' said they; 'they who would eat bread should first earn it; away with the kitchen-maid!' Then they took away her fine clothes, and gave her an old grey frock to put on, and laughed at her, and turned her into the kitchen.

There she was forced to do hard work; to rise early before daylight, to bring the water, to make the fire, to cook and to wash. Besides that, the sisters plagued her in all sorts of ways, and laughed at her. In the evening when she was tired, she had no bed to lie down on, but was made to lie by the hearth among the ashes; and as this, of course, made her always dusty and dirty, they called her Ashputtel.

It happened once that the father was going to the fair, and asked his wife's daughters what he should bring them.

'Fine clothes,' said the first; 'Pearls and diamonds,' cried the second. 'Now, child,' said he to his own daughter, 'what will you have?' 'The first twig, dear father, that brushes against your hat when you turn your face to come homewards,' said she. Then he bought for the first two the fine clothes and pearls and diamonds they had asked for: and on his way home, as he rode through a green copse, a hazel twig brushed against him, and almost pushed off his hat: so he broke it off and brought it away; and when he got home he gave it to his daughter. Then she took it, and went to her mother's grave and planted it there; and cried so much that it was watered with her tears; and there it grew and became a fine tree. Three times every day she went to it and cried; and soon a little bird came and built its nest upon the tree, and talked with her, and watched over her, and brought her whatever she wished for.

Now it happened that the king of that land held a feast, which was to last three days; and out of those who came to it his son was to choose a bride for himself. Ashputtel's two sisters were asked to come; so they called her up, and said, 'Now, comb our hair, brush our shoes, and tie our sashes for us, for we are going to dance at the king's feast.' Then she did as she was told; but when all was done she could not help crying, for she thought to herself, she should so have liked to have gone with them to the ball; and at last she begged her mother very hard to let her go. 'You, Ashputtel!' said she; 'you who have nothing to wear, no clothes at all, and who cannot even dance—you want to go to the ball? And when she kept on begging, she said at last, to get rid of her, 'I will throw this dishful of peas into the ash-heap, and if in two hours' time you have picked them all out, you shall go to the feast too.'

Then she threw the peas down among the ashes, but the little maiden ran out at the back door into the garden, and cried out:

'Hither, hither, through the sky,

Turtle-doves and linnets, fly!

Blackbird, thrush, and chaffinch gay,

Hither, hither, haste away!

One and all come help me, quick!

Haste ye, haste ye!—pick, pick, pick!'

Then first came two white doves, flying in at the kitchen window; next came two turtle-doves; and after them came all the little birds under heaven, chirping and fluttering in: and they flew down into the ashes. And the little doves stooped their heads down and set to work, pick, pick, pick; and then the others began to pick, pick, pick: and among them all they soon picked out all the good grain, and put it into a dish but left the ashes. Long before the end of the hour the work was quite done, and all flew out again at the windows.

Then Ashputtel brought the dish to her mother, overjoyed at the thought that now she should go to the ball. But the mother said, 'No, no! you slut, you have no clothes, and cannot dance; you shall not go.' And when Ashputtel begged very hard to go, she said, 'If you can in one hour's time pick two of those dishes of peas out of the ashes, you shall go too.' And thus she thought she should at least get rid of her. So she shook two dishes of peas into the ashes.

But the little maiden went out into the garden at the back of the house, and cried out as before:

'Hither, hither, through the sky,

Turtle-doves and linnets, fly!

Blackbird, thrush, and chaffinch gay,

Hither, hither, haste away!

One and all come help me, quick!

Haste ye, haste ye!—pick, pick, pick!'

Then first came two white doves in at the kitchen window; next came two turtle-doves; and after them came all the little birds under heaven, chirping and hopping about. And they flew down into the ashes; and the little doves put their heads down and set to work, pick, pick, pick; and then the others began pick, pick, pick; and they put all the good grain into the dishes, and left all the ashes. Before half an hour's time all was done, and out they flew again. And then Ashputtel took the dishes to her mother, rejoicing to think that she should now go to the ball. But her mother said, 'It is all of no use, you cannot go; you have no clothes, and cannot dance, and you would only put us to shame': and off she went with her two daughters to the ball.

Now when all were gone, and nobody left at home, Ashputtel went sorrowfully and sat down under the hazel-tree, and cried out:

'Shake, shake, hazel-tree,

Gold and silver over me!'

Then her friend the bird flew out of the tree, and brought a gold and silver dress for her, and slippers of spangled silk; and she put them on, and followed her sisters to the feast. But they did not know her, and thought it must be some strange princess, she looked so fine and beautiful in her rich clothes; and they never once thought of Ashputtel, taking it for granted that she was safe at home in the dirt.

The king's son soon came up to her, and took her by the hand and danced with her, and no one else: and he never left her hand; but when anyone else came to ask her to dance, he said, 'This lady is dancing with me.'

Thus they danced till a late hour of the night; and then she wanted to go home: and the king's son said, 'I shall go and take care of you to your home'; for he wanted to see where the beautiful maiden lived. But she slipped away from him, unawares, and ran off towards home; and as the prince followed her, she jumped up into the pigeon-house and shut the door. Then he waited till her father came home, and told him that the unknown maiden, who had been at the feast, had hid herself in the pigeon-house. But when they had broken open the door they found no one within; and as they came back into the house, Ashputtel was lying, as she always did, in her dirty frock by the ashes, and her dim little lamp was burning in the chimney. For she had run as quickly as she could through the pigeon-house and on to the hazel-tree, and had there taken off her beautiful clothes, and put them beneath the tree, that the bird might carry them away, and had lain down again amid the ashes in her little grey frock.

The next day when the feast was again held, and her father, mother, and sisters were gone, Ashputtel went to the hazel-tree, and said:

'Shake, shake, hazel-tree,

Gold and silver over me!'

And the bird came and brought a still finer dress than the one she had worn the day before. And when she came in it to the ball, everyone wondered at her beauty: but the king's son, who was waiting for her, took her by the hand, and danced with her; and when anyone asked her to dance, he said as before, 'This lady is dancing with me.'

When night came she wanted to go home; and the king's son followed here as before, that he might see into what house she went: but she sprang away from him all at once into the garden behind her father's house. In this garden stood a fine large pear-tree full of ripe fruit; and Ashputtel, not knowing where to hide herself, jumped up into it without being seen. Then the king's son lost sight of her, and could not find out where she was gone, but waited till her father came home, and said to him, 'The unknown lady who danced with me has slipped away, and I think she must have sprung into the pear-tree.' The father thought to himself, 'Can it be Ashputtel?' So he had an axe brought; and they cut down the tree, but found no one upon it. And when they came back into the kitchen, there lay Ashputtel among the ashes; for she had slipped down on the other side of the tree, and carried her beautiful clothes back to the bird at the hazel-tree, and then put on her little grey frock.

The third day, when her father and mother and sisters were gone, she went again into the garden, and said:

'Shake, shake, hazel-tree,

Gold and silver over me!'

Then her kind friend the bird brought a dress still finer than the former one, and slippers which were all of gold: so that when she came to the feast no one knew what to say, for wonder at her beauty: and the king's son danced with nobody but her; and when anyone else asked her to dance, he said, 'This lady is *my* partner, sir.'

When night came she wanted to go home; and the king's son would go with her, and said to himself, 'I will not lose her this time'; but, however, she again slipped away from him, though in such a hurry that she dropped her left golden slipper upon the stairs.

The prince took the shoe, and went the next day to the king his father, and said, 'I will take for my wife the lady that this golden slipper fits.' Then both the sisters were overjoyed to hear it; for they had beautiful feet, and had no doubt that they could wear the golden slipper. The eldest went first into the room where the slipper was, and wanted to try it on, and the mother stood by. But her great toe could not go into it, and the shoe was altogether much too small for her. Then the mother gave her a knife, and said, 'Never mind, cut it off; when you are queen you will not care about toes; you will not want to walk.' So the silly girl cut off her great toe, and thus squeezed on the shoe, and went to the king's son. Then he took her for his bride, and set her beside him on his horse, and rode away with her homewards.

But on their way home they had to pass by the hazel-tree that Ashputtel had planted; and on the branch sat a little dove singing:

'Back again! back again! look to the shoe!

The shoe is too small, and not made for you!

Prince! prince! look again for thy bride,

For she's not the true one that sits by thy side.'

Then the prince got down and looked at her foot; and he saw, by the blood that streamed from it, what a trick she had played him. So he turned his horse round, and brought the false bride back to her home, and said, 'This is not the right bride; let the other sister try and put on the slipper.' Then she went into the room and got her foot into the shoe, all but the heel, which was too large. But her mother squeezed it in till the blood came, and took her to the king's son: and he set her as his bride by his side on his horse, and rode away with her.

But when they came to the hazel-tree the little dove sat there still, and sang:

'Back again! back again! look to the shoe!

The shoe is too small, and not made for you!

Prince! prince! look again for thy bride,

For she's not the true one that sits by thy side.'

Then he looked down, and saw that the blood streamed so much from the shoe, that her white stockings were quite red. So he turned his horse and brought her also back again. 'This is not the true bride,' said he to the father; 'have you no other daughters?' 'No,' said he; 'there is only a little dirty Ashputtel here, the child of my first wife; I am sure she cannot be the bride.' The prince told him to send her. But the mother said, 'No, no, she is much too dirty; she will not dare to show herself.' However, the prince would have her come; and she first washed her face and hands, and then went in and curtsied to him, and he reached her the golden slipper. Then she took her clumsy shoe off her left foot, and put on the golden slipper; and it fitted her as if it had been made for her. And when he drew near and looked at her face he knew her, and said, 'This is the right bride.' But the mother and both the sisters were frightened, and turned pale with anger as he took Ashputtel on his horse, and rode away with her. And when they came to the hazel-tree, the white dove sang:

'Home! home! look at the shoe!

Princess! the shoe was made for you!

Prince! prince! take home thy bride,

For she is the true one that sits by thy side!'

And when the dove had done its song, it came flying, and perched upon her right shoulder, and so went home with her.

The Elves And The Shoemaker

There was once a shoemaker, who worked very hard and was very honest: but still he could not earn enough to live upon; and at last all he had in the world was gone, save just leather enough to make one pair of shoes.

Then he cut his leather out, all ready to make up the next day, meaning to rise early in the morning to his work. His conscience was clear and his heart light amidst all his troubles; so he went peaceably to bed, left all his cares to Heaven, and soon fell asleep. In the morning after he had said his prayers, he sat himself down to his work; when, to his great wonder, there stood the shoes all ready made, upon the table. The good man knew not what to say or think at such an odd thing happening. He looked at the workmanship; there was not one false stitch in the whole job; all was so neat and true, that it was quite a masterpiece.

The same day a customer came in, and the shoes suited him so well that he willingly paid a price higher than usual for them; and the poor shoemaker, with the money, bought leather enough to make two pairs more. In the evening he cut out the work, and went to bed early, that he might get up and begin betimes next day; but he was saved all the trouble, for when he got up in the morning the work was done ready to his hand. Soon in came buyers, who paid him handsomely for his goods, so that he bought leather enough for four pair more. He cut out the work again overnight and found it done in the morning, as before; and so it went on for some time: what was got ready in the evening was always done by daybreak, and the good man soon became thriving and well off again.

One evening, about Christmas-time, as he and his wife were sitting over the fire chatting together, he said to her, 'I should like to sit up and watch tonight, that we may see who it is that comes and does my work for me.' The wife liked the thought; so they left a light burning, and hid themselves in a corner of the room, behind a curtain that was hung up there, and watched what would happen.

As soon as it was midnight, there came in two little naked dwarfs; and they sat themselves upon the shoemaker's bench, took up all the work that was cut out, and began to ply with their little fingers, stitching and rapping and tapping away at such a rate, that the shoemaker was all wonder, and could not take his eyes off them. And on they went, till the job was quite done, and the shoes stood ready for use upon the table. This was long before daybreak; and then they bustled away as quick as lightning.

The next day the wife said to the shoemaker. 'These little wights have made us rich, and we ought to be thankful to them, and do them a good turn if we can. I am quite sorry to see them run about as they do; and indeed it is not very decent, for they have nothing upon their backs to keep off the cold. I'll tell you what, I will make each of them a shirt, and a coat and waistcoat, and a pair of pantaloons into the bargain; and do you make each of them a little pair of shoes.'

The thought pleased the good cobbler very much; and one evening, when all the things were ready, they laid them on the table, instead of the work that they used to cut out, and then went and hid themselves, to watch what the little elves would do.

About midnight in they came, dancing and skipping, hopped round the room, and then went to sit down to their work as usual; but when they saw the clothes lying for them, they laughed and chuckled, and seemed mightily delighted.

Then they dressed themselves in the twinkling of an eye, and danced and capered and sprang about, as merry as could be; till at last they danced out at the door, and away over the green.

The good couple saw them no more; but everything went well with them from that time forward, as long as they lived.

THE THREE BROTHERS

THERE was once a man who had three sons, and nothing else in the world but the house in which he lived. Now each of the sons wished to have the house after his father's death; but the father loved them all alike, and did not know what to do; he did not wish to sell the house, because it had belonged to his forefathers, else he might have divided the money amongst them. At last a plan came into his head, and he said to his sons, "Go into the world, and try each of you to learn a trade, and, when you all come back, he who makes the best masterpiece shall have the house."
The sons were well content with this, and the eldest determined to be a blacksmith, the second a barber, and the third a fencing-master. They fixed a time when they should all come home again, and then each went his way.

It chanced that they all found skilful masters, who taught them their trades well. The blacksmith had to shoe the King's horses, and he thought to himself, "The house is mine, without doubt." The barber only shaved great people, and he too already looked upon the house as his own. The fencing-master got many a blow, but he only bit his lip, and let nothing vex him; "for," said he to himself, "If you are afraid of a blow, you'll never win the house."

When the appointed time had gone by, the three brothers came back home to their father; but they did not know how to find the best opportunity for showing their skill, so they sat down and consulted together. As they were sitting thus, all at once a hare came running across the field. "Ah, ha, just in time!" said the barber. So he took his basin and soap, and lathered away until the hare came up; then he soaped and shaved off the hare's whiskers whilst he was running at the top of his speed, and did not even cut his skin or injure a hair on his body. "Well done!" said the old man. "your brothers will have to exert themselves wonderfully, or the house will be yours."

Soon after, up came a nobleman in his coach, dashing along at full speed. "Now you shall see what I can do, father," said the blacksmith; so away he ran after the coach, took all four shoes off the feet of one of the horses whilst he was galloping, and put him on four new shoes without stopping him. "You are a fine fellow, and as clever as your brother," said his father; "I do not know to which I ought to give the house."

Then the third son said, "Father, let me have my turn, if you please;" and, as it was beginning to rain, he drew his sword, and flourished it backwards and forwards above his head so fast that not a drop fell upon him. It rained still harder and harder, till at last it came down in torrents; but he only flourished his sword faster and faster, and remained as dry as if he were sitting in a house. When his father saw this he was amazed, and said, "This is the master-piece, the house is yours!"

His brothers were satisfied with this, as was agreed beforehand; and, as they loved one another very much, they all three stayed together in the house, followed their trades, and, as they had learnt them so well and were so clever, they earned a great deal of money. Thus they lived together happily until they grew old; and at last, when one of them fell sick and died, the two others grieved so sorely about it that they also fell ill, and soon after died. And because they had been so clever, and had loved one another so much, they were all laid in the same grave.

The Wishing-Table, The Gold-Ass, And The Cudgel In The Sack

THERE was once upon a time a tailor who had three sons, and only one goat. But as the goat supported the whole of them with her milk, she was obliged to have good food, and to be taken every day to pasture. The sons, therefore, did this, in turn. Once the eldest took her to the churchyard, where the finest herbs were to be found, and let her eat and run about there. At night when it was time to go home he asked, "Goat, hast thou had enough?" The goat answered,

"I have eaten so much,
Not a leaf more I'll touch, meh! meh!"

"Come home, then," said the youth, and took hold of the cord round her neck, led her into the stable and tied her up securely. "Well," said the old tailor, "has the goat had as much food as she ought?" "Oh," answered the son, "she has eaten so much, not a leaf more she'll touch." But the father wished to satisfy himself, and went down to the stable, stroked the dear animal and asked, "Goat, art thou satisfied?" The goat answered,

"Wherewithal should I be satisfied?
Among the graves I leapt about,
And found no food, so went without, meh! meh!"

"What do I hear?" cried the tailor, and ran upstairs and said to the youth, "Hollo, thou liar: thou saidest the goat had had enough, and hast let her hunger!" and in his anger he took the yard-measure from the wall, and drove him out with blows.

Next day it was the turn of the second son, who looked out for a place in the fence of the garden, where nothing but good herbs grew, and the goat cleared them all off. At night when he wanted to go home, he asked, "Goat, art thou satisfied?" The goat answered,

"I have eaten so much,
Not a leaf more I'll touch, meh! meh!"

"Come home, then," said the youth, and led her home, and tied her up in the stable. "Well," said the old tailor, "has the goat had as much food as she ought?" "Oh," answered the son, "she has eaten so much, not a leaf more she'll touch." The tailor would not rely on this, but went down to the stable and said, "Goat, hast thou had enough?" The goat answered,

"Wherewithal should I be satisfied?
Among the graves I leapt about,
And found no food, so went without, meh! meh!"

"The godless wretch!" cried the tailor, "to let such a good animal hunger," and he ran up and drove the youth out of doors with the yard-measure.

Now came the turn of the third son, who wanted to do the thing well, and sought out some bushes with the finest leaves, and let the goat devour them. In the evening when he wanted to go home, he asked, "Goat, hast thou had enough?" The goat answered,

"I have eaten so much,
Not a leaf more I'll touch, meh! meh!"

"Come home, then," said the youth, and led her into the stable, and tied her up. "Well," said the old tailor, "has the goat had a proper amount of food?" "She has eaten so much, not a leaf more she'll touch." The tailor did not trust to that, but went down and asked, "Goat, hast thou had enough?" The wicked beast answered,

"Wherewithal should I be satisfied?
Among the graves I leapt about,
And found no leaves, so went without, meh! meh!"

Oh, the brood of liars!" cried the tailor, "each as wicked and forgetful of his duty as the other! Ye shall no longer make a fool of me," and quite beside himself with anger, he ran upstairs and belabored the poor young fellow so vigorously with the yard-measure that he sprang out of the house.

The old tailor was now alone with his goat. Next morning he went down into the stable, caressed the goat and said, "Come, my dear little animal, I will take thee to feed myself." He took her by the rope and conducted her to green hedges, and amongst milfoil, and whatever else goats like to eat. "There thou mayest for once eat to thy heart's content," said he to her, and let her browse till evening. Then he asked, "Goat, art thou satisfied?" She replied,

"I have eaten so much,
Not a leaf more I'll touch, meh! meh!"
"Come home, then," said the tailor, and led her into the stable,

and tied her fast. When he was going away, he turned round again and said, "Well, art thou satisfied for once?" But the goat did not behave the better to him, and cried,

"Wherewithal should I be satisfied?
Among the graves I leapt about,
And found no leaves, so went without, meh! meh!"

When the tailor heard that, he was shocked, and saw clearly that he had driven away his three sons without cause. "Wait, thou ungrateful creature," cried he, "it is not enough to drive thee forth, I will mark thee so that thou wilt no more dare to show thyself amongst honest tailors." In great haste he ran upstairs, fetched his razor, lathered the goat's head, and shaved her as clean as the palm of his hand. And as the yard-measure would have been too good for her, he brought the horsewhip, and gave her such cuts with it that she ran away in violent haste.

When the tailor was thus left quite alone in his house he fell into great grief, and would gladly have had his sons back again, but no one knew whither they were gone. The eldest had apprenticed himself to a joiner, and learnt industriously and indefatigably, and when the time came for him to go travelling, his master presented him with a little table which had no particular appearance, and was made of common wood, but it had one good property; if anyone set it out, and said, "Little table, spread thyself," the good little table was at once covered with a clean little cloth, and a plate was there, and a knife and fork beside it, and dishes with boiled meats and roasted meats, as many as there was room for, and a great glass of red wine shone so that it made the heart glad. The young journeyman thought, "With this thou hast enough for thy whole life," and went joyously about the world and never troubled himself at all whether an inn was good or bad, or if anything was to be found in it or not. When it suited him he did not enter an inn at all, but either on the plain, in a wood, a meadow, or wherever he fancied, he took his little table off his back, set it down before him, and said, "Cover thyself," and then everything appeared that his heart desired. At length he took it into his head to go back to his father, whose anger would now be appeased, and who would now willingly receive him with his wishing-table. It came to pass that on his way home, he came one evening to an inn which was filled with guests. They bade him welcome, and invited him to sit and eat with them, for otherwise he would have difficulty in getting anything. "No," answered the joiner, "I will not take the few bites out of your mouths; rather than that, you shall be my guests." They laughed, and thought he was jesting with them; he, however, placed his wooden table in the middle of the room, and said, "Little table, cover thyself." Instantly it was covered with food, so good that the host could never have procured it, and the smell of it ascended pleasantly to the nostrils of the guests. "Fall to, dear friends," said the joiner; and the guests when they saw that he meant it, did not need to be asked twice, but drew near, pulled out their knives and attacked it valiantly. And what surprised them the most was that when a dish became empty, a full one instantly took its place of its own accord. The innkeeper stood in one corner and watched the affair; he did not at all know what to say, but thought, "Thou couldst easily find a use for such a cook as that in thy kitchen." The joiner and his comrades made merry until late into the night; at length they lay down to sleep, and the young apprentice also went to bed, and set his magic table against the wall. The host's thoughts, however, let him have no rest; it occurred to him that there was a little old table in his lumber-room which looked just like the apprentice's and he brought it out quite softly, and exchanged it for the wishing-table. Next morning, the joiner paid for his bed, took up his table, never thinking that he had got a false one, and went his way. At mid-day he reached his father, who received him with great joy. "Well, my dear son, what hast thou learnt?" said he to him. "Father, I have become a joiner."

"A good trade," replied the old man; "but what hast thou brought back with thee from thy apprenticeship?" "Father, the best thing which I have brought back with me is this little table." The tailor inspected it on all sides and said, "Thou didst not make a masterpiece when thou mad'st that; it is a bad old table." "But it is a table which furnishes itself," replied the son. "When I set it out, and tell it to cover itself, the most beautiful dishes stand on it, and a wine also, which gladdens the heart. Just invite all our relations and friends, they shall refresh and enjoy themselves for once, for the table will give them all they require." When the company was assembled, he put his table in the middle of the room and said, "Little table, cover thyself," but the little table did not bestir itself, and remained just as bare as any other table which did not understand language. Then the poor apprentice became aware that his table had been changed, and was ashamed at having to stand there like a liar. The relations, however, mocked him, and were forced to go home without having eaten or drunk. The father brought out his patches again, and went on tailoring, but the son went to a master in the craft.

The second son had gone to a miller and had apprenticed himself to him. When his years were over, the master said, "As thou hast conducted thyself so well, I give thee an ass of a peculiar kind, which neither draws a cart nor carries a sack." "To what use is he put, then?" asked the young apprentice. "He lets gold drop from his mouth," answered the miller. "If thou settest him on a cloth and sayest 'Bricklebrit,' the good animal will drop gold pieces for thee." "That is a fine thing," said the apprentice, and thanked the master, and went out into the world. When he had need of gold, he had only to say "Bricklebrit" to his ass, and it rained gold pieces, and he had nothing to do but pick them off the ground. Wheresoever he went, the best of everything was good enough for him, and the dearer the better, for he had always a full purse. When he had looked about the world for some time, he thought, "Thou must seek out thy father; if thou goest to him with the gold-ass he will forget his anger, and receive thee well." It came to pass that he came to the same public-house in which his brother's table had been exchanged. He led his ass by the bridle, and the host was about to take the animal from him and tie him up, but the young apprentice said, "Don't trouble yourself, I will take my grey horse into the stable, and tie him up myself too, for I must know where he stands." This struck the host as odd, and he thought that a man who was forced to look after his ass himself, could not have much to spend; but when the stranger put his hand in his pocket and brought out two gold pieces, and said he was to provide something good for him, the host opened his eyes wide, and ran and sought out the best he could muster. After dinner the guest asked what he owed. The host did not see why he should not double the reckoning, and said the apprentice must give two more gold pieces. He felt in his pocket, but his gold was just at an end. "Wait an instant, sir host," said he, "I will go and fetch some money;" but he took the table-cloth with him. The host could not imagine what this could mean, and being curious, stole after him, and as the guest bolted the stable-door, he peeped through a hole left by a knot in the wood. The stranger spread out the cloth under the animal and cried, "Bricklebrit," and immediately the beast began to let gold pieces fall, so that it fairly rained down money on the ground. "Eh, my word," said the host, "ducats are quickly coined there! A purse like that is not amiss." The guest paid his score, and went to bed, but in the night the host stole down into the stable, led away the master of the mint, and tied up another ass in his place. Early next morning the apprentice travelled away with his ass, and thought that he had his gold-ass. At mid-day he reached his father, who rejoiced to see him again, and gladly took him in. "What hast thou made of thyself, my son?" asked the old man. "A miller," dear father, he answered. "What hast thou brought back with thee from thy travels?" "Nothing else but an ass." "There are asses enough here," said the father, "I would rather have had a good goat." "Yes," replied the son, "but it is no common ass, but a gold-ass, when I say 'Bricklebrit,' the good beast opens its mouth and drops a whole sheetful of gold pieces. Just summon all our relations hither, and I will make them rich folks." "That suits me well," said the tailor, "for then I shall have no need to torment myself any longer with the needle," and ran out himself and called the relations together. As soon as they were assembled, the miller bade them make way, spread out his cloth, and brought the ass into the room. "Now watch," said he, and cried, "Bricklebrit," but no gold pieces fell, and it was clear that the animal knew nothing of the art, for every ass does not attain such perfection. Then the poor miller pulled a long face, saw that he was betrayed, and begged pardon of the relatives, who went home as poor as they came. There was no help for it, the old man had to betake him to his needle once more, and the youth hired himself to a miller.

The third brother had apprenticed himself to a turner, and as that is skilled labour, he was the longest in learning. His brothers, however, told him in a letter how badly things had gone with them, and how the innkeeper had cheated them of their beautiful wishing-gifts on the last evening before they reached home. When the turner had served his time, and had to set out on his travels, as he had conducted himself so well, his master presented him with a sack and said, "There is a cudgel in it." "I can put on the sack," said he, "and it may be of good service to me, but why should the cudgel be in it? It only makes it heavy." "I will tell thee why," replied the master; "if any one has done anything to injure thee, do but say, 'Out of the sack, Cudgel!' and the cudgel will leap forth among the people, and play such a dance on their backs that they will not be able to stir or move for a week, and it will not leave off until thou sayest, "Into the sack, Cudgel!" The apprentice thanked him, and put the sack on his back, and when any one came too near him, and wished to attack him, he said, "Out of the sack, Cudgel!" and instantly the cudgel sprang out, and dusted the coat or jacket of one after the other on their backs, and never stopped until it had stripped it off them, and it was done so quickly, that before anyone was aware, it was already his own turn. In the evening the young turner reached the inn where his brothers had been cheated. He laid his sack on the table before him, and began to talk of all the wonderful things which he had seen in the world. "Yes," said he, "people may easily find a table which will cover itself, a gold-ass, and things of that kind -- extremely good things which I by no means despise -- but these are nothing in comparison with the treasure which I have won for myself, and am carrying about with me in my sack there." The inn-keeper pricked up his ears, "What in the world can that be?" thought he; "the sack must be filled with nothing but jewels; I ought to get them cheap too, for all good things go in threes." When it was time for sleep, the guest stretched himself on the bench, and laid his sack beneath him for a pillow. When the inn-keeper thought his guest was lying in a sound sleep, he went to him and pushed and pulled quite gently and carefully at the sack to see if he could possibly draw it away and lay another in its place. The turner had, however, been waiting for this for a long time, and now just as the inn-keeper was about to give a hearty tug, he cried, "Out of the sack, Cudgel!" Instantly the little cudgel came forth, and fell on the inn-keeper and gave him a sound thrashing.

The host cried for mercy; but the louder he cried, so much more heavily the cudgel beat the time on his back, until at length he fell to the ground exhausted. Then the turner said, "If thou dost not give back the table which covers itself, and the gold-ass, the dance shall begin afresh." "Oh, no," cried the host, quite humbly, "I will gladly produce everything, only make the accursed kobold creep back into the sack." Then said the apprentice, "I will let mercy take the place of justice, but beware of getting into mischief again!" So he cried, "Into the sack, Cudgel!" and let him have rest.

Next morning the turner went home to his father with the wishing-table, and the gold-ass. The tailor rejoiced when he saw him once more, and asked him likewise what he had learned in foreign parts. "Dear father," said he, "I have become a turner." "A skilled trade," said the father. "What hast thou brought back with thee from thy travels?"

"A precious thing, dear father," replied the son, "a cudgel in the sack."

"What!" cried the father, "a cudgel! That's worth thy trouble, indeed! From every tree thou can cut thyself one." "But not one like this, dear father. If I say, 'Out of the sack, Cudgel!' the cudgel springs out and leads any one who means ill with me a weary dance, and never stops until he lies on the ground and prays for fair weather. Look you, with this cudgel have I got back the wishing-table and the gold-ass which the thievish inn-keeper took away from my brothers. Now let them both be sent for, and invite all our kinsmen. I will give them to eat and to drink, and will fill their pockets with gold into the bargain." The old tailor would not quite believe, but nevertheless got the relatives together. Then the turner spread a cloth in the room and led in the gold-ass, and said to his brother, "Now, dear brother, speak to him." The miller said, "Bricklebrit," and instantly the gold pieces fell down on the cloth like a thunder-shower, and the ass did not stop until every one of them had so much that he could carry no more. (I can see in thy face that thou also wouldst like to be there.)

Then the turner brought the little table, and said, "Now dear brother, speak to it." And scarcely had the carpenter said, "Table, cover thyself," than it was spread and amply covered with the most exquisite dishes. Then such a meal took place as the good tailor had never yet known in his house, and the whole party of kinsmen stayed together till far in the night, and were all merry and glad. The tailor locked away needle and thread, yard-measure and goose, in a press, and lived with his three sons in joy and splendour. (What, however, has become of the goat who was to blame for the tailor driving out his three sons? That I will tell thee. She was ashamed that she had a bald head, and ran to a fox's hole and crept into it. When the fox came home, he was met by two great eyes shining out of the darkness, and was terrified and ran away. A bear met him, and as the fox looked quite disturbed, he said, "What is the matter with thee, brother Fox, why dost thou look like that?" "Ah," answered Redskin, "a fierce beast is in my cave and stared at me with its fiery eyes." "We will soon drive him out," said the bear, and went with him to the cave and looked in, but when he saw the fiery eyes, fear seized on him likewise; he would have nothing to do with the furious beast, and took to his heels. The bee met him, and as she saw that he was ill at ease, she said, "Bear, thou art really pulling a very pitiful face; what has become of all thy gaiety?" "It is all very well for thee to talk," replied the bear, "a furious beast with staring eyes is in Redskin's house, and we can't drive him out." The bee said, "Bear I pity thee, I am a poor weak creature whom thou wouldst not turn aside to look at, but still, I believe, I can help thee." She flew into the fox's cave, lighted on the goat's smoothly-shorn head, and stung her so violently, that she sprang up, crying "Meh, meh," and ran forth into the world as if mad, and to this hour no one knows where she has gone.)

Iron Hans

There was once upon a time a king who had a great forest near his palace, full of all kinds of wild animals. One day he sent out a huntsman to shoot him a roe, but he did not come back. 'Perhaps some accident has befallen him,' said the king, and the next day he sent out two more huntsmen who were to search for him, but they too stayed away. Then on the third day, he sent for all his huntsmen, and said: 'Scour the whole forest through, and do not give up until you have found all three.' But of these also, none came home again, none were seen again. From that time forth, no one would any longer venture into the forest, and it lay there in deep stillness and solitude, and nothing was seen of it, but sometimes an eagle or a hawk flying over it. This lasted for many years, when an unknown huntsman announced himself to the king as seeking a situation, and offered to go into the dangerous forest. The king, however, would not give his consent, and said: 'It is not safe in there; I fear it would fare with you no better than with the others, and you would never come out again.' The huntsman replied: 'Lord, I will venture it at my own risk, of fear I know nothing.'

The huntsman therefore betook himself with his dog to the forest. It was not long before the dog fell in with some game on the way, and wanted to pursue it; but hardly had the dog run two steps when it stood before a deep pool, could go no farther, and a naked arm stretched itself out of the water, seized it, and drew it under. When the huntsman saw that, he went back and fetched three men to come with buckets and bale out the water. When they could see to the bottom there lay a wild man whose body was brown like rusty iron, and whose hair hung over his face down to his knees. They bound him with cords, and led him away to the castle. There was great astonishment over the wild man; the king, however, had him put in an iron cage in his courtyard, and forbade the door to be opened on pain of death, and the queen herself was to take the key into her keeping. And from this time forth everyone could again go into the forest with safety.

The king had a son of eight years, who was once playing in the courtyard, and while he was playing, his golden ball fell into the cage. The boy ran thither and said: 'Give me my ball out.' 'Not till you have opened the door for me,' answered the man. 'No,' said the boy, 'I will not do that; the king has forbidden it,' and ran away. The next day he again went and asked for his ball; the wild man said: 'Open my door,' but the boy would not. On the third day the king had ridden out hunting, and the boy went once more and said: 'I cannot open the door even if I wished, for I have not the key.' Then the wild man said: 'It lies under your mother's pillow, you can get it there.' The boy, who wanted to have his ball back, cast all thought to the winds, and brought the key. The door opened with difficulty, and the boy pinched his fingers. When it was open the wild man stepped out, gave him the golden ball, and hurried away. The boy had become afraid; he called and cried after him: 'Oh, wild man, do not go away, or I shall be beaten!' The wild man turned back, took him up, set him on his shoulder, and went with hasty steps into the forest. When the king came home, he observed the empty cage, and asked the queen how that had happened. She knew nothing about it, and sought the key, but it was gone. She called the boy, but no one answered. The king sent out people to seek for him in the fields, but they did not find him. Then he could easily guess what had happened, and much grief reigned in the royal court.

When the wild man had once more reached the dark forest, he took the boy down from his shoulder, and said to him: 'You will never see your father and mother again, but I will keep you with me, for you have set me free, and I have compassion on you. If you do all I bid you, you shall fare well. Of treasure and gold have I enough, and more than anyone in the world.' He made a bed of moss for the boy on which he slept, and the next morning the man took him to a well, and said: 'Behold, the gold well is as bright and clear as crystal, you shall sit beside it, and take care that nothing falls into it, or it will be polluted. I will come every evening to see if you have obeyed my order.' The boy placed himself by the brink of the well, and often saw a golden fish or a golden snake show itself therein, and took care that nothing fell in. As he was thus sitting, his finger hurt him so violently that he involuntarily put it in the water. He drew it quickly out again, but saw that it was quite gilded, and whatsoever pains he took to wash the gold off again, all was to no purpose. In the evening Iron Hans came back, looked at the boy, and said: 'What has happened to the well?' 'Nothing nothing,' he answered, and held his finger behind his back, that the man might not see it. But he said: 'You have dipped your finger into the water, this time it may pass, but take care you do not again let anything go in.' By daybreak the boy was already sitting by the well and watching it. His finger hurt him again and he passed it over his head, and then unhappily a hair fell down into the well. He took it quickly out, but it was already quite gilded. Iron Hans came, and already knew what had happened. 'You have let a hair fall into the well,' said he. 'I will allow you to watch by it once more, but if this happens for the third time then the well is polluted and you can no longer remain with me.'

On the third day, the boy sat by the well, and did not stir his finger, however much it hurt him. But the time was long to him, and he looked at the reflection of his face on the surface of the water. And as he still bent down more and more while he was doing so, and trying to look straight into the eyes, his long hair fell down from his shoulders into the water. He raised himself up quickly, but the whole of the hair of his head was already golden and shone like the sun. You can imagine how terrified the poor boy was! He took his pocket-handkerchief and tied it round his head, in order that the man might not see it. When he came he already knew everything, and said: 'Take the handkerchief off.' Then the golden hair streamed forth, and let the boy excuse himself as he might, it was of no use. 'You have not stood the trial and can stay here no longer. Go forth into the world, there you will learn what poverty is. But as you have not a bad heart, and as I mean well by you, there is one thing I will grant you; if you fall into any difficulty, come to the forest and cry: "Iron Hans," and then I will come and help you. My power is great, greater than you think, and I have gold and silver in abundance.'

Then the king's son left the forest, and walked by beaten and unbeaten paths ever onwards until at length he reached a great city. There he looked for work, but could find none, and he learnt nothing by which he could help himself. At length he went to the palace, and asked if they would take him in. The people about court did not at all know what use they could make of him, but they liked him, and told him to stay. At length the cook took him into his service, and said he might carry wood and water, and rake the cinders together. Once when it so happened that no one else was at hand, the cook ordered him to carry the food to the royal table, but as he did not like to let his golden hair be seen, he kept his little cap on. Such a thing as that had never yet come under the king's notice, and he said: 'When you come to the royal table you must take your hat off.' He answered: 'Ah, Lord, I cannot; I have a bad sore place on my head.' Then the king had the cook called before him and scolded him, and asked how he could take such a boy as that into his service; and that he was to send him away at once. The cook, however, had pity on him, and exchanged him for the gardener's boy.

And now the boy had to plant and water the garden, hoe and dig, and bear the wind and bad weather. Once in summer when he was working alone in the garden, the day was so warm he took his little cap off that the air might cool him. As the sun shone on his hair it glittered and flashed so that the rays fell into the bedroom of the king's daughter, and up she sprang to see what that could be. Then she saw the boy, and cried to him: 'Boy, bring me a wreath of flowers.' He put his cap on with all haste, and gathered wild field-flowers and bound them together. When he was ascending the stairs with them, the gardener met him, and said: 'How can you take the king's daughter a garland of such common flowers? Go quickly, and get another, and seek out the prettiest and rarest.' 'Oh, no,' replied the boy, 'the wild ones have more scent, and will please her better.' When he got into the room, the king's daughter said: 'Take your cap off, it is not seemly to keep it on in my presence.' He again said: 'I may not, I have a sore head.' She, however, caught at his cap and pulled it off, and then his golden hair rolled down on his shoulders, and it was splendid to behold. He wanted to run out, but she held him by the arm, and gave him a handful of ducats. With these he departed, but he cared nothing for the gold pieces. He took them to the gardener, and said: 'I present them to your children, they can play with them.' The following day the king's daughter again called to him that he was to bring her a wreath of field-flowers, and then he went in with it, she instantly snatched at his cap, and wanted to take it away from him, but he held it fast with both hands. She again gave him a handful of ducats, but he would not keep them, and gave them to the gardener for playthings for his children. On the third day things went just the same; she could not get his cap away from him, and he would not have her money.

Not long afterwards, the country was overrun by war. The king gathered together his people, and did not know whether or not he could offer any opposition to the enemy, who was superior in strength and had a mighty army. Then said the gardener's boy: 'I am grown up, and will go to the wars also, only give me a horse.' The others laughed, and said: 'Seek one for yourself when we are gone, we will leave one behind us in the stable for you.' When they had gone forth, he went into the stable, and led the horse out; it was lame of one foot, and limped hobblety jib, hobblety jib; nevertheless he mounted it, and rode away to the dark forest. When he came to the outskirts, he called 'Iron Hans' three times so loudly that it echoed through the trees. Thereupon the wild man appeared immediately, and said: 'What do you desire?' 'I want a strong steed, for I am going to the wars.' 'That you shall have, and still more than you ask for.' Then the wild man went back into the forest, and it was not long before a stable-boy came out of it, who led a horse that snorted with its nostrils, and could hardly be restrained, and behind them followed a great troop of warriors entirely equipped in iron, and their swords flashed in the sun. The youth made over his three-legged horse to the stable-boy, mounted the other, and rode at the head of the soldiers. When he got near the battlefield a great part of the king's men had already fallen, and little was wanting to make the rest give way. Then the youth galloped thither with his iron soldiers, broke like a hurricane over the enemy, and beat down all who opposed him. They began to flee, but the youth pursued, and never stopped, until there was not a single man left. Instead of returning to the king, however, he conducted his troop by byways back to the forest, and called forth Iron Hans. 'What do you desire?' asked the wild man. 'Take back your horse and your troops, and give me my three-legged horse again.' All that he asked was done, and soon he was riding on his three-legged horse. When the king returned to his palace, his daughter went to meet him, and wished him joy of his victory. 'I am not the one who carried away the victory,' said he, 'but a strange knight who came to my assistance with his soldiers.' The daughter wanted to hear who the strange knight was, but the king did not know, and said: 'He followed the enemy, and I did not see him again.' She inquired of the gardener where his boy was, but he smiled, and said: 'He has just come home on his three-legged horse, and the others have been mocking him, and crying: "Here comes our hobblety jib back again!" They asked, too: "Under what hedge have you been lying sleeping all the time?" So he said: "I did the best of all, and it would have gone badly without me." And then he was still more ridiculed.'

The king said to his daughter: 'I will proclaim a great feast that shall last for three days, and you shall throw a golden apple. Perhaps the unknown man will show himself.' When the feast was announced, the youth went out to the forest, and called Iron Hans. 'What do you desire?' asked he. 'That I may catch the king's daughter's golden apple.' 'It is as safe as if you had it already,' said Iron Hans. 'You shall likewise have a suit of red armour for the occasion, and ride on a spirited chestnut-horse.' When the day came, the youth galloped to the spot, took his place amongst the knights, and was recognized by no one. The king's daughter came forward, and threw a golden apple to the knights, but none of them caught it but he, only as soon as he had it he galloped away.

On the second day Iron Hans equipped him as a white knight, and gave him a white horse. Again he was the only one who caught the apple, and he did not linger an instant, but galloped off with it. The king grew angry, and said: 'That is not allowed; he must appear before me and tell his name.' He gave the order that if the knight who caught the apple, should go away again they should pursue him, and if he would not come back willingly, they were to cut him down and stab him.

On the third day, he received from Iron Hans a suit of black armour and a black horse, and again he caught the apple. But when he was riding off with it, the king's attendants pursued him, and one of them got so near him that he wounded the youth's leg with the point of his sword. The youth nevertheless escaped from them, but his horse leapt so violently that the helmet fell from the youth's head, and they could see that he had golden hair. They rode back and announced this to the king.

The following day the king's daughter asked the gardener about his boy. 'He is at work in the garden; the queer creature has been at the festival too, and only came home yesterday evening; he has likewise shown my children three golden apples which he has won.'

The king had him summoned into his presence, and he came and again had his little cap on his head. But the king's daughter went up to him and took it off, and then his golden hair fell down over his shoulders, and he was so handsome that all were amazed. 'Are you the knight who came every day to the festival, always in different colours, and who caught the three golden apples?' asked the king. 'Yes,' answered he, 'and here the apples are,' and he took them out of his pocket, and returned them to the king. 'If you desire further proof, you may see the wound which your people gave me when they followed me. But I am likewise the knight who helped you to your victory over your enemies.' 'If you can perform such deeds as that, you are no gardener's boy; tell me, who is your father?' 'My father is a mighty king, and gold have I in plenty as great as I require.' 'I well see,' said the king, 'that I owe my thanks to you; can I do anything to please you?' 'Yes,' answered he, 'that indeed you can. Give me your daughter to wife.' The maiden laughed, and said: 'He does not stand much on ceremony, but I have already seen by his golden hair that he was no gardener's boy,' and then she went and kissed him. His father and mother came to the wedding, and were in great delight, for they had given up all hope of ever seeing their dear son again. And as they were sitting at the marriage-feast, the music suddenly stopped, the doors opened, and a stately king came in with a great retinue. He went up to the youth, embraced him and said: 'I am Iron Hans, and was by enchantment a wild man, but you have set me free; all the treasures which I possess, shall be your property.'

CLEVER ELSIE

There was once a man who had a daughter who was called Clever Elsie. And when she had grown up her father said: 'We will get her married.' 'Yes,' said the mother, 'if only someone would come who would have her.' At length a man came from a distance and wooed her, who was called Hans; but he stipulated that Clever Elsie should be really smart. 'Oh,' said the father, 'she has plenty of good sense'; and the mother said: 'Oh, she can see the wind coming up the street, and hear the flies coughing.' 'Well,' said Hans, 'if she is not really smart, I won't have her.' When they were sitting at dinner and had eaten, the mother said: 'Elsie, go into the cellar and fetch some beer.' Then Clever Elsie took the pitcher from the wall, went into the cellar, and tapped the lid briskly as she went, so that the time might not appear long. When she was below she fetched herself a chair, and set it before the barrel so that she had no need to stoop, and did not hurt her back or do herself any unexpected injury. Then she placed the can before her, and turned the tap, and while the beer was running she would not let her eyes be idle, but looked up at the wall, and after much peering here and there, saw a pick-axe exactly above her, which the masons had accidentally left there.

Then Clever Elsie began to weep and said: 'If I get Hans, and we have a child, and he grows big, and we send him into the cellar here to draw beer, then the pick-axe will fall on his head and kill him.' Then she sat and wept and screamed with all the strength of her body, over the misfortune which lay before her. Those upstairs waited for the drink, but Clever Elsie still did not come. Then the woman said to the servant: 'Just go down into the cellar and see where Elsie is.' The maid went and found her sitting in front of the barrel, screaming loudly. 'Elsie why do you weep?' asked the maid. 'Ah,' she answered, 'have I not reason to weep? If I get Hans, and we have a child, and he grows big, and has to draw beer here, the pick-axe will perhaps fall on his head, and kill him.' Then said the maid: 'What a clever Elsie we have!' and sat down beside her and began loudly to weep over the misfortune. After a while, as the maid did not come back, and those upstairs were thirsty for the beer, the man said to the boy: 'Just go down into the cellar and see where Elsie and the girl are.' The boy went down, and there sat Clever Elsie and the girl both weeping together. Then he asked: 'Why are you weeping?' 'Ah,' said Elsie, 'have I not reason to weep? If I get Hans, and we have a child, and he grows big, and has to draw beer here, the pick-axe will fall on his head and kill him.' Then said the boy: 'What a clever Elsie we have!' and sat down by her, and likewise began to howl loudly. Upstairs they waited for the boy, but as he still did not return, the man said to the woman: 'Just go down into the cellar and see where Elsie is!' The woman went down, and found all three in the midst of their lamentations, and inquired what was the cause; then Elsie told her also that her future child was to be killed by the pick-axe, when it grew big and had to draw beer, and the pick-axe fell down. Then said the mother likewise: 'What a clever Elsie we have!' and sat down and wept with them. The man upstairs waited a short time, but as his wife did not come back and his thirst grew ever greater, he said: 'I must go into the cellar myself and see where Elsie is.' But when he got into the cellar, and they were all sitting together crying, and he heard the reason, and that Elsie's child was the cause, and the Elsie might perhaps bring one into the world some day, and that he might be killed by the pick-axe, if he should happen to be sitting beneath it, drawing beer just at the very time when it fell down, he cried: 'Oh, what a clever Elsie!' and sat down, and likewise wept with them. The bridegroom stayed upstairs alone for a long time; then as no one would come back he thought: 'They must be waiting for me below: I too must go there and see what they are about.' When he got down, the five of them were sitting screaming and lamenting quite piteously, each out-doing the other. 'What misfortune has happened then?' asked he. 'Ah, dear Hans,' said Elsie, 'if we marry each other and have a child, and he is big, and we perhaps send him here to draw something to drink, then the pick-axe which has been left up there might dash his brains out if it were to fall down, so have we not reason to weep?' 'Come,' said Hans, 'more understanding than that is not needed for my household, as you are such a clever Elsie, I will have you,' and seized her hand, took her upstairs with him, and married her.

After Hans had had her some time, he said: 'Wife, I am going out to work and earn some money for us; go into the field and cut the corn that we may have some bread.' 'Yes, dear Hans, I will do that.' After Hans had gone away, she cooked herself some good broth and took it into the field with her. When she came to the field she said to herself: 'What shall I do; shall I cut first, or shall I eat first? Oh, I will eat first.' Then she drank her cup of broth and when she was fully satisfied, she once more said: 'What shall I do? Shall I cut first, or shall I sleep first? I will sleep first.' Then she lay down among the corn and fell asleep. Hans had been at home for a long time, but Elsie did not come; then said he: 'What a clever Elsie I have; she is so industrious that she does not even come home to eat.' But when evening came and she still stayed away, Hans went out to see what she had cut, but nothing was cut, and she was lying among the corn asleep. Then Hans hastened home and brought a fowler's net with little bells and hung it round about her, and she still went on sleeping. Then he ran home, shut the house-door, and sat down in his chair and worked. At length, when it was quite dark, Clever Elsie awoke and when she got up there was a jingling all round about her, and the bells rang at each step which she took. Then she was alarmed, and became uncertain whether she really was Clever Elsie or not, and said: 'Is it I, or is it not I?' But she knew not what answer to make to this, and stood for a time in doubt; at length she thought: 'I will go home and ask if it be I, or if it be not I, they will be sure to know.' She ran to the door of her own house, but it was shut; then she knocked at the window and cried: 'Hans, is Elsie within?' 'Yes,' answered Hans, 'she is within.' Hereupon she was terrified, and said: 'Ah, heavens! Then it is not I,' and went to another door; but when the people heard the jingling of the bells they would not open it, and she could get in nowhere. Then she ran out of the village, and no one has seen her since.

THE BREMEN TOWN MUSICIANS

A CERTAIN man had a donkey, which had carried the corn-sacks to the mill indefatigably for many a long year; but his strength was going, and he was growing more and more unfit for work. Then his master began to consider how he might best save his keep; but the donkey, seeing that no good wind was blowing, ran away and set out on the road to Bremen. "There," he thought, "I can surely be town-musician." When he had walked some distance, he found a hound lying on the road, gasping like one who had run till he was tired. "What are you gasping so for, you big fellow?" asked the donkey.

"Ah," replied the hound, "as I am old, and daily grow weaker, and no longer can hunt, my master wanted to kill me, so I took to flight; but now how am I to earn my bread?"

"I tell you what," said the donkey, "I am going to Bremen, and shall be town-musician there; go with me and engage yourself also as a musician. I will play the lute, and you shall beat the kettledrum."

The hound agreed, and on they went.

Before long they came to a cat, sitting on the path, with a face like three rainy days! "Now then, old shaver, what has gone askew with you?" asked the donkey.

"Who can be merry when his neck is in danger?" answered the cat. "Because I am now getting old, and my teeth are worn to stumps, and I prefer to sit by the fire and spin, rather than hunt about after mice, my mistress wanted to drown me, so I ran away. But now good advice is scarce. Where am I to go?"

"Go with us to Bremen. You understand night-music, you can be a town-musician."

The cat thought well of it, and went with them. After this the three fugitives came to a farm-yard, where the cock was sitting upon the gate, crowing with all his might. "Your crow goes through and through one," said the donkey. "What is the matter?"

"I have been foretelling fine weather, because it is the day on which Our Lady washes the Christ-child's little shirts, and wants to dry them," said the cock; "but guests are coming for Sunday, so the housewife has no pity, and has told the cook that she intends to eat me in the soup to-morrow, and this evening I am to have my head cut off. Now I am crowing at full pitch while I can."

"Ah, but red-comb," said the donkey, "you had better come away with us. We are going to Bremen; you can find something better than death everywhere: you have a good voice, and if we make music together it must have some quality!"

The cock agreed to this plan, and all four went on together. They could not, however, reach the city of Bremen in one day, and in the evening they came to a forest where they meant to pass the night. The donkey and the hound laid themselves down under a large tree, the cat and the cock settled themselves in the branches; but the cock flew right to the top, where he was most safe. Before he went to sleep he looked round on all four sides, and thought he saw in the distance a little spark burning; so he called out to his companions that there must be a house not far off, for he saw a light. The donkey said, "If so, we had better get up and go on, for the shelter here is bad." The hound thought that a few bones with some meat on would do him good too!

So they made their way to the place where the light was, and soon saw it shine brighter and grow larger, until they came to a well-lighted robber's house. The donkey, as the biggest, went to the window and looked in.

"What do you see, my grey-horse?" asked the cock. "What do I see?" answered the donkey; "a table covered with good things to eat and drink, and robbers sitting at it enjoying themselves." "That would be the sort of thing for us," said the cock. "Yes, yes; ah, how I wish we were there!" said the donkey.

Then the animals took counsel together how they should manage to drive away the robbers, and at last they thought of a plan. The donkey was to place himself with his fore-feet upon the window-ledge, the hound was to jump on the donkey's back, the cat was to climb upon the dog, and lastly the cock was to fly up and perch upon the head of the cat.

When this was done, at a given signal, they began to perform their music together: the donkey brayed, the hound barked, the cat mewed, and the cock crowed; then they burst through the window into the room, so that the glass clattered! At this horrible din, the robbers sprang up, thinking no otherwise than that a ghost had come in, and fled in a great fright out into the forest. The four companions now sat down at the table, well content with what was left, and ate as if they were going to fast for a month.

As soon as the four minstrels had done, they put out the light, and each sought for himself a sleeping-place according to his nature and to what suited him. The donkey laid himself down upon some straw in the yard, the hound behind the door, the cat upon the hearth near the warm ashes, and the cock perched himself upon a beam of the roof; and being tired from their long walk, they soon went to sleep.

When it was past midnight, and the robbers saw from afar that the light was no longer burning in their house, and all appeared quiet, the captain said, "We ought not to have let ourselves be frightened out of our wits;" and ordered one of them to go and examine the house.

The messenger finding all still, went into the kitchen to light a candle, and, taking the glistening fiery eyes of the cat for live coals, he held a lucifer-match to them to light it. But the cat did not understand the joke, and flew in his face, spitting and scratching. He was dreadfully frightened, and ran to the back-door, but the dog, who lay there sprang up and bit his leg; and as he ran across the yard by the straw-heap, the donkey gave him a smart kick with its hind foot. The cock, too, who had been awakened by the noise, and had become lively, cried down from the beam, "Cock-a-doodle-doo!"

Then the robber ran back as fast as he could to his captain, and said, "Ah, there is a horrible witch sitting in the house, who spat on me and scratched my face with her long claws; and by the door stands a man with a knife, who stabbed me in the leg; and in the yard there lies a black monster, who beat me with a wooden club; and above, upon the roof, sits the judge, who called out, 'Bring the rogue here to me!' so I got away as well as I could."

After this the robbers did not trust themselves in the house again; but it suited the four musicians of Bremen so well that they did not care to leave it any more. And the mouth of him who last told this story is still warm.

THE SIX SWANS

ONCE upon a time, a certain King was hunting in a great forest, and he chased a wild beast so eagerly that none of his attendants could follow him. When evening drew near he stopped and looked around him, and then he saw that he had lost his way. He sought a way out, but could find none. Then he perceived an aged woman with a head which nodded perpetually, who came towards him, but she was a witch. "Good woman," said he to her, "Can you not show me the way through the forest?" "Oh, yes, Lord King," she answered, "that I certainly can, but on one condition, and if you do not fulfil that, you will never get out of the forest, and will die of hunger in it."

"What kind of condition is it?" asked the King.

"I have a daughter," said the old woman, "who is as beautiful as any one in the world, and well deserves to be your consort, and if you will make her your Queen, I will show you the way out of the forest." In the anguish of his heart the King consented, and the old woman led him to her little hut, where her daughter was sitting by the fire. She received the King as if she had been expecting him, and he saw that she was very beautiful, but still she did not please him, and he could not look at her without secret horror. After he had taken the maiden up on his horse, the old woman showed him the way, and the King reached his royal palace again, where the wedding was celebrated.

The King had already been married once, and had by his first wife, seven children, six boys and a girl, whom he loved better than anything else in the world. As he now feared that the step-mother might not treat them well, and even do them some injury, he took them to a lonely castle which stood in the midst of a forest. It lay so concealed, and the way was so difficult to find that he himself would not have found it, if a wise woman had not given him a ball of yarn with wonderful properties. When he threw it down before him, it unrolled itself and showed him his path. The King, however, went so frequently away to his dear children that the Queen observed his absence; she was curious and wanted to know what he did when he was quite alone in the forest. She gave a great deal of money to his servants, and they betrayed the secret to her, and told her likewise of the ball which alone could point out the way. And now she knew no rest until she had learnt where the King kept the ball of yarn, and then she made little shirts of white silk, and as she had learnt the art of witchcraft from her mother, she sewed a charm inside them. And once when the King had ridden forth to hunt, she took the little shirts and went into the forest, and the ball showed her the way. The children, who saw from a distance that some one was approaching, thought that their dear father was coming to them, and full of joy, ran to meet him. Then she threw one of the little shirts over each of them, and no sooner had the shirts touched their bodies than they were changed into swans, and flew away over the forest. The Queen went home quite delighted, and thought she had got rid of her step-children, but the girl had not run out with her brothers, and the Queen knew nothing about her. Next day the King went to visit his children, but he found no one but the little girl. "Where are thy brothers?' asked the King. "Alas, dear father," she answered, "they have gone away and left me alone!" and she told him that she had seen from her little window how her brothers had flown away over the forest in the shape of swans, and she showed him the feathers, which they had let fall in the courtyard, and which she had picked up. The King mourned, but he did not think that the Queen had done this wicked deed, and as he feared that the girl would also be stolen away from him, he wanted to take her away with him. But she was afraid of her step-mother, and entreated the King to let her stay just this one night more in the forest castle.

The poor girl thought, "I can no longer stay here. I will go and seek my brothers." And when night came, she ran away, and went straight into the forest. She walked the whole night long, and next day also without stopping, until she could go no farther for weariness. Then she saw a forest-hut, and went into it, and found a room with six little beds, but she did not venture to get into one of them, but crept under one, and lay down on the hard ground, intending to pass the night there. Just before sunset, however, she heard a rustling, and saw six swans come flying in at the window. They alighted on the ground and blew at each other, and blew all the feathers off, and their swan's skins stripped off like a shirt. Then the maiden looked at them and recognized her brothers, was glad and crept forth from beneath the bed. The brothers were not less delighted to see their little sister, but their joy was of short duration. "Here canst thou not abide," they said to her. "This is a shelter for robbers, if they come home and find thee, they will kill thee." "But can you not protect me?" asked the little sister. "No," they replied, "only for one quarter of an hour each evening can we lay aside our swan's skins and have during that time our human form;

after that, we are once more turned into swans." The little sister wept and said, "Can you not be set free?" "Alas, no," they answered, "the conditions are too hard! For six years thou mayst neither speak nor laugh, and in that time thou must sew together six little shirts of starwort for us. And if one single word falls from thy lips, all thy work will be lost." And when the brothers had said this, the quarter of an hour was over, and they flew out of the window again as swans.

The maiden, however, firmly resolved to deliver her brothers, even if it should cost her her life. She left the hut, went into the midst of the forest, seated herself on a tree, and there passed the night. Next morning she went out and gathered starwort and began to sew. She could not speak to any one, and she had no inclination to laugh; she sat there and looked at nothing but her work. When she had already spent a long time there it came to pass that the King of the country was hunting in the forest, and his huntsmen came to the tree on which the maiden was sitting. They called to her and said, "Who art thou?" But she made no answer. "Come down to us," said they. "We will not do thee any harm." She only shook her head. As they pressed her further with questions she threw her golden necklace down to them, and thought to content them thus. They, however, did not cease, and then she threw her girdle down to them, and as this also was to no purpose, her garters, and by degrees everything that she had on that she could do without until she had nothing left but her shift. The huntsmen, however, did not let themselves be turned aside by that, but climbed the tree and fetched the maiden down and led her before the King.

The King asked, "Who art thou? What art thou doing on the tree?" But she did not answer. He put the question in every language that he knew, but she remained as mute as a fish. As she was so beautiful, the King's heart was touched, and he was smitten with a great love for her. He put his mantle on her, took her before him on his horse, and carried her to his castle. Then he caused her to be dressed in rich garments, and she shone in her beauty like bright daylight, but no word could be drawn from her. He placed her by his side at table, and her modest bearing and courtesy pleased him so much that he said, "She is the one whom I wish to marry, and no other woman in the world." And after some days he united himself to her.

The King, however, had a wicked mother who was dissatisfied with this marriage and spoke ill of the young Queen. "Who knows," said she, "from whence the creature who can't speak, comes? She is not worthy of a king!" After a year had passed, when the Queen brought her first child into the world, the old woman took it away from her, and smeared her mouth with blood as she slept. Then she went to the King and accused the Queen of being a man-eater. The King would not believe it, and would not suffer any one to do her any injury. She, however, sat continually sewing at the shirts, and cared for nothing else. The next time, when she again bore a beautiful boy, the false step-mother used the same treachery, but the King could not bring himself to give credit to her words. He said, "She is too pious and good to do anything of that kind; if she were not dumb, and could defend herself, her innocence would come to light." But when the old woman stole away the newly-born child for the third time, and accused the Queen, who did not utter one word of defence, the King could do no otherwise than deliver her over to justice, and she was sentenced to suffer death by fire.

When the day came for the sentence to be executed, it was the last day of the six years during which she was not to speak or laugh, and she had delivered her dear brothers from the power of the enchantment. The six shirts were ready, only the left sleeve of the sixth was wanting. When, therefore, she was led to the stake, she laid the shirts on her arm, and when she stood on high and the fire was just going to be lighted, she looked around and six swans came flying through the air towards her. Then she saw that her deliverance was near, and her heart leapt with joy. The swans swept towards her and sank down so that she could throw the shirts over them, and as they were touched by them, their swan's skins fell off, and her brothers stood in their own bodily form before her, and were vigorous and handsome. The youngest only lacked his left arm, and had in the place of it a swan's wing on his shoulder. They embraced and kissed each other, and the Queen went to the King, who was greatly moved, and she began to speak and said, "Dearest husband, now I may speak and declare to thee that I am innocent, and falsely accused." And she told him of the treachery of the old woman who had taken away her three children and hidden them. Then to the great joy of the King they were brought thither, and as a punishment, the wicked step-mother was bound to the stake, and burnt to ashes. But the King and the Queen with their six brothers lived many years in happiness and peace.

The Poor Miller's Boy And The Cat

IN a certain mill lived an old miller who had neither wife nor child, and three apprentices served under him. As they had been with him several years, he one day said to them, "I am old, and want to sit in the chimney-corner, go out, and whichsoever of you brings me the best horse home, to him will I give the mill, and in return for it he shall take care of me till my death."

The third of the boys was, however, the drudge, who was looked on as foolish by the others; they begrudged the mill to him, and afterwards he would not have it.

Then all three went out together, and when they came to the village, the two said to stupid Hans, "Thou mayst just as well stay here, as long as thou livest thou wilt never get a horse." Hans, however, went with them, and when it was night they came to a cave in which they lay down to sleep. The two sharp ones waited until Hans had fallen asleep, then they got up, and went away leaving him where he was. And they thought they had done a very clever thing, but it was certain to turn out ill for them.

When the sun arose, and Hans woke up, he was lying in a deep cavern. He looked around on every side and exclaimed, "Oh, heavens, where am I?" Then he got up and clambered out of the cave, went into the forest, and thought, "Here I am quite alone and deserted, how shall I obtain a horse now?"

Whilst he was thus walking full of thought, he met a small tabby-cat which said quite kindly, "Hans, where are you going?" "Alas, thou canst not help me." "I well know your desire," said the cat. "You wish to have a beautiful horse. Come with me, and be my faithful servant for seven years long, and then I will give you one more beautiful than any you have ever seen in your whole life." "Well, this is a wonderful cat!" thought Hans, "but I am determined to see if she is telling the truth." So she took him with her into her enchanted castle, where there were nothing but cats who were her servants. They leapt nimbly upstairs and downstairs, and were merry and happy. In the evening when they sat down to dinner, three of them had to make music.

One played the bassoon, the other the fiddle, and the third put the trumpet to his lips, and blew out his cheeks as much as he possibly could. When they had dined, the table was carried away, and the cat said, "Now, Hans, come and dance with me."

"No," said he, "I won't dance with a pussy cat. I have never done that yet."

"Then take him to bed," said she to the cats. So one of them lighted him to his bed-room, one pulled his shoes off, one his stockings, and at last one of them blew out the candle. Next morning they returned and helped him out of bed, one put his stockings on for him, one tied his garters, one brought his shoes, one washed him, and one dried his face with her tail.

"That feels very soft!" said Hans. He, however, had to serve the cat, and chop some wood every day, and to do that, he had an axe of silver, and the wedge and saw were of silver and the mallet of copper. So he chopped the wood small; stayed there in the house and had good meat and drink, but never saw anyone but the tabby-cat and her servants.

Once she said to him, "Go and mow my meadow, and dry the grass," and gave him a scythe of silver, and a whetstone of gold, but bade him deliver them up again carefully. So Hans went thither, and did what he was bidden, and when he had finished the work, he carried the scythe, whetstone, and hay to the house, and asked if it was not yet time for her to give him his reward.

"No," said the cat, "you must first do something more for me of the same kind. There is timber of silver, carpenter's axe, square, and everything that is needful, all of silver, with these build me a small house." Then Hans built the small house, and said that he had now done everything, and still he had no horse. Nevertheless the seven years had gone by with him as if they were six months. The cat asked him if he would like to see her horses? "Yes," said Hans. Then she opened the door of the small house, and when she had opened it, there stood twelve horses, such horses, so bright and shining, that his heart rejoiced at the sight of them.

And now she gave him to eat and drink, and said, "Go home, I will not give thee thy horse away with thee; but in three days' time I will follow thee and bring it."

So Hans set out, and she showed him the way to the mill. She had, however, never once given him a new coat, and he had been obliged to keep on his dirty old smock-frock, which he had brought with him, and which during the seven years had everywhere become too small for him.

When he reached home, the two other apprentices were there again as well, and each of them certainly had brought a horse with him, but one of them was a blind one, and the other lame. They asked Hans where his horse was. "It will follow me in three days' time." Then they laughed and said, "Indeed, stupid Hans, where wilt thou get a horse?" "It will be a fine one!"

Hans went into the parlour, but the miller said he should not sit down to table, for he was so ragged and torn, that they would all be ashamed of him if any one came in. So they gave him a mouthful of food outside, and at night, when they went to rest, the two others would not let him have a bed, and at last he was forced to creep into the goose-house, and lie down on a little hard straw. In the morning when he awoke, the three days had passed, and a coach came with six horses and they shone so bright that it was delightful to see them! and a servant brought a seventh as well, which was for the poor miller's boy. And a magnificent princess alighted from the coach and went into the mill, and this princess was the little tabby-cat whom poor Hans had served for seven years.

She asked the miller where the miller's boy and drudge was? Then the miller said, "We cannot have him here in the mill, for he is so ragged; he is lying in the goose-house." Then the King's daughter said that they were to bring him immediately. So they brought him out, and he had to hold his little smock-frock together to cover himself. The servants unpacked splendid garments, and washed him and dressed him, and when that was done, no King could have looked more handsome. Then the maiden desired to see the horses which the other apprentices had brought home with them, and one of them was blind and the other lame. So she ordered the servant to bring the seventh horse, and when the miller saw it, he said that such a horse as that had never yet entered his yard.

"And that is for the third miller's boy," said she.

"Then he must have the mill," said the miller, but the King's daughter said that the horse was there, and that he was to keep his mill as well, and took her faithful Hans and set him in the coach, and drove away with him. They first drove to the little house which he had built with the silver tools, and behold it was a great castle, and everything inside it was of silver and gold; and then she married him, and he was rich, so rich that he had enough for all the rest of his life. After this, let no one ever say that anyone who is silly can never become a person of importance.

Little Red-Cap [Little Red Riding Hood]

Once upon a time there was a dear little girl who was loved by everyone who looked at her, but most of all by her grandmother, and there was nothing that she would not have given to the child. Once she gave her a little cap of red velvet, which suited her so well that she would never wear anything else; so she was always called 'Little Red-Cap.'

One day her mother said to her: 'Come, Little Red-Cap, here is a piece of cake and a bottle of wine; take them to your grandmother, she is ill and weak, and they will do her good. Set out before it gets hot, and when you are going, walk nicely and quietly and do not run off the path, or you may fall and break the bottle, and then your grandmother will get nothing; and when you go into her room, don't forget to say, "Good morning", and don't peep into every corner before you do it.'

'I will take great care,' said Little Red-Cap to her mother, and gave her hand on it.

The grandmother lived out in the wood, half a league from the village, and just as Little Red-Cap entered the wood, a wolf met her. Red-Cap did not know what a wicked creature he was, and was not at all afraid of him.

'Good day, Little Red-Cap,' said he.

'Thank you kindly, wolf.'

'Whither away so early, Little Red-Cap?'

'To my grandmother's.'

'What have you got in your apron?'

'Cake and wine; yesterday was baking-day, so poor sick grandmother is to have something good, to make her stronger.'

'Where does your grandmother live, Little Red-Cap?'

'A good quarter of a league farther on in the wood; her house stands under the three large oak-trees, the nut-trees are just below; you surely must know it,' replied Little Red-Cap.

The wolf thought to himself: 'What a tender young creature! what a nice plump mouthful—she will be better to eat than the old woman. I must act craftily, so as to catch both.' So he walked for a short time by the side of Little Red-Cap, and then he said: 'See, Little Red-Cap, how pretty the flowers are about here—why do you not look round? I believe, too, that you do not hear how sweetly the little birds are singing; you walk gravely along as if you were going to school, while everything else out here in the wood is merry.'

Little Red-Cap raised her eyes, and when she saw the sunbeams dancing here and there through the trees, and pretty flowers growing everywhere, she thought: 'Suppose I take grandmother a fresh nosegay; that would please her too. It is so early in the day that I shall still get there in good time'; and so she ran from the path into the wood to look for flowers. And whenever she had picked one, she fancied that she saw a still prettier one farther on, and ran after it, and so got deeper and deeper into the wood.

Meanwhile the wolf ran straight to the grandmother's house and knocked at the door.

'Who is there?'

'Little Red-Cap,' replied the wolf. 'She is bringing cake and wine; open the door.'

'Lift the latch,' called out the grandmother, 'I am too weak, and cannot get up.'

The wolf lifted the latch, the door sprang open, and without saying a word he went straight to the grandmother's bed, and devoured her. Then he put on her clothes, dressed himself in her cap laid himself in bed and drew the curtains.

Little Red-Cap, however, had been running about picking flowers, and when she had gathered so many that she could carry no more, she remembered her grandmother, and set out on the way to her.

She was surprised to find the cottage-door standing open, and when she went into the room, she had such a strange feeling that she said to herself: 'Oh dear! how uneasy I feel today, and at other times I like being with grandmother so much.' She called out: 'Good morning,' but received no answer; so she went to the bed and drew back the curtains. There lay her grandmother with her cap pulled far over her face, and looking very strange.

'Oh! grandmother,' she said, 'what big ears you have!'

'The better to hear you with, my child,' was the reply.

'But, grandmother, what big eyes you have!' she said.

'The better to see you with, my dear.'

'But, grandmother, what large hands you have!'

'The better to hug you with.'

'Oh! but, grandmother, what a terrible big mouth you have!'

'The better to eat you with!'

And scarcely had the wolf said this, than with one bound he was out of bed and swallowed up Red-Cap.

When the wolf had appeased his appetite, he lay down again in the bed, fell asleep and began to snore very loud. The huntsman was just passing the house, and thought to himself: 'How the old woman is snoring! I must just see if she wants anything.' So he went into the room, and when he came to the bed, he saw that the wolf was lying in it. 'Do I find you here, you old sinner!' said he. 'I have long sought you!' Then just as he was going to fire at him, it occurred to him that the wolf might have devoured the grandmother, and that she might still be saved, so he did not fire, but took a pair of scissors, and began to cut open the stomach of the sleeping wolf. When he had made two snips, he saw the little Red-Cap shining, and then he made two snips more, and the little girl sprang out, crying: 'Ah, how frightened I have been! How dark it was inside the wolf'; and after that the aged grandmother came out alive also, but scarcely able to breathe. Red-Cap, however, quickly fetched great stones with which they filled the wolf's belly, and when he awoke, he wanted to run away, but the stones were so heavy that he collapsed at once, and fell dead.

Then all three were delighted. The huntsman drew off the wolf's skin and went home with it; the grandmother ate the cake and drank the wine which Red-Cap had brought, and revived, but Red-Cap thought to herself: 'As long as I live, I will never by myself leave the path, to run into the wood, when my mother has forbidden me to do so.'

It also related that once when Red-Cap was again taking cakes to the old grandmother, another wolf spoke to her, and tried to entice her from the path. Red-Cap, however, was on her guard, and went straight forward on her way, and told her grandmother that she had met the wolf, and that he had said 'good morning' to her, but with such a wicked look in his eyes, that if they had not been on the public road she was certain he would have eaten her up. 'Well,' said the grandmother, 'we will shut the door, that he may not come in.'

Soon afterwards the wolf knocked, and cried: 'Open the door, grandmother, I am Little Red-Cap, and am bringing you some cakes.' But they did not speak, or open the door, so the grey-beard stole twice or thrice round the house, and at last jumped on the roof, intending to wait until Red-Cap went home in the evening, and then to steal after her and devour her in the darkness. But the grandmother saw what was in his thoughts.

In front of the house was a great stone trough, so she said to the child: 'Take the pail, Red-Cap; I made some sausages yesterday, so carry the water in which I boiled them to the trough.' Red-Cap carried until the great trough was quite full. Then the smell of the sausages reached the wolf, and he sniffed and peeped down, and at last stretched out his neck so far that he could no longer keep his footing and began to slip, and slipped down from the roof straight into the great trough, and was drowned. But Red-Cap went joyously home, and no one ever did anything to harm her again.

King Grisly-Beard

A great king of a land far away in the East had a daughter who was very beautiful, but so proud, and haughty, and conceited, that none of the princes who came to ask her in marriage was good enough for her, and she only made sport of them.

Once upon a time the king held a great feast, and asked thither all her suitors; and they all sat in a row, ranged according to their rank—kings, and princes, and dukes, and earls, and counts, and barons, and knights. Then the princess came in, and as she passed by them she had something spiteful to say to every one. The first was too fat: 'He's as round as a tub,' said she. The next was too tall: 'What a maypole!' said she. The next was too short: 'What a dumpling!' said she. The fourth was too pale, and she called him 'Wallface.' The fifth was too red, so she called him 'Coxcomb.' The sixth was not straight enough; so she said he was like a green stick, that had been laid to dry over a baker's oven. And thus she had some joke to crack upon every one: but she laughed more than all at a good king who was there. 'Look at him,' said she; 'his beard is like an old mop; he shall be called Grisly-beard.' So the king got the nickname of Grisly-beard.

But the old king was very angry when he saw how his daughter behaved, and how she ill-treated all his guests; and he vowed that, willing or unwilling, she should marry the first man, be he prince or beggar, that came to the door.

Two days after there came by a travelling fiddler, who began to play under the window and beg alms; and when the king heard him, he said, 'Let him come in.' So they brought in a dirty-looking fellow; and when he had sung before the king and the princess, he begged a boon. Then the king said, 'You have sung so well, that I will give you my daughter for your wife.' The princess begged and prayed; but the king said, 'I have sworn to give you to the first comer, and I will keep my word.' So words and tears were of no avail; the parson was sent for, and she was married to the fiddler. When this was over the king said, 'Now get ready to go—you must not stay here—you must travel on with your husband.'

Then the fiddler went his way, and took her with him, and they soon came to a great wood. 'Pray,' said she, 'whose is this wood?' 'It belongs to King Grisly-beard,' answered he; 'hadst thou taken him, all had been thine.' 'Ah! unlucky wretch that I am!' sighed she; 'would that I had married King Grisly-beard!' Next they came to some fine meadows. 'Whose are these beautiful green meadows?' said she. 'They belong to King Grisly-beard, hadst thou taken him, they had all been thine.' 'Ah! unlucky wretch that I am!' said she; 'would that I had married King Grisly-beard!'

Then they came to a great city. 'Whose is this noble city?' said she. 'It belongs to King Grisly-beard; hadst thou taken him, it had all been thine.' 'Ah! wretch that I am!' sighed she; 'why did I not marry King Grisly-beard?' 'That is no business of mine,' said the fiddler: 'why should you wish for another husband? Am not I good enough for you?'

At last they came to a small cottage. 'What a paltry place!' said she; 'to whom does that little dirty hole belong?' Then the fiddler said, 'That is your and my house, where we are to live.' 'Where are your servants?' cried she. 'What do we want with servants?' said he; 'you must do for yourself whatever is to be done. Now make the fire, and put on water and cook my supper, for I am very tired.' But the princess knew nothing of making fires and cooking, and the fiddler was forced to help her. When they had eaten a very scanty meal they went to bed; but the fiddler called her up very early in the morning to clean the house. Thus they lived for two days: and when they had eaten up all there was in the cottage, the man said, 'Wife, we can't go on thus, spending money and earning nothing. You must learn to weave baskets.' Then he went out and cut willows, and brought them home, and she began to weave; but it made her fingers very sore. 'I see this work won't do,' said he: 'try and spin; perhaps you will do that better.' So she sat down and tried to spin; but the threads cut her tender fingers till the blood ran. 'See now,' said the fiddler, 'you are good for nothing; you can do no work: what a bargain I have got! However, I'll try and set up a trade in pots and pans, and you shall stand in the market and sell them.' 'Alas!' sighed she, 'if any of my father's court should pass by and see me standing in the market, how they will laugh at me!'

But her husband did not care for that, and said she must work, if she did not wish to die of hunger. At first the trade went well; for many people, seeing such a beautiful woman, went to buy her wares, and paid their money without thinking of taking away the goods. They lived on this as long as it lasted; and then her husband bought a fresh lot of ware, and she sat herself down with it in the corner of the market; but a drunken soldier soon came by, and rode his horse against her stall, and broke all her goods into a thousand pieces. Then she began to cry, and knew not what to do. 'Ah! what will become of me?' said she; 'what will my husband say?' So she ran home and told him all. 'Who would have thought you would have been so silly,' said he, 'as to put an earthenware stall in the corner of the market, where everybody passes? but let us have no more crying; I see you are not fit for this sort of work, so I have been to the king's palace, and asked if they did not want a kitchen-maid; and they say they will take you, and there you will have plenty to eat.'

Thus the princess became a kitchen-maid, and helped the cook to do all the dirtiest work; but she was allowed to carry home some of the meat that was left, and on this they lived.

She had not been there long before she heard that the king's eldest son was passing by, going to be married; and she went to one of the windows and looked out. Everything was ready, and all the pomp and brightness of the court was there. Then she bitterly grieved for the pride and folly which had brought her so low. And the servants gave her some of the rich meats, which she put into her basket to take home.

All on a sudden, as she was going out, in came the king's son in golden clothes; and when he saw a beautiful woman at the door, he took her by the hand, and said she should be his partner in the dance; but she trembled for fear, for she saw that it was King Grisly-beard, who was making sport of her. However, he kept fast hold, and led her in; and the cover of the basket came off, so that the meats in it fell about. Then everybody laughed and jeered at her; and she was so abashed, that she wished herself a thousand feet deep in the earth. She sprang to the door to run away; but on the steps King Grisly-beard overtook her, and brought her back and said, 'Fear me not! I am the fiddler who has lived with you in the hut. I brought you there because I really loved you. I am also the soldier that overset your stall. I have done all this only to cure you of your silly pride, and to show you the folly of your ill-treatment of me. Now all is over: you have learnt wisdom, and it is time to hold our marriage feast.'

Then the chamberlains came and brought her the most beautiful robes; and her father and his whole court were there already, and welcomed her home on her marriage. Joy was in every face and every heart. The feast was grand; they danced and sang; all were merry; and I only wish that you and I had been of the party.

THE GOLD-CHILDREN

THERE was once a poor man and a poor woman who had nothing but a little cottage, and who earned their bread by fishing, and always lived from hand to mouth. But it came to pass one day when the man was sitting by the water-side, and casting his net, that he drew out a fish entirely of gold. As he was looking at the fish, full of astonishment, it began to speak and said, "Hark you, fisherman, if you will throw me back again into the water, I will change your little hut into a splendid castle." Then the fisherman answered, "Of what use is a castle to me, if I have nothing to eat?" The gold fish continued, "That shall be taken care of, there will be a cupboard in the castle in which, when you open it, shall be dishes of the most delicate meats, and as many of them as you can desire." "If that be true," said the man, "then I can well do you a favour." "Yes," said the fish, "there is, however, the condition that you shall disclose to no one in the world, whosoever he may be, whence your good luck has come, if you speak but one single word, all will be over." Then the man threw the wonderful fish back again into the water, and went home. But where his hovel had formerly stood, now stood a great castle. He opened wide his eyes, entered, and saw his wife dressed in beautiful clothes, sitting in a splendid room, and she was quite delighted, and said, "Husband, how has all this come to pass? It suits me very well." "Yes," said the man, "it suits me too, but I am frightfully hungry, just give me something to eat." Said the wife, "But I have got nothing and don't know where to find anything in this new house." "There is no need of your knowing," said the man, "for I see yonder a great cupboard, just unlock it." When she opened it, there stood cakes, meat, fruit, wine, quite a bright prospect.

Then the woman cried joyfully, "What more can you want, my dear?" and they sat down, and ate and drank together. When they had had enough, the woman said, "But husband, whence come all these riches?" "Alas," answered he, "do not question me about it, for I dare not tell you anything; if I disclose it to any one, then all our good fortune will fly." "Very good," said she, "if I am not to know anything, then I do not want to know anything." However, she was not in earnest; she never rested day or night, and she goaded her husband until in his impatience he revealed that all was owing to a wonderful golden fish which he had caught, and to which in return he had given its liberty. And as soon as the secret was out, the splendid castle with the cupboard immediately disappeared, they were once more in the old fisherman's hut, and the man was obliged to follow his former trade and fish. But fortune would so have it, that he once more drew out the golden fish. "Listen," said the fish, "if you will throw me back into the water again, I will once more give you the castle with the cupboard full of roast and boiled meats; only be firm, for your life's sake don't reveal from whom you have it, or you will lose it all again!" "I will take good care," answered the fisherman, and threw the fish back into the water. Now at home everything was once more in its former magnificence, and the wife was overjoyed at their good fortune, but curiosity left her no peace, so that after a couple of days she began to ask again how it had come to pass, and how he had managed to secure it. The man kept silence for a short time, but at last she made him so angry that he broke out, and betrayed the secret. In an instant the castle disappeared, and they were back again in their old hut. "Now you have got what you want," said he; "and we can gnaw at a bare bone again." "Ah," said the woman, "I had rather not have riches if I am not to know from whom they come, for then I have no peace."

The man went back to fish, and after a while he chanced to draw out the gold fish for a third time. "Listen," said the fish, "I see very well that I am fated to fall into your hands, take me home and cut me into six pieces; give your wife two of them to eat, two to your horse and bury two of them in the ground, then they will bring you a blessing." The fisherman took the fish home with him, and did as it had bidden him. It came to pass, however, that from the two pieces that were buried in the ground two golden lilies sprang up, that the horse had two golden foals, and the fisherman's wife bore two children who were made entirely of gold. The children grew up, became tall and handsome, and the lilies and horses grew likewise. Then they said, "Father, we want to mount our golden steeds and travel out in the world." But he answered sorrowfully, "How shall I bear it if you go away, and I know not how it fares with you?" Then they said, "The two golden lilies remain here. By them you can see how it is with us; if they are fresh, then we are in health; if they are withered, we are ill; if they perish, then we are dead." So they rode forth and came to an inn, in which were many people, and when they perceived the gold-children they began to laugh, and jeer. When one of them heard the mocking he felt ashamed and would not go out into the world, but turned back and went home again to his father. But the other rode forward and reached a great forest. As he was about to enter it, the people said, It is not safe for you to ride through, the wood is full of robbers who would treat you badly. You will fare ill, and when they see that you are all of gold, and your horse likewise, they will assuredly kill you.'

But he would not allow himself to be frightened, and said, "I must and will ride through it." Then he took bear-skins and covered himself and his horse with them, so that the gold was no more to be seen, and rode fearlessly into the forest. When he had ridden onward a little he heard a rustling in the bushes, and heard voices speaking together. From one side came cries of, "There is one," but from the other, "Let him go, 'tis an idle fellow, as poor and bare as a church-mouse, what should we gain from him?"

So the gold-child rode joyfully through the forest, and no evil befell him. One day he entered a village wherein he saw a maiden, who was so beautiful that he did not believe that any more beautiful than she existed in the world. And as such a mighty love took possession of him, he went up to her and said, "I love thee with my whole heart, wilt thou be my wife?" He, too, pleased the maiden so much that she agreed and said, "Yes, I will be thy wife, and be true to thee my whole life long." Then they were married, and just as they were in the greatest happiness, home came the father of the bride, and when he saw that his daughter's wedding was being celebrated, he was astonished, and said, "Where is the bridegroom?" They showed him the gold-child, who, however, still wore his bear-skins. Then the father said wrathfully, "A vagabond shall never have my daughter!" and was about to kill him. Then the bride begged as hard as she could, and said, "He is my husband, and I love him with all my heart!" until at last he allowed himself to be appeased. Nevertheless the idea never left his thoughts, so that next morning he rose early, wishing to see whether his daughter's husband was a common ragged beggar. But when he peeped in, he saw a magnificent golden man in the bed, and the cast-off bear-skins lying on the ground. Then he went back and thought, "What a good thing it was that I restrained my anger! I should have committed a great crime." But the gold-child dreamed that he rode out to hunt a splendid stag, and when he awoke in the morning, he said to his wife, "I must go out hunting." She was uneasy, and begged him to stay there, and said, "You might easily meet with a great misfortune," but he answered, "I must and will go."

Thereupon he got up, and rode forth into the forest, and it was not long before a fine stag crossed his path exactly according to his dream. He aimed and was about to shoot it, when the stag ran away.

He gave chase over hedges and ditches for the whole day without feeling tired, but in the evening the stag vanished from his sight, and when the gold-child looked round him, he was standing before a little house, wherein was a witch.

He knocked, and a little old woman came out and asked, "What are you doing so late in the midst of the great forest?" "Have you not seen a stag?" "Yes," answered she, "I know the stag well," and thereupon a little dog which had come out of the house with her, barked at the man violently. "Wilt thou be silent, thou odious toad," said he, "or I will shoot thee dead." Then the witch cried out in a passion, "What! will you slay my little dog?" and immediately transformed him, so that he lay like a stone, and his bride awaited him in vain and thought, "That which I so greatly dreaded, which lay so heavily on my heart, has come upon him!"

But at home the other brother was standing by the gold-lilies, when one of them suddenly drooped. "Good heavens!" said he, "my brother has met with some great misfortune! I must away to see if I can possibly rescue him." Then the father said, "Stay here, if I lose you also, what shall I do?" But he answered, "I must and will go forth!"

Then he mounted his golden horse, and rode forth and entered the great forest, where his brother lay turned to stone. The old witch came out of her house and called him, wishing to entrap him also, but he did not go near her, and said, "I will shoot you, if you will not bring my brother to life again." She touched the stone, though very unwillingly, with her forefinger, and he was immediately restored to his human shape. But the two gold-children rejoiced when they saw each other again, kissed and caressed each other, and rode away together out of the forest, the one home to his bride, and the other to his father. The father then said, "I knew well that you had rescued your brother, for the golden lily suddenly rose up and blossomed out again." Then they lived happily, and all prospered with them until their death.

SNOWDROP

It was the middle of winter, when the broad flakes of snow were falling around, that the queen of a country many thousand miles off sat working at her window. The frame of the window was made of fine black ebony, and as she sat looking out upon the snow, she pricked her finger, and three drops of blood fell upon it. Then she gazed thoughtfully upon the red drops that sprinkled the white snow, and said, 'Would that my little daughter may be as white as that snow, as red as that blood, and as black as this ebony windowframe!' And so the little girl really did grow up; her skin was as white as snow, her cheeks as rosy as the blood, and her hair as black as ebony; and she was called Snowdrop.

But this queen died; and the king soon married another wife, who became queen, and was very beautiful, but so vain that she could not bear to think that anyone could be handsomer than she was. She had a fairy looking-glass, to which she used to go, and then she would gaze upon herself in it, and say:

'Tell me, glass, tell me true!

Of all the ladies in the land,

Who is fairest, tell me, who?'

And the glass had always answered:

'Thou, queen, art the fairest in all the land.'

But Snowdrop grew more and more beautiful; and when she was seven years old she was as bright as the day, and fairer than the queen herself. Then the glass one day answered the queen, when she went to look in it as usual:

'Thou, queen, art fair, and beauteous to see,

But Snowdrop is lovelier far than thee!'

When she heard this she turned pale with rage and envy, and called to one of her servants, and said, 'Take Snowdrop away into the wide wood, that I may never see her any more.' Then the servant led her away; but his heart melted when Snowdrop begged him to spare her life, and he said, 'I will not hurt you, thou pretty child.' So he left her by herself; and though he thought it most likely that the wild beasts would tear her in pieces, he felt as if a great weight were taken off his heart when he had made up his mind not to kill her but to leave her to her fate, with the chance of someone finding and saving her.

Then poor Snowdrop wandered along through the wood in great fear; and the wild beasts roared about her, but none did her any harm. In the evening she came to a cottage among the hills, and went in to rest, for her little feet would carry her no further. Everything was spruce and neat in the cottage: on the table was spread a white cloth, and there were seven little plates, seven little loaves, and seven little glasses with wine in them; and seven knives and forks laid in order; and by the wall stood seven little beds. As she was very hungry, she picked a little piece of each loaf and drank a very little wine out of each glass; and after that she thought she would lie down and rest. So she tried all the little beds; but one was too long, and another was too short, till at last the seventh suited her: and there she laid herself down and went to sleep.

By and by in came the masters of the cottage. Now they were seven little dwarfs, that lived among the mountains, and dug and searched for gold. They lighted up their seven lamps, and saw at once that all was not right. The first said, 'Who has been sitting on my stool?' The second, 'Who has been eating off my plate?' The third, 'Who has been picking my bread?' The fourth, 'Who has been meddling with my spoon?' The fifth, 'Who has been handling my fork?' The sixth, 'Who has been cutting with my knife?' The seventh, 'Who has been drinking my wine?' Then the first looked round and said, 'Who has been lying on my bed?' And the rest came running to him, and everyone cried out that somebody had been upon his bed. But the seventh saw Snowdrop, and called all his brethren to come and see her; and they cried out with wonder and astonishment and brought their lamps to look at her, and said, 'Good heavens! what a lovely child she is!' And they were very glad to see her, and took care not to wake her; and the seventh dwarf slept an hour with each of the other dwarfs in turn, till the night was gone.

In the morning Snowdrop told them all her story; and they pitied her, and said if she would keep all things in order, and cook and wash and knit and spin for them, she might stay where she was, and they would take good care of her. Then they went out all day long to their work, seeking for gold and silver in the mountains: but Snowdrop was left at home; and they warned her, and said, 'The queen will soon find out where you are, so take care and let no one in.'

But the queen, now that she thought Snowdrop was dead, believed that she must be the handsomest lady in the land; and she went to her glass and said:

'Tell me, glass, tell me true!

Of all the ladies in the land,

Who is fairest, tell me, who?'

And the glass answered:

'Thou, queen, art the fairest in all this land:

But over the hills, in the greenwood shade,

Where the seven dwarfs their dwelling have made,

There Snowdrop is hiding her head; and she

Is lovelier far, O queen!
than thee.'

Then the queen was very much frightened; for she knew that the glass always spoke the truth, and was sure that the servant had betrayed her. And she could not bear to think that anyone lived who was more beautiful than she was; so she dressed herself up as an old pedlar, and went her way over the hills, to the place where the dwarfs dwelt. Then she knocked at the door, and cried, 'Fine wares to sell!' Snowdrop looked out at the window, and said, 'Good day, good woman! what have you to sell?' 'Good wares, fine wares,' said she; 'laces and bobbins of all colours.' 'I will let the old lady in; she seems to be a very good sort of body,' thought Snowdrop, as she ran down and unbolted the door. 'Bless me!' said the old woman, 'how badly your stays are laced! Let me lace them up with one of my nice new laces.' Snowdrop did not dream of any mischief; so she stood before the old woman; but she set to work so nimbly, and pulled the lace so tight, that Snowdrop's breath was stopped, and she fell down as if she were dead. 'There's an end to all thy beauty,' said the spiteful queen, and went away home.

In the evening the seven dwarfs came home; and I need not say how grieved they were to see their faithful Snowdrop stretched out upon the ground, as if she was quite dead. However, they lifted her up, and when they found what ailed her, they cut the lace; and in a little time she began to breathe, and very soon came to life again. Then they said, 'The old woman was the queen herself; take care another time, and let no one in when we are away.'

When the queen got home, she went straight to her glass, and spoke to it as before; but to her great grief it still said:

'Thou, queen, art the fairest in all this land:

But over the hills, in the greenwood shade,

Where the seven dwarfs their dwelling have made,

There Snowdrop is hiding her head; and she

Is lovelier far, O queen!
than thee.'

Then the blood ran cold in her heart with spite and malice, to see that Snowdrop still lived; and she dressed herself up again, but in quite another dress from the one she wore before, and took with her a poisoned comb. When she reached the dwarfs' cottage, she knocked at the door, and cried, 'Fine wares to sell!' But Snowdrop said, 'I dare not let anyone in.' Then the queen said, 'Only look at my beautiful combs!' and gave her the poisoned one. And it looked so pretty, that she took it up and put it into her hair to try it; but the moment it touched her head, the poison was so powerful that she fell down senseless. 'There you may lie,' said the queen, and went her way. But by good luck the dwarfs came in very early that evening; and when they saw Snowdrop lying on the ground, they thought what had happened, and soon found the poisoned comb. And when they took it away she got well, and told them all that had passed; and they warned her once more not to open the door to anyone.

Meantime the queen went home to her glass, and shook with rage when she read the very same answer as before; and she said, 'Snowdrop shall die, if it cost me my life.' So she went by herself into her chamber, and got ready a poisoned apple: the outside looked very rosy and tempting, but whoever tasted it was sure to die. Then she dressed herself up as a peasant's wife, and travelled over the hills to the dwarfs' cottage, and knocked at the door; but Snowdrop put her head out of the window and said, 'I dare not let anyone in, for the dwarfs have told me not.' 'Do as you please,' said the old woman, 'but at any rate take this pretty apple; I will give it you.' 'No,' said Snowdrop, 'I dare not take it.' 'You silly girl!' answered the other, 'what are you afraid of? Do you think it is poisoned? Come! do you eat one part, and I will eat the other.' Now the apple was so made up that one side was good, though the other side was poisoned. Then Snowdrop was much tempted to taste, for the apple looked so very nice; and when she saw the old woman eat, she could wait no longer. But she had scarcely put the piece into her mouth, when she fell down dead upon the ground. 'This time nothing will save thee,' said the queen; and she went home to her glass, and at last it said:

'Thou, queen, art the fairest of all the fair.'

And then her wicked heart was glad, and as happy as such a heart could be.

When evening came, and the dwarfs had gone home, they found Snowdrop lying on the ground: no breath came from her lips, and they were afraid that she was quite dead. They lifted her up, and combed her hair, and washed her face with wine and water; but all was in vain, for the little girl seemed quite dead. So they laid her down upon a bier, and all seven watched and bewailed her three whole days; and then they thought they would bury her: but her cheeks were still rosy; and her face looked just as it did while she was alive; so they said, 'We will never bury her in the cold ground.' And they made a coffin of glass, so that they might still look at her, and wrote upon it in golden letters what her name was, and that she was a king's daughter. And the coffin was set among the hills, and one of the dwarfs always sat by it and watched. And the birds of the air came too, and bemoaned Snowdrop; and first of all came an owl, and then a raven, and at last a dove, and sat by her side.

And thus Snowdrop lay for a long, long time, and still only looked as though she was asleep; for she was even now as white as snow, and as red as blood, and as black as ebony. At last a prince came and called at the dwarfs' house; and he saw Snowdrop, and read what was written in golden letters. Then he offered the dwarfs money, and prayed and besought them to let him take her away; but they said, 'We will not part with her for all the gold in the world.' At last, however, they had pity on him, and gave him the coffin; but the moment he lifted it up to carry it home with him, the piece of apple fell from between her lips, and Snowdrop awoke, and said, 'Where am I?' And the prince said, 'Thou art quite safe with me.'

Then he told her all that had happened, and said, 'I love you far better than all the world; so come with me to my father's palace, and you shall be my wife.' And Snowdrop consented, and went home with the prince; and everything was got ready with great pomp and splendour for their wedding.

To the feast was asked, among the rest, Snowdrop's old enemy the queen; and as she was dressing herself in fine rich clothes, she looked in the glass and said:

'Tell me, glass, tell me true!

Of all the ladies in the land,

Who is fairest, tell me, who?'

And the glass answered:

'Thou, lady, art loveliest here, I ween;

But lovelier far is the new-made queen.'

When she heard this she started with rage; but her envy and curiosity were so great, that she could not help setting out to see the bride.

And when she got there, and saw that it was no other than Snowdrop, who, as she thought, had been dead a long while, she choked with rage, and fell down and died: but Snowdrop and the prince lived and reigned happily over that land many, many years; and sometimes they went up into the mountains, and paid a visit to the little dwarfs, who had been so kind to Snowdrop in her time of need.

RUMPELSTILTSKIN

By the side of a wood, in a country a long way off, ran a fine stream of water; and upon the stream there stood a mill. The miller's house was close by, and the miller, you must know, had a very beautiful daughter. She was, moreover, very shrewd and clever; and the miller was so proud of her, that he one day told the king of the land, who used to come and hunt in the wood, that his daughter could spin gold out of straw. Now this king was very fond of money; and when he heard the miller's boast his greediness was raised, and he sent for the girl to be brought before him. Then he led her to a chamber in his palace where there was a great heap of straw, and gave her a spinning-wheel, and said, 'All this must be spun into gold before morning, as you love your life.' It was in vain that the poor maiden said that it was only a silly boast of her father, for that she could do no such thing as spin straw into gold: the chamber door was locked, and she was left alone.

She sat down in one corner of the room, and began to bewail her hard fate; when on a sudden the door opened, and a droll-looking little man hobbled in, and said, 'Good morrow to you, my good lass; what are you weeping for?' 'Alas!' said she, 'I must spin this straw into gold, and I know not how.' 'What will you give me,' said the hobgoblin, 'to do it for you?' 'My necklace,' replied the maiden. He took her at her word, and sat himself down to the wheel, and whistled and sang:

'Round about, round about,

Lo and behold!

Reel away, reel away,

Straw into gold!'

And round about the wheel went merrily; the work was quickly done, and the straw was all spun into gold.

When the king came and saw this, he was greatly astonished and pleased; but his heart grew still more greedy of gain, and he shut up the poor miller's daughter again with a fresh task. Then she knew not what to do, and sat down once more to weep; but the dwarf soon opened the door, and said, 'What will you give me to do your task?' 'The ring on my finger,' said she. So her little friend took the ring, and began to work at the wheel again, and whistled and sang:

'Round about, round about,

Lo and behold!

Reel away, reel away,

Straw into gold!'

till, long before morning, all was done again.

The king was greatly delighted to see all this glittering treasure; but still he had not enough: so he took the miller's daughter to a yet larger heap, and said, 'All this must be spun tonight; and if it is, you shall be my queen.' As soon as she was alone that dwarf came in, and said, 'What will you give me to spin gold for you this third time?' 'I have nothing left,' said she. 'Then say you will give me,' said the little man, 'the first little child that you may have when you are queen.' 'That may never be,' thought the miller's daughter: and as she knew no other way to get her task done, she said she would do what he asked. Round went the wheel again to the old song, and the manikin once more spun the heap into gold. The king came in the morning, and, finding all he wanted, was forced to keep his word; so he married the miller's daughter, and she really became queen.

At the birth of her first little child she was very glad, and forgot the dwarf, and what she had said. But one day he came into her room, where she was sitting playing with her baby, and put her in mind of it. Then she grieved sorely at her misfortune, and said she would give him all the wealth of the kingdom if he would let her off, but in vain; till at last her tears softened him, and he said, 'I will give you three days' grace, and if during that time you tell me my name, you shall keep your child.'

Now the queen lay awake all night, thinking of all the odd names that she had ever heard; and she sent messengers all over the land to find out new ones. The next day the little man came, and she began with TIMOTHY, ICHABOD, BENJAMIN, JEREMIAH, and all the names she could remember; but to all and each of them he said, 'Madam, that is not my name.'

The second day she began with all the comical names she could hear of, BANDY-LEGS, HUNCHBACK, CROOK-SHANKS, and so on; but the little gentleman still said to every one of them, 'Madam, that is not my name.'

The third day one of the messengers came back, and said, 'I have travelled two days without hearing of any other names; but yesterday, as I was climbing a high hill, among the trees of the forest where the fox and the hare bid each other good night, I saw a little hut; and before the hut burnt a fire; and round about the fire a funny little dwarf was dancing upon one leg, and singing:

"Merrily the feast I'll make.

Today I'll brew, tomorrow bake;

Merrily I'll dance and sing,

For next day will a stranger bring.

Little does my lady dream

Rumpelstiltskin is my name!"

When the queen heard this she jumped for joy, and as soon as her little friend came she sat down upon her throne, and called all her court round to enjoy the fun; and the nurse stood by her side with the baby in her arms, as if it was quite ready to be given up. Then the little man began to chuckle at the thought of having the poor child, to take home with him to his hut in the woods; and he cried out, 'Now, lady, what is my name?' 'Is it JOHN?' asked she. 'No, madam!' 'Is it TOM?' 'No, madam!' 'Is it JEMMY?' 'It is not.' 'Can your name be RUMPELSTILTSKIN?' said the lady slyly. 'Some witch told you that!—some witch told you that!' cried the little man, and dashed his right foot in a rage so deep into the floor, that he was forced to lay hold of it with both hands to pull it out.

Then he made the best of his way off, while the nurse laughed and the baby crowed; and all the court jeered at him for having had so much trouble for nothing, and said, 'We wish you a very good morning, and a merry feast, Mr RUMPLESTILTSKIN!'

BRIAR ROSE

A king and queen once upon a time reigned in a country a great way off, where there were in those days fairies. Now this king and queen had plenty of money, and plenty of fine clothes to wear, and plenty of good things to eat and drink, and a coach to ride out in every day: but though they had been married many years they had no children, and this grieved them very much indeed. But one day as the queen was walking by the side of the river, at the bottom of the garden, she saw a poor little fish, that had thrown itself out of the water, and lay gasping and nearly dead on the bank. Then the queen took pity on the little fish, and threw it back again into the river; and before it swam away it lifted its head out of the water and said, 'I know what your wish is, and it shall be fulfilled, in return for your kindness to me—you will soon have a daughter.' What the little fish had foretold soon came to pass; and the queen had a little girl, so very beautiful that the king could not cease looking on it for joy, and said he would hold a great feast and make merry, and show the child to all the land. So he asked his kinsmen, and nobles, and friends, and neighbours. But the queen said, 'I will have the fairies also, that they might be kind and good to our little daughter.' Now there were thirteen fairies in the kingdom; but as the king and queen had only twelve golden dishes for them to eat out of, they were forced to leave one of the fairies without asking her. So twelve fairies came, each with a high red cap on her head, and red shoes with high heels on her feet, and a long white wand in her hand: and after the feast was over they gathered round in a ring and gave all their best gifts to the little princess. One gave her goodness, another beauty, another riches, and so on till she had all that was good in the world.

Just as eleven of them had done blessing her, a great noise was heard in the courtyard, and word was brought that the thirteenth fairy was come, with a black cap on her head, and black shoes on her feet, and a broomstick in her hand: and presently up she came into the dining-hall. Now, as she had not been asked to the feast she was very angry, and scolded the king and queen very much, and set to work to take her revenge. So she cried out, 'The king's daughter shall, in her fifteenth year, be wounded by a spindle, and fall down dead.' Then the twelfth of the friendly fairies, who had not yet given her gift, came forward, and said that the evil wish must be fulfilled, but that she could soften its mischief; so her gift was, that the king's daughter, when the spindle wounded her, should not really die, but should only fall asleep for a hundred years.

However, the king hoped still to save his dear child altogether from the threatened evil; so he ordered that all the spindles in the kingdom should be bought up and burnt. But all the gifts of the first eleven fairies were in the meantime fulfilled; for the princess was so beautiful, and well behaved, and good, and wise, that everyone who knew her loved her.

It happened that, on the very day she was fifteen years old, the king and queen were not at home, and she was left alone in the palace. So she roved about by herself, and looked at all the rooms and chambers, till at last she came to an old tower, to which there was a narrow staircase ending with a little door. In the door there was a golden key, and when she turned it the door sprang open, and there sat an old lady spinning away very busily. 'Why, how now, good mother,' said the princess; 'what are you doing there?' 'Spinning,' said the old lady, and nodded her head, humming a tune, while buzz! went the wheel. 'How prettily that little thing turns round!' said the princess, and took the spindle and began to try and spin. But scarcely had she touched it, before the fairy's prophecy was fulfilled; the spindle wounded her, and she fell down lifeless on the ground.

However, she was not dead, but had only fallen into a deep sleep; and the king and the queen, who had just come home, and all their court, fell asleep too; and the horses slept in the stables, and the dogs in the court, the pigeons on the house-top, and the very flies slept upon the walls. Even the fire on the hearth left off blazing, and went to sleep; the jack stopped, and the spit that was turning about with a goose upon it for the king's dinner stood still; and the cook, who was at that moment pulling the kitchen-boy by the hair to give him a box on the ear for something he had done amiss, let him go, and both fell asleep; the butler, who was slyly tasting the ale, fell asleep with the jug at his lips: and thus everything stood still, and slept soundly.

A large hedge of thorns soon grew round the palace, and every year it became higher and thicker; till at last the old palace was surrounded and hidden, so that not even the roof or the chimneys could be seen. But there went a report through all the land of the beautiful sleeping Briar Rose (for so the king's daughter was called): so that, from time to time, several kings' sons came, and tried to break through the thicket into the palace. This, however, none of them could ever do; for the thorns and bushes laid hold of them, as it were with hands; and there they stuck fast, and died wretchedly.

After many, many years there came a king's son into that land: and an old man told him the story of the thicket of thorns; and how a beautiful palace stood behind it, and how a wonderful princess, called Briar Rose, lay in it asleep, with all her court. He told, too, how he had heard from his grandfather that many, many princes had come, and had tried to break through the thicket, but that they had all stuck fast in it, and died. Then the young prince said, 'All this shall not frighten me; I will go and see this Briar Rose.' The old man tried to hinder him, but he was bent upon going.

Now that very day the hundred years were ended; and as the prince came to the thicket he saw nothing but beautiful flowering shrubs, through which he went with ease, and they shut in after him as thick as ever. Then he came at last to the palace, and there in the court lay the dogs asleep; and the horses were standing in the stables; and on the roof sat the pigeons fast asleep, with their heads under their wings. And when he came into the palace, the flies were sleeping on the walls; the spit was standing still; the butler had the jug of ale at his lips, going to drink a draught; the maid sat with a fowl in her lap ready to be plucked; and the cook in the kitchen was still holding up her hand, as if she was going to beat the boy.

Then he went on still farther, and all was so still that he could hear every breath he drew; till at last he came to the old tower, and opened the door of the little room in which Briar Rose was; and there she lay, fast asleep on a couch by the window. She looked so beautiful that he could not take his eyes off her, so he stooped down and gave her a kiss. But the moment he kissed her she opened her eyes and awoke, and smiled upon him; and they went out together; and soon the king and queen also awoke, and all the court, and gazed on each other with great wonder. And the horses shook themselves, and the dogs jumped up and barked; the pigeons took their heads from under their wings, and looked about and flew into the fields; the flies on the walls buzzed again; the fire in the kitchen blazed up; round went the jack, and round went the spit, with the goose for the king's dinner upon it; the butler finished his draught of ale; the maid went on plucking the fowl; and the cook gave the boy the box on his ear.

And then the prince and Briar Rose were married, and the wedding feast was given; and they lived happily together all their lives long.

The Three Little Men In The Wood

THERE was once a man whose wife died, and a woman whose husband died, and the man had a daughter, and the woman also had a daughter. The girls were acquainted with each other, and went out walking together, and afterwards came to the woman in her house. Then said she to the man's daughter, "Listen, tell thy father that I would like to marry him, and then thou shalt wash thyself in milk every morning, and drink wine, but my own daughter shall wash herself in water and drink water." The girl went home, and told her father what the woman had said. The man said, "What shall I do? Marriage is a joy and also a torment." At length as he could come to no decision, he pulled off his boot, and said, "Take this boot, it has a hole in the sole of it. Go with it up to the loft, hang it on the big nail, and then pour water into it. If it hold the water, then I will again take a wife, but if it run through, I will not." The girl did as she was ordered, but the water drew the hole together, and the boot became full to the top. She informed her father how it had turned out. Then he himself went up, and when he saw that she was right, he went to the widow and wooed her, and the wedding was celebrated.

The next morning, when the two girls got up, there stood before the man's daughter milk for her to wash in and wine for her to drink, but before the woman's daughter stood water to wash herself with and water for drinking.

On the second morning, stood water for washing and water for drinking before the man's daughter as well as before the woman's daughter. And on the third morning stood water for washing and water for drinking before the man's daughter, and milk for washing and wine for drinking, before the woman's daughter, and so it continued. The woman became bitterly unkind to her step-daughter, and day by day did her best to treat her still worse. She was also envious because her step-daughter was beautiful and lovable, and her own daughter ugly and repulsive.

Once, in winter, when everything was frozen as hard as a stone, and hill and vale lay covered with snow, the woman made a frock of paper, called her step-daughter, and said, "Here, put on this dress and go out into the wood, and fetch me a little basketful of strawberries, -- I have a fancy for some." "Good heavens!" said the girl, "no strawberries grow in winter! The ground is frozen, and besides the snow has covered everything. And why am I to go in this paper frock? It is so cold outside that one's very breath freezes! The wind will blow through the frock, and the thorns will tear it off my body." "Wilt thou contradict me again?" said the stepmother, "See that thou goest, and do not show thy face again until thou hast the basketful of strawberries!" Then she gave her a little piece of hard bread, and said, "This will last thee the day," and thought, "Thou wilt die of cold and hunger outside, and wilt never be seen again by me."

Then the maiden was obedient, and put on the paper frock, and went out with the basket. Far and wide there was nothing but snow, and not a green blade to be seen. When she got into the wood she saw a small house out of which peeped three dwarfs. She wished them good day, and knocked modestly at the door. They cried, "Come in," and she entered the room and seated herself on the bench by the stove, where she began to warm herself and eat her breakfast. The elves said, "Give us, too, some of it." "Willingly," she said, and divided her bit of bread in two and gave them the half. They asked, "What dost thou here in the forest in the winter time, in thy thin dress?" "Ah," she answered, "I am to look for a basketful of strawberries, and am not to go home until I can take them with me." When she had eaten her bread, they gave her a broom and said, "Sweep away the snow at the back door with it." But when she was outside, the three little men said to each other, "What shall we give her as she is so good, and has shared her bread with us?" Then said the first, "My gift is, that she shall every day grow more beautiful." The second said, "My gift is, that gold pieces shall fall out of her mouth every time she speaks." The third said, "My gift is, that a king shall come and take her to wife."

The girl, however, did as the little men had bidden her, swept away the snow behind the little house with the broom, and what did she find but real ripe strawberries, which came up quite dark-red out of the snow! In her joy she hastily gathered her basket full, thanked the little men, shook hands with each of them, and ran home to take her step-mother what she had longed for so much. When she went in and said good-evening, a piece of gold at once fell from her mouth. Thereupon she related what had happened to her in the wood, but with every word she spoke, gold pieces fell from her mouth, until very soon the whole room was covered with them. "Now look at her arrogance," cried the step-sister, "to throw about gold in that way!" but she was secretly envious of it, and wanted to go into the forest also to seek strawberries. The mother said, "No, my dear little daughter, it is too cold, thou mightest die of cold." However, as her daughter let her have no peace, the mother at last yielded, made her a magnificent dress of fur, which she was obliged to put on, and gave her bread-and-butter and cake with her.

The girl went into the forest and straight up to the little house. The three little elves peeped out again, but she did not greet them, and without looking round at them and without speaking to them, she went awkwardly into the room, seated herself by the stove, and began to eat her bread-and-butter and cake. "Give us some of it," cried the little men; but she replied, "There is not enough for myself, so how can I give it away to other people?" When she had done eating, they said, "There is a broom for thee, sweep all clean for us outside by the back-door." "Humph! Sweep for yourselves," she answered, "I am not your servant." When she saw that they were not going to give her anything, she went out by the door. Then the little men said to each other, "What shall we give her as she is so naughty, and has a wicked envious heart, that will never let her do a good turn to any one?" The first said, "I grant that she may grow uglier every day." The second said, "I grant that at every word she says, a toad shall spring out of her mouth." The third said, "I grant that she may die a miserable death." The maiden looked for strawberries outside, but as she found none, she went angrily home. And when she opened her mouth, and was about to tell her mother what had happened to her in the wood, with every word she said, a toad sprang out of her mouth, so that every one was seized with horror of her.

Then the step-mother was still more enraged, and thought of nothing but how to do every possible injury to the man's daughter, whose beauty, however, grew daily greater. At length she took a cauldron, set it on the fire, and boiled yarn in it. When it was boiled, she flung it on the poor girl's shoulder, and gave her an axe in order that she might go on the frozen river, cut a hole in the ice, and rinse the yarn. She was obedient, went thither and cut a hole in the ice; and while she was in the midst of her cutting, a splendid carriage came driving up, in which sat the King. The carriage stopped, and the King asked,"My child, who are thou, and what art thou doing here?" "I am a poor girl, and I am rinsing yarn." Then the King felt compassion, and when he saw that she was so very beautiful, he said to her, "Wilt thou go away with me?" "Ah, yes, with all my heart," she answered, for she was glad to get away from the mother and sister.

So she got into the carriage and drove away with the King, and when they arrived at his palace, the wedding was celebrated with great pomp, as the little men had granted to the maiden. When a year was over, the young Queen bore a son, and as the step-mother had heard of her great good-fortune, she came with her daughter to the palace and pretended that she wanted to pay her a visit. Once, however, when the King had gone out, and no one else was present, the wicked woman seized the Queen by the head, and her daughter seized her by the feet, and they lifted her out of the bed, and threw her out of the window into the stream which flowed by. Then the ugly daughter laid herself in the bed, and the old woman covered her up over her head. When the King came home again and wanted to speak to his wife, the old woman cried, "Hush, hush, that can't be now, she is lying in a violent perspiration; you must let her rest to-day." The King suspected no evil, and did not come back again till next morning; and as he talked with his wife and she answered him, with every word a toad leaped out, whereas formerly a piece of gold had fallen out. Then he asked what that could be, but the old woman said that she had got that from the violent perspiration, and would soon lose it again. During the night, however, the scullion saw a duck come swimming up the gutter, and it said,

"King, what art thou doing now?
Sleepest thou, or wakest thou?"

And as he returned no answer, it said,

"And my guests, What may they do?"

The scullion said,

"They are sleeping soundly, too."

Then it asked again,

"What does little baby mine?"

He answered,

"Sleepeth in her cradle fine."

Then she went upstairs in the form of the Queen, nursed the baby, shook up its little bed, covered it over, and then swam away again down the gutter in the shape of a duck. She came thus for two nights; on the third, she said to the scullion, "Go and tell the King to take his sword and swing it three times over me on the threshold." Then the scullion ran and told this to the King, who came with his sword and swung it thrice over the spirit, and at the third time, his wife stood before him strong, living, and healthy as she had been before. Thereupon the King was full of great joy, but he kept the Queen hidden in a chamber until the Sunday, when the baby was to be christened. And when it was christened he said, "What does a person deserve who drags another out of bed and throws him in the water?" "The wretch deserves nothing better," answered the old woman, "than to be taken and put in a barrel stuck full of nails, and rolled down hill into the water." "Then," said the King, "Thou hast pronounced thine own sentence;" and he ordered such a barrel to be brought, and the old woman to be put into it with her daughter, and then the top was hammered on, and the barrel rolled down hill until it went into the river.

The Golden Bird

A certain king had a beautiful garden, and in the garden stood a tree which bore golden apples. These apples were always counted, and about the time when they began to grow ripe it was found that every night one of them was gone. The king became very angry at this, and ordered the gardener to keep watch all night under the tree. The gardener set his eldest son to watch; but about twelve o'clock he fell asleep, and in the morning another of the apples was missing. Then the second son was ordered to watch; and at midnight he too fell asleep, and in the morning another apple was gone. Then the third son offered to keep watch; but the gardener at first would not let him, for fear some harm should come to him: however, at last he consented, and the young man laid himself under the tree to watch. As the clock struck twelve he heard a rustling noise in the air, and a bird came flying that was of pure gold; and as it was snapping at one of the apples with its beak, the gardener's son jumped up and shot an arrow at it. But the arrow did the bird no harm; only it dropped a golden feather from its tail, and then flew away. The golden feather was brought to the king in the morning, and all the council was called together. Everyone agreed that it was worth more than all the wealth of the kingdom: but the king said, 'One feather is of no use to me, I must have the whole bird.'

Then the gardener's eldest son set out and thought to find the golden bird very easily; and when he had gone but a little way, he came to a wood, and by the side of the wood he saw a fox sitting; so he took his bow and made ready to shoot at it. Then the fox said, 'Do not shoot me, for I will give you good counsel; I know what your business is, and that you want to find the golden bird.

You will reach a village in the evening; and when you get there, you will see two inns opposite to each other, one of which is very pleasant and beautiful to look at: go not in there, but rest for the night in the other, though it may appear to you to be very poor and mean.' But the son thought to himself, 'What can such a beast as this know about the matter?' So he shot his arrow at the fox; but he missed it, and it set up its tail above its back and ran into the wood. Then he went his way, and in the evening came to the village where the two inns were; and in one of these were people singing, and dancing, and feasting; but the other looked very dirty, and poor. 'I should be very silly,' said he, 'if I went to that shabby house, and left this charming place'; so he went into the smart house, and ate and drank at his ease, and forgot the bird, and his country too.

Time passed on; and as the eldest son did not come back, and no tidings were heard of him, the second son set out, and the same thing happened to him. He met the fox, who gave him the good advice: but when he came to the two inns, his eldest brother was standing at the window where the merrymaking was, and called to him to come in; and he could not withstand the temptation, but went in, and forgot the golden bird and his country in the same manner.

Time passed on again, and the youngest son too wished to set out into the wide world to seek for the golden bird;

but his father would not listen to it for a long while, for he was very fond of his son, and was afraid that some ill luck might happen to him also, and prevent his coming back. However, at last it was agreed he should go, for he would not rest at home; and as he came to the wood, he met the fox, and heard the same good counsel. But he was thankful to the fox, and did not attempt his life as his brothers had done; so the fox said, 'Sit upon my tail, and you will travel faster.' So he sat down, and the fox began to run, and away they went over stock and stone so quick that their hair whistled in the wind.

When they came to the village, the son followed the fox's counsel, and without looking about him went to the shabby inn and rested there all night at his ease. In the morning came the fox again and met him as he was beginning his journey, and said, 'Go straight forward, till you come to a castle, before which lie a whole troop of soldiers fast asleep and snoring: take no notice of them, but go into the castle and pass on and on till you come to a room, where the golden bird sits in a wooden cage; close by it stands a beautiful golden cage; but do not try to take the bird out of the shabby cage and put it into the handsome one, otherwise you will repent it.' Then the fox stretched out his tail again, and the young man sat himself down, and away they went over stock and stone till their hair whistled in the wind.

Before the castle gate all was as the fox had said: so the son went in and found the chamber where the golden bird hung in a wooden cage, and below stood the golden cage, and the three golden apples that had been lost were lying close by it. Then thought he to himself, 'It will be a very droll thing to bring away such a fine bird in this shabby cage'; so he opened the door and took hold of it and put it into the golden cage. But the bird set up such a loud scream that all the soldiers awoke, and they took him prisoner and carried him before the king. The next morning the court sat to judge him; and when all was heard, it sentenced him to die, unless he should bring the king the golden horse which could run as swiftly as the wind; and if he did this, he was to have the golden bird given him for his own.

So he set out once more on his journey, sighing, and in great despair, when on a sudden his friend the fox met him, and said, 'You see now what has happened on account of your not listening to my counsel. I will still, however, tell you how to find the golden horse, if you will do as I bid you. You must go straight on till you come to the castle where the horse stands in his stall: by his side will lie the groom fast asleep and snoring: take away the horse quietly, but be sure to put the old leathern saddle upon him, and not the golden one that is close by it.' Then the son sat down on the fox's tail, and away they went over stock and stone till their hair whistled in the wind.

All went right, and the groom lay snoring with his hand upon the golden saddle. But when the son looked at the horse, he thought it a great pity to put the leathern saddle upon it. 'I will give him the good one,' said he; 'I am sure he deserves it.' As he took up the golden saddle the groom awoke and cried out so loud, that all the guards ran in and took him prisoner, and in the morning he was again brought before the court to be judged, and was sentenced to die. But it was agreed, that, if he could bring thither the beautiful princess, he should live, and have the bird and the horse given him for his own.

Then he went his way very sorrowful; but the old fox came and said, 'Why did not you listen to me? If you had, you would have carried away both the bird and the horse; yet will I once more give you counsel. Go straight on, and in the evening you will arrive at a castle. At twelve o'clock at night the princess goes to the bathing-house: go up to her and give her a kiss, and she will let you lead her away; but take care you do not suffer her to go and take leave of her father and mother.' Then the fox stretched out his tail, and so away they went over stock and stone till their hair whistled again.

As they came to the castle, all was as the fox had said, and at twelve o'clock the young man met the princess going to the bath and gave her the kiss, and she agreed to run away with him, but begged with many tears that he would let her take leave of her father. At first he refused, but she wept still more and more, and fell at his feet, till at last he consented; but the moment she came to her father's house the guards awoke and he was taken prisoner again.

Then he was brought before the king, and the king said, 'You shall never have my daughter unless in eight days you dig away the hill that stops the view from my window.' Now this hill was so big that the whole world could not take it away: and when he had worked for seven days, and had done very little, the fox came and said. 'Lie down and go to sleep; I will work for you.' And in the morning he awoke and the hill was gone; so he went merrily to the king, and told him that now that it was removed he must give him the princess.

Then the king was obliged to keep his word, and away went the young man and the princess; and the fox came and said to him, 'We will have all three, the princess, the horse, and the bird.' 'Ah!' said the young man, 'that would be a great thing, but how can you contrive it?'

'If you will only listen,' said the fox, 'it can be done. When you come to the king, and he asks for the beautiful princess, you must say, "Here she is!" Then he will be very joyful; and you will mount the golden horse that they are to give you, and put out your hand to take leave of them; but shake hands with the princess last. Then lift her quickly on to the horse behind you; clap your spurs to his side, and gallop away as fast as you can.'

All went right: then the fox said, 'When you come to the castle where the bird is, I will stay with the princess at the door, and you will ride in and speak to the king; and when he sees that it is the right horse, he will bring out the bird; but you must sit still, and say that you want to look at it, to see whether it is the true golden bird; and when you get it into your hand, ride away.'

This, too, happened as the fox said; they carried off the bird, the princess mounted again, and they rode on to a great wood. Then the fox came, and said, 'Pray kill me, and cut off my head and my feet.' But the young man refused to do it: so the fox said, 'I will at any rate give you good counsel: beware of two things; ransom no one from the gallows, and sit down by the side of no river.' Then away he went. 'Well,' thought the young man, 'it is no hard matter to keep that advice.'

He rode on with the princess, till at last he came to the village where he had left his two brothers. And there he heard a great noise and uproar; and when he asked what was the matter, the people said, 'Two men are going to be hanged.' As he came nearer, he saw that the two men were his brothers, who had turned robbers; so he said, 'Cannot they in any way be saved?' But the people said 'No,' unless he would bestow all his money upon the rascals and buy their liberty. Then he did not stay to think about the matter, but paid what was asked, and his brothers were given up, and went on with him towards their home.

And as they came to the wood where the fox first met them, it was so cool and pleasant that the two brothers said, 'Let us sit down by the side of the river, and rest a while, to eat and drink.' So he said, 'Yes,' and forgot the fox's counsel, and sat down on the side of the river; and while he suspected nothing, they came behind, and threw him down the bank, and took the princess, the horse, and the bird, and went home to the king their master, and said. 'All this have we won by our labour.' Then there was great rejoicing made; but the horse would not eat, the bird would not sing, and the princess wept.

The youngest son fell to the bottom of the river's bed: luckily it was nearly dry, but his bones were almost broken, and the bank was so steep that he could find no way to get out. Then the old fox came once more, and scolded him for not following his advice; otherwise no evil would have befallen him: 'Yet,' said he, 'I cannot leave you here, so lay hold of my tail and hold fast.' Then he pulled him out of the river, and said to him, as he got upon the bank, 'Your brothers have set watch to kill you, if they find you in the kingdom.' So he dressed himself as a poor man, and came secretly to the king's court, and was scarcely within the doors when the horse began to eat, and the bird to sing, and the princess left off weeping. Then he went to the king, and told him all his brothers' roguery; and they were seized and punished, and he had the princess given to him again; and after the king's death he was heir to his kingdom.

A long while after, he went to walk one day in the wood, and the old fox met him, and besought him with tears in his eyes to kill him, and cut off his head and feet. And at last he did so, and in a moment the fox was changed into a man, and turned out to be the brother of the princess, who had been lost a great many many years.

THE QUEEN BEE

Two kings' sons once upon a time went into the world to seek their fortunes; but they soon fell into a wasteful foolish way of living, so that they could not return home again. Then their brother, who was a little insignificant dwarf, went out to seek for his brothers: but when he had found them they only laughed at him, to think that he, who was so young and simple, should try to travel through the world, when they, who were so much wiser, had been unable to get on. However, they all set out on their journey together, and came at last to an ant-hill. The two elder brothers would have pulled it down, in order to see how the poor ants in their fright would run about and carry off their eggs. But the little dwarf said, 'Let the poor things enjoy themselves, I will not suffer you to trouble them.'

So on they went, and came to a lake where many many ducks were swimming about. The two brothers wanted to catch two, and roast them. But the dwarf said, 'Let the poor things enjoy themselves, you shall not kill them.' Next they came to a bees'-nest in a hollow tree, and there was so much honey that it ran down the trunk; and the two brothers wanted to light a fire under the tree and kill the bees, so as to get their honey. But the dwarf held them back, and said, 'Let the pretty insects enjoy themselves, I cannot let you burn them.'

At length the three brothers came to a castle: and as they passed by the stables they saw fine horses standing there, but all were of marble, and no man was to be seen. Then they went through all the rooms, till they came to a door on which were three locks: but in the middle of the door was a wicket, so that they could look into the next room. There they saw a little grey old man sitting at a table; and they called to him once or twice, but he did not hear: however, they called a third time, and then he rose and came out to them.

He said nothing, but took hold of them and led them to a beautiful table covered with all sorts of good things: and when they had eaten and drunk, he showed each of them to a bed-chamber.

The next morning he came to the eldest and took him to a marble table, where there were three tablets, containing an account of the means by which the castle might be disenchanted. The first tablet said: 'In the wood, under the moss, lie the thousand pearls belonging to the king's daughter; they must all be found: and if one be missing by set of sun, he who seeks them will be turned into marble.'

The eldest brother set out, and sought for the pearls the whole day: but the evening came, and he had not found the first hundred: so he was turned into stone as the tablet had foretold.

The next day the second brother undertook the task; but he succeeded no better than the first; for he could only find the second hundred of the pearls; and therefore he too was turned into stone.

At last came the little dwarf's turn; and he looked in the moss; but it was so hard to find the pearls, and the job was so tiresome!—so he sat down upon a stone and cried.

And as he sat there, the king of the ants (whose life he had saved) came to help him, with five thousand ants; and it was not long before they had found all the pearls and laid them in a heap.

The second tablet said: 'The key of the princess's bed-chamber must be fished up out of the lake.'

And as the dwarf came to the brink of it, he saw the two ducks whose lives he had saved swimming about; and they dived down and soon brought in the key from the bottom.

The third task was the hardest. It was to choose out the youngest and the best of the king's three daughters. Now they were all beautiful, and all exactly alike: but he was told that the eldest had eaten a piece of sugar, the next some sweet syrup, and the youngest a spoonful of honey; so he was to guess which it was that had eaten the honey.

Then came the queen of the bees, who had been saved by the little dwarf from the fire, and she tried the lips of all three; but at last she sat upon the lips of the one that had eaten the honey: and so the dwarf knew which was the youngest.

Thus the spell was broken, and all who had been turned into stones awoke, and took their proper forms. And the dwarf married the youngest and the best of the princesses, and was king after her father's death; but his two brothers married the other two sisters.

Foundling-Bird

THERE was once a forester who went into the forest to hunt, and as he entered it he heard a sound of screaming as if a little child were there. He followed the sound, and at last came to a high tree, and at the top of this a little child was sitting, for the mother had fallen asleep under the tree with the child, and a bird of prey had seen it in her arms, had flown down, snatched it away, and set it on the high tree.

The forester climbed up, brought the child down, and thought to himself, "Thou wilt take him home with thee, and bring him up with thy Lina." He took it home, therefore, and the two children grew up together. The one, however, which he had found on a tree was called Fundevogel, because a bird had carried it away. Fundevogel and Lina loved each other so dearly that when they did not see each other they were sad.

The forester, however, had an old cook, who one evening took two pails and began to fetch water, and did not go once only, but many times, out to the spring. Lina saw this and said, "Hark you, old Sanna, why are you fetching so much water?" "If thou wilt never repeat it to anyone, I will tell thee why." So Lina said, no, she would never repeat it to anyone, and then the cook said, "Early to-morrow morning, when the forester is out hunting, I will heat the water, and when it is boiling in the kettle, I will throw in Fundevogel, and will boil him in it."

Betimes next morning the forester got up and went out hunting, and when he was gone the children were still in bed. Then Lina said to Fundevogel, "If thou wilt never leave me, I too will never leave thee." Fundevogel said, "Neither now, nor ever will I leave thee." Then said Lina, "Then I will tell thee. Last night, old Sanna carried so many buckets of water into the house that I asked her why she was doing that, and she said that if I would promise not to tell any one she would tell me, and I said I would be sure not to tell any one, and she said that early to-morrow morning when father was out hunting, she would set the kettle full of water, throw thee into it and boil thee; but we will get up quickly, dress ourselves, and go away together."

The two children therefore got up, dressed themselves quickly, and went away. When the water in the kettle was boiling, the cook went into the bed-room to fetch Fundevogel and throw him into it. But when she came in, and went to the beds, both the children were gone. Then she was terribly alarmed, and she said to herself, "What shall I say now when the forester comes home and sees that the children are gone? They must be followed instantly to get them back again."

Then the cook sent three servants after them, who were to run and overtake the children. The children, however, were sitting outside the forest, and when they saw from afar the three servants running, Lina said to Fundevogel, "Never leave me, and I will never leave thee." Fundevogel said, "Neither now, nor ever." Then said Lina, "Do thou become a rose-tree, and I the rose upon it." When the three servants came to the forest, nothing was there but a rose-tree and one rose on it, but the children were nowhere. Then said they, "There is nothing to be done here," and they went home and told the cook that they had seen nothing in the forest but a little rose-bush with one rose on it. Then the old cook scolded and said, "You simpletons, you should have cut the rose-bush in two, and have broken off the rose and brought it home with you; go, and do it once." They had therefore to go out and look for the second time. The children, however, saw them coming from a distance. Then Lina said, "Fundevogel, never leave me, and I will never leave thee." Fundevogel said, "Neither now, nor ever." Said Lina, "Then do thou become a church, and I'll be the chandelier in it." So when the three servants came, nothing was there but a church, with a chandelier in it. They said therefore to each other, "What can we do here, let us go home." When they got home, the cook asked if they had not found them; so they said no, they had found nothing but a church, and that there was a chandelier in it. And the cook scolded them and said, "You fools! why did you not pull the church to pieces, and bring the chandelier home with you?" And now the old cook herself got on her legs, and went with the three servants in pursuit of the children. The children, however, saw from afar that the three servants were coming, and the cook waddling after them. Then said Lina, "Fundevogel, never leave me, and I will never leave thee." Then said Fundevogel, "Neither now, nor ever." Said Lina, "Be a fishpond, and I will be the duck upon it." The cook, however, came up to them, and when she saw the pond she lay down by it, and was about to drink it up. But the duck swam quickly to her, seized her head in its beak and drew her into the water, and there the old witch had to drown. Then the children went home together, and were heartily delighted, and if they are not dead, they are living still.

THE GOLDEN GOOSE

There was a man who had three sons, the youngest of whom was called Dummling, and was despised, mocked, and sneered at on every occasion.

It happened that the eldest wanted to go into the forest to hew wood, and before he went his mother gave him a beautiful sweet cake and a bottle of wine in order that he might not suffer from hunger or thirst.

When he entered the forest he met a little grey-haired old man who bade him good day, and said: 'Do give me a piece of cake out of your pocket, and let me have a draught of your wine; I am so hungry and thirsty.' But the clever son answered: 'If I give you my cake and wine, I shall have none for myself; be off with you,' and he left the little man standing and went on.

But when he began to hew down a tree, it was not long before he made a false stroke, and the axe cut him in the arm, so that he had to go home and have it bound up. And this was the little grey man's doing.

After this the second son went into the forest, and his mother gave him, like the eldest, a cake and a bottle of wine. The little old grey man met him likewise, and asked him for a piece of cake and a drink of wine. But the second son, too, said sensibly enough: 'What I give you will be taken away from myself; be off!' and he left the little man standing and went on. His punishment, however, was not delayed; when he had made a few blows at the tree he struck himself in the leg, so that he had to be carried home.

Then Dummling said: 'Father, do let me go and cut wood.' The father answered: 'Your brothers have hurt themselves with it, leave it alone, you do not understand anything about it.' But Dummling begged so long that at last he said: 'Just go then, you will get wiser by hurting yourself.' His mother gave him a cake made with water and baked in the cinders, and with it a bottle of sour beer.

When he came to the forest the little old grey man met him likewise, and greeting him, said: 'Give me a piece of your cake and a drink out of your bottle; I am so hungry and thirsty.' Dummling answered: 'I have only cinder-cake and sour beer; if that pleases you, we will sit down and eat.' So they sat down, and when Dummling pulled out his cinder-cake, it was a fine sweet cake, and the sour beer had become good wine. So they ate and drank, and after that the little man said: 'Since you have a good heart, and are willing to divide what you have, I will give you good luck. There stands an old tree, cut it down, and you will find something at the roots.' Then the little man took leave of him.

Dummling went and cut down the tree, and when it fell there was a goose sitting in the roots with feathers of pure gold. He lifted her up, and taking her with him, went to an inn where he thought he would stay the night. Now the host had three daughters, who saw the goose and were curious to know what such a wonderful bird might be, and would have liked to have one of its golden feathers.

The eldest thought: 'I shall soon find an opportunity of pulling out a feather,' and as soon as Dummling had gone out she seized the goose by the wing, but her finger and hand remained sticking fast to it.

The second came soon afterwards, thinking only of how she might get a feather for herself, but she had scarcely touched her sister than she was held fast.

At last the third also came with the like intent, and the others screamed out: 'Keep away; for goodness' sake keep away!' But she did not understand why she was to keep away. 'The others are there,' she thought, 'I may as well be there too,' and ran to them; but as soon as she had touched her sister, she remained sticking fast to her. So they had to spend the night with the goose.

The next morning Dummling took the goose under his arm and set out, without troubling himself about the three girls who were hanging on to it. They were obliged to run after him continually, now left, now right, wherever his legs took him.

In the middle of the fields the parson met them, and when he saw the procession he said: 'For shame, you good-for-nothing girls, why are you running across the fields after this young man? Is that seemly?' At the same time he seized the youngest by the hand in order to pull her away, but as soon as he touched her he likewise stuck fast, and was himself obliged to run behind.

Before long the sexton came by and saw his master, the parson, running behind three girls. He was astonished at this and called out: 'Hi! your reverence, whither away so quickly? Do not forget that we have a christening today!' and running after him he took him by the sleeve, but was also held fast to it.

Whilst the five were trotting thus one behind the other, two labourers came with their hoes from the fields; the parson called out to them and begged that they would set him and the sexton free. But they had scarcely touched the sexton when they were held fast, and now there were seven of them running behind Dummling and the goose.

Soon afterwards he came to a city, where a king ruled who had a daughter who was so serious that no one could make her laugh. So he had put forth a decree that whosoever should be able to make her laugh should marry her. When Dummling heard this, he went with his goose and all her train before the king's daughter, and as soon as she saw the seven people running on and on, one behind the other, she began to laugh quite loudly, and as if she would never stop. Thereupon Dummling asked to have her for his wife; but the king did not like the son-in-law, and made all manner of excuses and said he must first produce a man who could drink a cellarful of wine. Dummling thought of the little grey man, who could certainly help him; so he went into the forest, and in the same place where he had felled the tree, he saw a man sitting, who had a very sorrowful face. Dummling asked him what he was taking to heart so sorely, and he answered: 'I have such a great thirst and cannot quench it; cold water I cannot stand, a barrel of wine I have just emptied, but that to me is like a drop on a hot stone!'

'There, I can help you,' said Dummling, 'just come with me and you shall be satisfied.'

He led him into the king's cellar, and the man bent over the huge barrels, and drank and drank till his loins hurt, and before the day was out he had emptied all the barrels.

Then Dummling asked once more for his bride, but the king was vexed that such an ugly fellow, whom everyone called Dummling, should take away his daughter, and he made a new condition; he must first find a man who could eat a whole mountain of bread. Dummling did not think long, but went straight into the forest, where in the same place there sat a man who was tying up his body with a strap, and making an awful face, and saying: 'I have eaten a whole ovenful of rolls, but what good is that when one has such a hunger as I? My stomach remains empty, and I must tie myself up if I am not to die of hunger.'

At this Dummling was glad, and said: 'Get up and come with me; you shall eat yourself full.' He led him to the king's palace where all the flour in the whole Kingdom was collected, and from it he caused a huge mountain of bread to be baked. The man from the forest stood before it, began to eat, and by the end of one day the whole mountain had vanished. Then Dummling for the third time asked for his bride; but the king again sought a way out, and ordered a ship which could sail on land and on water. 'As soon as you come sailing back in it,' said he, 'you shall have my daughter for wife.'

Dummling went straight into the forest, and there sat the little grey man to whom he had given his cake.

When he heard what Dummling wanted, he said: 'Since you have given me to eat and to drink, I will give you the ship; and I do all this because you once were kind to me.'

Then he gave him the ship which could sail on land and water, and when the king saw that, he could no longer prevent him from having his daughter.

The wedding was celebrated, and after the king's death, Dummling inherited his kingdom and lived for a long time contentedly with his wife.

Mother Holle

Once upon a time there was a widow who had two daughters; one of them was beautiful and industrious, the other ugly and lazy. The mother, however, loved the ugly and lazy one best, because she was her own daughter, and so the other, who was only her stepdaughter, was made to do all the work of the house, and was quite the Cinderella of the family. Her stepmother sent her out every day to sit by the well in the high road, there to spin until she made her fingers bleed. Now it chanced one day that some blood fell on to the spindle, and as the girl stopped over the well to wash it off, the spindle suddenly sprang out of her hand and fell into the well. She ran home crying to tell of her misfortune, but her stepmother spoke harshly to her, and after giving her a violent scolding, said unkindly, 'As you have let the spindle fall into the well you may go yourself and fetch it out.'

The girl went back to the well not knowing what to do, and at last in her distress she jumped into the water after the spindle.

She remembered nothing more until she awoke and found herself in a beautiful meadow, full of sunshine, and with countless flowers blooming in every direction.

She walked over the meadow, and presently she came upon a baker's oven full of bread, and the loaves cried out to her, 'Take us out, take us out, or alas! we shall be burnt to a cinder; we were baked through long ago.' So she took the bread-shovel and drew them all out.

She went on a little farther, till she came to a tree full of apples. 'Shake me, shake me, I pray,' cried the tree; 'my apples, one and all, are ripe.' So she shook the tree, and the apples came falling down upon her like rain; but she continued shaking until there was not a single apple left upon it. Then she carefully gathered the apples together in a heap and walked on again.

The next thing she came to was a little house, and there she saw an old woman looking out, with such large teeth, that she was terrified, and turned to run away. But the old woman called after her, 'What are you afraid of, dear child? Stay with me; if you will do the work of my house properly for me, I will make you very happy. You must be very careful, however, to make my bed in the right way, for I wish you always to shake it thoroughly, so that the feathers fly about; then they say, down there in the world, that it is snowing; for I am Mother Holle.' The old woman spoke so kindly, that the girl summoned up courage and agreed to enter into her service.

She took care to do everything according to the old woman's bidding and every time she made the bed she shook it with all her might, so that the feathers flew about like so many snowflakes. The old woman was as good as her word: she never spoke angrily to her, and gave her roast and boiled meats every day.

So she stayed on with Mother Holle for some time, and then she began to grow unhappy. She could not at first tell why she felt sad, but she became conscious at last of great longing to go home; then she knew she was homesick, although she was a thousand times better off with Mother Holle than with her mother and sister. After waiting awhile, she went to Mother Holle and said, 'I am so homesick, that I cannot stay with you any longer, for although I am so happy here, I must return to my own people.'

Then Mother Holle said, 'I am pleased that you should want to go back to your own people, and as you have served me so well and faithfully, I will take you home myself.'

Thereupon she led the girl by the hand up to a broad gateway. The gate was opened, and as the girl passed through, a shower of gold fell upon her, and the gold clung to her, so that she was covered with it from head to foot.

'That is a reward for your industry,' said Mother Holle, and as she spoke she handed her the spindle which she had dropped into the well.

The gate was then closed, and the girl found herself back in the old world close to her mother's house. As she entered the courtyard, the cock who was perched on the well, called out:

'Cock-a-doodle-doo!

Your golden daughter's come back to you.'

Then she went in to her mother and sister, and as she was so richly covered with gold, they gave her a warm welcome. She related to them all that had happened, and when the mother heard how she had come by her great riches, she thought she should like her ugly, lazy daughter to go and try her fortune. So she made the sister go and sit by the well and spin, and the girl pricked her finger and thrust her hand into a thorn-bush, so that she might drop some blood on to the spindle; then she threw it into the well, and jumped in herself.

Like her sister she awoke in the beautiful meadow, and walked over it till she came to the oven. 'Take us out, take us out, or alas! we shall be burnt to a cinder; we were baked through long ago,' cried the loaves as before. But the lazy girl answered, 'Do you think I am going to dirty my hands for you?' and walked on.

Presently she came to the apple-tree. 'Shake me, shake me, I pray; my apples, one and all, are ripe,' it cried. But she only answered, 'A nice thing to ask me to do, one of the apples might fall on my head,' and passed on.

At last she came to Mother Holle's house, and as she had heard all about the large teeth from her sister, she was not afraid of them, and engaged herself without delay to the old woman.

The first day she was very obedient and industrious, and exerted herself to please Mother Holle, for she thought of the gold she should get in return. The next day, however, she began to dawdle over her work, and the third day she was more idle still; then she began to lie in bed in the mornings and refused to get up. Worse still, she neglected to make the old woman's bed properly, and forgot to shake it so that the feathers might fly about. So Mother Holle very soon got tired off her, and told her she might go. The lazy girl was delighted at this, and thought to herself, 'The gold will soon be mine.' Mother Holle led her, as she had led her sister, to the broad gateway; but as she was passing through, instead of the shower of gold, a great bucketful of pitch came pouring over her.

'That is in return for your services,' said the old woman, and she shut the gate.

So the lazy girl had to go home covered with pitch, and the cock on the well called out as she saw her:

'Cock-a-doodle-doo!

Your dirty daughter's come back to you.'

But, try what she would, she could not get the pitch off and it stuck to her as long as she lived.

The Two Travellers

HILL and vale do not come together, but the children of men do, good and bad. In this way a shoemaker and a tailor once met with each other in their travels. The tailor was a handsome little fellow who was always merry and full of enjoyment. He saw the shoemaker coming towards him from the other side, and as he observed by his bag what kind of a trade he plied, he sang a little mocking song to him,

"Sew me the seam,
Draw me the thread,
Spread it over with pitch,
Knock the nail on the head."

The shoemaker, however, could not endure a joke; he pulled a face as if he had drunk vinegar, and made a gesture as if he were about to seize the tailor by the throat. But the little fellow began to laugh, reached him his bottle, and said, "No harm was meant, take a drink, and swallow your anger down." The shoemaker took a very hearty drink, and the storm on his face began to clear away. He gave the bottle back to the tailor, and said, "I spoke civilly to you; one speaks well after much drinking, but not after much thirst. Shall we travel together?" "All right," answered the tailor, "if only it suits you to go into a big town where there is no lack of work." "That is just where I want to go," answered the shoemaker. "In a small nest there is nothing to earn, and in the country, people like to go barefoot." They travelled therefore onwards together, and always set one foot before the other like a weasel in the snow.

Both of them had time enough, but little to bite and to break. When they reached a town they went about and paid their respects to the tradesmen, and because the tailor looked so lively and merry, and had such pretty red cheeks, every one gave him work willingly, and when luck was good the master's daughters gave him a kiss beneath the porch, as well. When he again fell in with the shoemaker, the tailor had always the most in his bundle. The ill-tempered shoemaker made a wry face, and thought, "The greater the rascal the more the luck," but the tailor began to laugh and to sing, and shared all he got with his comrade. If a couple of pence jingled in his pockets, he ordered good cheer, and thumped the table in his joy till the glasses danced, and it was lightly come, lightly go, with him.

When they had travelled for some time, they came to a great forest through which passed the road to the capital. Two foot-paths, however, led through it, one of which was a seven days' journey, and the other only two, but neither of the travellers knew which way was the short one. They seated themselves beneath an oak-tree, and took counsel together how they should forecast, and for how many days they should provide themselves with bread. The shoemaker said, "One must look before one leaps, I will take with me bread for a week." "What!" said the tailor, "drag bread for seven days on one's back like a beast of burden, and not be able to look about. I shall trust in God, and not trouble myself about anything! The money I have in my pocket is as good in summer as in winter, but in hot weather bread gets dry, and mouldy into the bargain; even my coat does not go as far as it might. Besides, why should we not find the right way? Bread for two days, and that's enough." Each, therefore, bought his own bread, and then they tried their luck in the forest.

It was as quiet there as in a church. No wind stirred, no brook murmured, no bird sang, and through the thickly-leaved branches no sunbeam forced its way. The shoemaker spoke never a word, the heavy bread weighed down his back until the perspiration streamed down his cross and gloomy face. The tailor, however, was quite merry, he jumped about, whistled on a leaf, or sang a song, and thought to himself, "God in heaven must be pleased to see me so happy."

This lasted two days, but on the third the forest would not come to an end, and the tailor had eaten up all his bread, so after all his heart sank down a yard deeper. In the meantime he did not lose courage, but relied on God and on his luck. On the third day he lay down in the evening hungry under a tree, and rose again next morning hungry still; so also passed the fourth day, and when the shoemaker seated himself on a fallen tree and devoured his dinner, the tailor was only a looker-on. If he begged for a little piece of bread the other laughed mockingly, and said, "Thou hast always been so merry, now thou canst try for once what it is to be sad: the birds which sing too early in the morning are struck by the hawk in the evening," In short he was pitiless. But on the fifth morning the poor tailor could no longer stand up, and was hardly able to utter one word for weakness; his cheeks were white, and his eyes red. Then the shoemaker said to him, "I will give thee a bit of bread to-day, but in return for it, I will put out thy right eye." The unhappy tailor who still wished to save his life, could not do it in any other way; he wept once more with both eyes, and then held them out, and the shoemaker, who had a heart of stone, put out his right eye with a sharp knife. The tailor called to remembrance what his mother had formerly said to him when he had been eating secretly in the pantry. "Eat what one can, and suffer what one must." When he had consumed his dearly-bought bread, he got on his legs again, forgot his misery and comforted himself with the thought that he could always see enough with one eye. But on the sixth day, hunger made itself felt again, and gnawed him almost to the heart. In the evening he fell down by a tree, and on the seventh morning he could not raise himself up for faintness, and death was close at hand. Then said the shoemaker, "I will show mercy and give thee bread once more, but thou shalt not have it for nothing, I shall put out thy other eye for it." And now the tailor felt how thoughtless his life had been, prayed to God for forgiveness, and said, "Do what thou wilt, I will bear what I must, but remember that our Lord God does not always look on passively, and that an hour will come when the evil deed which thou hast done to me, and which I have not deserved of thee, will be requited. When times were good with me, I shared what I had with thee. My trade is of that kind that each stitch must always be exactly like the other. If I no longer have my eyes and can sew no more I must go a-begging. At any rate do not leave me here alone when I am blind, or I shall die of hunger." The shoemaker, however, who had driven God out of his heart, took the knife and put out his left eye. Then he gave him a bit of bread to eat, held out a stick to him, and drew him on behind him.

When the sun went down, they got out of the forest, and before them in the open country stood the gallows. Thither the shoemaker guided the blind tailor, and then left him alone and went his way. Weariness, pain, and hunger made the wretched man fall asleep, and he slept the whole night. When day dawned he awoke, but knew not where he lay. Two poor sinners were hanging on the gallows, and a crow sat on the head of each of them. Then one of the men who had been hanged began to speak, and said, "Brother, art thou awake?" "Yes, I am awake," answered the second. "Then I will tell thee something," said the first; "the dew which this night has fallen down over us from the gallows, gives every one who washes himself with it his eyes again. If blind people did but know this, how many would regain their sight who do not believe that to be possible."

When the tailor heard that, he took his pocket-handkerchief, pressed it on the grass, and when it was moist with dew, washed the sockets of his eyes with it. Immediately was fulfilled what the man on the gallows had said, and a couple of healthy new eyes filled the sockets. It was not long before the tailor saw the sun rise behind the mountains; in the plain before him lay the great royal city with its magnificent gates and hundred towers, and the golden balls and crosses which were on the spires began to shine. He could distinguish every leaf on the trees, saw the birds which flew past, and the midges which danced in the air. He took a needle out of his pocket, and as he could thread it as well as ever he had done, his heart danced with delight. He threw himself on his knees, thanked God for the mercy he had shown him, and said his morning prayer. He did not forget also to pray for the poor sinners who were hanging there swinging against each other in the wind like the pendulums of clocks. Then he took his bundle on his back and soon forgot the pain of heart he had endured, and went on his way singing and whistling.

The first thing he met was a brown foal running about the fields at large. He caught it by the mane, and wanted to spring on it and ride into the town. The foal, however, begged to be set free. "I am still too young," it said, "even a light tailor such as thou art would break my back in two let me go till I have grown strong. A time may perhaps come when I may reward thee for it." "Run off," said the tailor, "I see thou art still a giddy thing." He gave it a touch with a switch over its back, whereupon it kicked up its hind legs for joy, leapt over hedges and ditches, and galloped away into the open country.

But the little tailor had eaten nothing since the day before. "The sun to be sure fills my eyes," said he, "but the bread does not fill my mouth. The first thing that comes across me and is even half edible will have to suffer for it." In the meantime a stork stepped solemnly over the meadow towards him. "Halt, halt!" cried the tailor, and seized him by the leg. "I don't know if thou art good to eat or not, but my hunger leaves me no great choice. I must cut thy head off, and roast thee." "Don't do that," replied the stork; "I am a sacred bird which brings mankind great profit, and no one does me an injury. Leave me my life, and I may do thee good in some other way." "Well, be off, Cousin Longlegs," said the tailor. The stork rose up, let its long legs hang down, and flew gently away.

"What's to be the end of this?" said the tailor to himself at last, "my hunger grows greater and greater, and my stomach more and more empty. Whatsoever comes in my way now is lost." At this moment he saw a couple of young ducks which were on a pond come swimming towards him. "You come just at the right moment," said he, and laid hold of one of them and was about to wring its neck. On this an old duck which was hidden among the reeds, began to scream loudly, and swam to him with open beak, and begged him urgently to spare her dear children. "Canst thou not imagine," said she, "how thy mother would mourn if any one wanted to carry thee off, and give thee thy finishing stroke?" "Only be quiet," said the good-tempered tailor, "thou shalt keep thy children," and put the prisoner back into the water.

When he turned round, he was standing in front of an old tree which was partly hollow, and saw some wild bees flying in and out of it. "There I shall at once find the reward of my good deed," said the tailor, "the honey will refresh me." But the Queen-bee came out, threatened him and said, "If thou touchest my people, and destroyest my nest, our stings shall pierce thy skin like ten thousand red-hot needles. But if thou wilt leave us in peace and go thy way, we will do thee a service for it another time."

The little tailor saw that here also nothing was to be done. "Three dishes empty and nothing on the fourth is a bad dinner!" He dragged himself therefore with his starved-out stomach into the town, and as it was just striking twelve, all was ready-cooked for him in the inn, and he was able to sit down at once to dinner. When he was satisfied he said, "Now I will get to work." He went round the town, sought a master, and soon found a good situation. As, however, he had thoroughly learnt his trade, it was not long before he became famous, and every one wanted to have his new coat made by the little tailor, whose importance increased daily. "I can go no further in skill," said he, "and yet things improve every day." At last the King appointed him court-tailor.

But how things do happen in the world! On the very same day his former comrade the shoemaker also became court-shoemaker. When the latter caught sight of the tailor, and saw that he had once more two healthy eyes, his conscience troubled him. "Before he takes revenge on me," thought he to himself, "I must dig a pit for him." He, however, who digs a pit for another, falls into it himself. In the evening when work was over and it had grown dusk, he stole to the King and said, "Lord King, the tailor is an arrogant fellow and has boasted that he will get the gold crown back again which was lost in ancient times." "That would please me very much," said the King, and he caused the tailor to be brought before him next morning, and ordered him to get the crown back again, or to leave the town for ever. "Oho!" thought the tailor, "a rogue gives more than he has got. If the surly King wants me to do what can be done by no one, I will not wait till morning, but will go out of the town at once, to-day." He packed up his bundle, therefore, but when he was without the gate he could not help being sorry to give up his good fortune, and turn his back on the town in which all had gone so well with him. He came to the pond where he had made the acquaintance of the ducks; at that very moment the old one whose young ones he had spared, was sitting there by the shore, pluming herself with her beak. She knew him again instantly, and asked why he was hanging his head so? "Thou wilt not be surprised when thou hearest what has befallen me," replied the tailor, and told her his fate. "If that be all," said the duck, "we can help thee. The crown fell into the water, and lies down below at the bottom; we will soon bring it up again for thee. In the meantime just spread out thy handkerchief on the bank." She dived down with her twelve young ones, and in five minutes she was up again and sat with the crown resting on her wings, and the twelve young ones were swimming round about and had put their beaks under it, and were helping to carry it. They swam to the shore and put the crown on the handkerchief. No one can imagine how magnificent the crown was; when the sun shone on it, it gleamed like a hundred thousand carbuncles. The tailor tied his handkerchief together by the four corners, and carried it to the King, who was full of joy, and put a gold chain round the tailor's neck.

When the shoemaker saw that one stroke had failed, he contrived a second, and went to the King and said, "Lord King, the tailor has become insolent again; he boasts that he will copy in wax the whole of the royal palace, with everything that pertains to it, loose or fast, inside and out." The King sent for the tailor and ordered him to copy in wax the whole of the royal palace, with everything that pertained to it, movable or immovable, within and without, and if he did not succeed in doing this, or if so much as one nail on the wall were wanting, he should be imprisoned for his whole life under ground.

The tailor thought, "It gets worse and worse! No one can endure that?" and threw his bundle on his back, and went forth. When he came to the hollow tree, he sat down and hung his head. The bees came flying out, and the Queen-bee asked him if he had a stiff neck, since he held his head so awry? "Alas, no," answered the tailor, "something quite different weighs me down," and he told her what the King had demanded of him. The bees began to buzz and hum amongst themselves, and the Queen-bee said, "Just go home again, but come back to-morrow at this time, and bring a large sheet with you, and then all will be well." So he turned back again, but the bees flew to the royal palace and straight into it through the open windows, crept round about into every corner, and inspected everything most carefully. Then they hurried back and modelled the palace in wax with such rapidity that any one looking on would have thought it was growing before his eyes. By the evening all was ready, and when the tailor came next morning, the whole of the splendid building was there, and not one nail in the wall or tile of the roof was wanting, and it was delicate withal, and white as snow, and smelt sweet as honey. The tailor wrapped it carefully in his cloth and took it to the King, who could not admire it enough, placed it in his largest hall, and in return for it presented the tailor with a large stone house.

The shoemaker, however, did not give up, but went for the third time to the King and said, "Lord King, it has come to the tailor's ears that no water will spring up in the court-yard of the castle, and he has boasted that it shall rise up in the midst of the court-yard to a man's height and be clear as crystal." Then the King ordered the tailor to be brought before him and said, "If a stream of water does not rise in my court-yard by to-morrow as thou hast promised, the executioner shall in that very place make thee shorter by the head." The poor tailor did not take long to think about it, but hurried out to the gate, and because this time it was a matter of life and death to him, tears rolled down his face. Whilst he was thus going forth full of sorrow, the foal to which he had formerly given its liberty, and which had now become a beautiful chestnut horse, came leaping towards him. "The time has come," it said to the tailor, "when I can repay thee for thy good deed. I know already what is needful to thee, but thou shalt soon have help; get on me, my back can carry two such as thou." The tailor's courage came back to him; he jumped up in one bound, and the horse went full speed into the town, and right up to the court-yard of the castle. It galloped as quick as lightning thrice round it, and at the third time it fell violently down. At the same instant, however, there was a terrific clap of thunder, a fragment of earth in the middle of the court-yard sprang like a cannon-ball into the air, and over the castle, and directly after it a jet of water rose as high as a man on horseback, and the water was as pure as crystal, and the sunbeams began to dance on it. When the King saw that he arose in amazement, and went and embraced the tailor in the sight of all men.

But good fortune did not last long. The King had daughters in plenty, one still prettier than the other, but he had no son. So the malicious shoemaker betook himself for the fourth time to the King, and said, "Lord King, the tailor has not given up his arrogance. He has now boasted that if he liked, he could cause a son to be brought to the Lord king through the air." The King commanded the tailor to be summoned, and said, "If thou causest a son to be brought to me within nine days, thou shalt have my eldest daughter to wife." "The reward is indeed great," thought the little tailor; "one would willingly do something for it, but the cherries grow too high for me, if I climb for them, the bough will break beneath me, and I shall fall."

He went home, seated himself cross-legged on his work-table, and thought over what was to be done. "It can't be managed," cried he at last, "I will go away; after all I can't live in peace here." He tied up his bundle and hurried away to the gate. When he got to the meadow, he perceived his old friend the stork, who was walking backwards and forwards like a philosopher. Sometimes he stood still, took a frog into close consideration, and at length swallowed it down. The stork came to him and greeted him. "I see," he began, "that thou hast thy pack on thy back. Why art thou leaving the town?" The tailor told him what the King had required of him, and how he could not perform it, and lamented his misfortune. "Don't let thy hair grow grey about that," said the stork, "I will help thee out of thy difficulty. For a long time now, I have carried the children in swaddling-clothes into the town, so for once in a way I can fetch a little prince out of the well. Go home and be easy. In nine days from this time repair to the royal palace, and there will I come." The little tailor went home, and at the appointed time was at the castle. It was not long before the stork came flying thither and tapped at the window. The tailor opened it, and cousin Longlegs came carefully in, and walked with solemn steps over the smooth marble pavement. He had, moreover, a baby in his beak that was as lovely as an angel, and stretched out its little hands to the Queen. The stork laid it in her lap, and she caressed it and kissed it, and was beside herself with delight. Before the stork flew away, he took his travelling bag off his back and handed it over to the Queen. In it there were little paper parcels with colored sweetmeats, and they were divided amongst the little princesses. The eldest, however, had none of them, but got the merry tailor for a husband. "It seems to me," said he, "just as if I had won the highest prize. My mother was if right after all, she always said that whoever trusts in God and only has good luck, can never fail."

The shoemaker had to make the shoes in which the little tailor danced at the wedding festival, after which he was commanded to quit the town for ever. The road to the forest led him to the gallows. Worn out with anger, rage, and the heat of the day, he threw himself down. When he had closed his eyes and was about to sleep, the two crows flew down from the heads of the men who were hanging there, and pecked his eyes out. In his madness he ran into the forest and must have died there of hunger, for no one has ever either seen him again or heard of him.

JORINDA AND JORINDEL

There was once an old castle, that stood in the middle of a deep gloomy wood, and in the castle lived an old fairy. Now this fairy could take any shape she pleased. All the day long she flew about in the form of an owl, or crept about the country like a cat; but at night she always became an old woman again. When any young man came within a hundred paces of her castle, he became quite fixed, and could not move a step till she came and set him free; which she would not do till he had given her his word never to come there again: but when any pretty maiden came within that space she was changed into a bird, and the fairy put her into a cage, and hung her up in a chamber in the castle. There were seven hundred of these cages hanging in the castle, and all with beautiful birds in them.

Now there was once a maiden whose name was Jorinda. She was prettier than all the pretty girls that ever were seen before, and a shepherd lad, whose name was Jorindel, was very fond of her, and they were soon to be married. One day they went to walk in the wood, that they might be alone; and Jorindel said, 'We must take care that we don't go too near to the fairy's castle.' It was a beautiful evening; the last rays of the setting sun shone bright through the long stems of the trees upon the green underwood beneath, and the turtle-doves sang from the tall birches.

Jorinda sat down to gaze upon the sun; Jorindel sat by her side; and both felt sad, they knew not why; but it seemed as if they were to be parted from one another for ever. They had wandered a long way; and when they looked to see which way they should go home, they found themselves at a loss to know what path to take.

The sun was setting fast, and already half of its circle had sunk behind the hill: Jorindel on a sudden looked behind him, and saw through the bushes that they had, without knowing it, sat down close under the old walls of the castle. Then he shrank for fear, turned pale, and trembled. Jorinda was just singing,

'The ring-dove sang from the willow spray,

Well-a-day! Well-a-day!

He
mourn'd for the fate of his darling mate,

Well-a-day!'

when her song stopped suddenly. Jorindel turned to see the reason, and beheld his Jorinda changed into a nightingale, so that her song ended with a mournful *jug, jug*. An owl with fiery eyes flew three times round them, and three times screamed:

'Tu whu! Tu whu! Tu whu!'

Jorindel could not move; he stood fixed as a stone, and could neither weep, nor speak, nor stir hand or foot. And now the sun went quite down; the gloomy night came; the owl flew into a bush; and a moment after the old fairy came forth pale and meagre, with staring eyes, and a nose and chin that almost met one another.

She mumbled something to herself, seized the nightingale, and went away with it in her hand. Poor Jorindel saw the nightingale was gone—but what could he do? He could not speak, he could not move from the spot where he stood. At last the fairy came back and sang with a hoarse voice:

'Till the prisoner is fast,

And her doom is cast,

There stay! Oh, stay!

When the charm is around her,

And the spell has bound her,

Hie away! away!'

On a sudden Jorindel found himself free. Then he fell on his knees before the fairy, and prayed her to give him back his dear Jorinda: but she laughed at him, and said he should never see her again; then she went her way.

He prayed, he wept, he sorrowed, but all in vain. 'Alas!' he said, 'what will become of me?' He could not go back to his own home, so he went to a strange village, and employed himself in keeping sheep. Many a time did he walk round and round as near to the hated castle as he dared go, but all in vain; he heard or saw nothing of Jorinda.

At last he dreamt one night that he found a beautiful purple flower, and that in the middle of it lay a costly pearl; and he dreamt that he plucked the flower, and went with it in his hand into the castle, and that everything he touched with it was disenchanted, and that there he found his Jorinda again.

In the morning when he awoke, he began to search over hill and dale for this pretty flower; and eight long days he sought for it in vain: but on the ninth day, early in the morning, he found the beautiful purple flower; and in the middle of it was a large dewdrop, as big as a costly pearl. Then he plucked the flower, and set out and travelled day and night, till he came again to the castle.

He walked nearer than a hundred paces to it, and yet he did not become fixed as before, but found that he could go quite close up to the door. Jorindel was very glad indeed to see this. Then he touched the door with the flower, and it sprang open; so that he went in through the court, and listened when he heard so many birds singing. At last he came to the chamber where the fairy sat, with the seven hundred birds singing in the seven hundred cages. When she saw Jorindel she was very angry, and screamed with rage; but she could not come within two yards of him, for the flower he held in his hand was his safeguard. He looked around at the birds, but alas! there were many, many nightingales, and how then should he find out which was his Jorinda? While he was thinking what to do, he saw the fairy had taken down one of the cages, and was making the best of her way off through the door. He ran or flew after her, touched the cage with the flower, and Jorinda stood before him, and threw her arms round his neck looking as beautiful as ever, as beautiful as when they walked together in the wood.

Then he touched all the other birds with the flower, so that they all took their old forms again; and he took Jorinda home, where they were married, and lived happily together many years: and so did a good many other lads, whose maidens had been forced to sing in the old fairy's cages by themselves, much longer than they liked.

How Six Men Got On In The World

THERE was once a man who understood all kinds of arts; he served in war, and behaved well and bravely, but when the war was over he received his dismissal, and three farthings for his expenses on the way. "Stop," said he, "I shall not be content with this. If I can only meet with the right people, the King will yet have to give me all the treasure of the country." Then full of anger he went into the forest, and saw a man standing therein who had plucked up six trees as if they were blades of corn. He said to him, "Wilt thou be my servant and go with me?" "Yes," he answered, "but, first, I will take this little bundle of sticks home to my mother," and he took one of the trees, and wrapped it round the five others, lifted the bundle on his back, and carried it away. Then he returned and went with his master, who said, "We two ought to be able to get through the world very well," and when they had walked on for a short while they found a huntsman who was kneeling, had shouldered his gun, and was about to fire. The master said to him, "Huntsman, what art thou going to shoot?" He answered, "Two miles from here a fly is sitting on the branch of an oak-tree, and I want to shoot its left eye out." "Oh, come with me," said the man, "if we three are together, we certainly ought to be able to get on in the world!" The huntsman was ready, and went with him, and they came to seven windmills whose sails were turning round with great speed, and yet no wind was blowing either on the right or the left, and no leaf was stirring. Then said the man, "I know not what is driving the windmills, not a breath of air is stirring," and he went onwards with his servants, and when they had walked two miles they saw a man sitting on a tree who was shutting one nostril, and blowing out of the other. "Good gracious! what are you doing up there?" He answered, "Two miles from here are seven windmills; look, I am blowing them till they turn round." "Oh, come with me," said the man. "If we four are together, we shall carry the whole world before us!" Then the blower came down and went with him, and after a while they saw a man who was standing on one leg and had taken off the other, and laid it beside him. Then the master said, "You have arranged things very comfortably to have a rest." "I am a runner," he replied, "and to stop myself running far too fast, I have taken off one of my legs, for if I run with both, I go quicker than any bird can fly." "Oh, go with me. If we five are together, we shall carry the whole world before us." So he went with them, and it was not long before they met a man who wore a cap, but had put it quite on one ear. Then the master said to him, "Gracefully, gracefully, don't stick your cap on one ear, you look just like a tom-fool!" "I must not wear it otherwise," said he, "for if I set my hat straight, a terrible frost comes on, and all the birds in the air are frozen, and drop dead on the ground." "Oh, come with me," said the master. "If we six are together, we can carry the whole world before us."

Now the six came to a town where the King had proclaimed that whosoever ran a race with his daughter and won the victory, should be her husband, but whosoever lost it, must lose his head. Then the man presented himself and said, "I will, however, let my servant run for me." The King replied, "Then his life also must be staked, so that his head and thine are both set on the victory." When that was settled and made secure, the man buckled the other leg on the runner, and said to him, "Now be nimble, and help us to win." It was fixed that the one who was first to bring some water from a far distant well was to be the victor. The runner received a pitcher, and the King's daughter one too, and they began to run at the same time, but in an instant, when the King's daughter had got a very little way, the people who were looking on could see no more of the runner, and it was just as if the wind had whistled by. In a short time he reached the well, filled his pitcher with water, and turned back. Half-way home, however, he was overcome with fatigue, and set his pitcher down, lay down himself, and fell asleep. He had, however, made a pillow of a horse's skull which was lying on the ground, in order that he might lie uncomfortably, and soon wake up again. In the meantime the King's daughter, who could also run very well quite as well as any ordinary mortal can had reached the well, and was hurrying back with her pitcher full of water, and when she saw the runner lying there asleep, she was glad and said, "My enemy is delivered over into my hands," emptied his pitcher, and ran on. And now all would have been lost if by good luck the huntsman had not been standing at the top of the castle, and had not seen everything with his sharp eyes. Then said he, "The King's daughter shall still not prevail against us;" and he loaded his gun, and shot so cleverly, that he shot the horse's skull away from under the runner's head without hurting him. Then the runner awoke, leapt up, and saw that his pitcher was empty, and that the King's daughter was already far in advance. He did not lose heart, however, but ran back to the well with his pitcher, again drew some water, and was at home again, ten minutes before the King's daughter. "Behold!" said he, "I have not bestirred myself till now, it did not deserve to be called running before."

But it pained the King, and still more his daughter, that she should be carried off by a common disbanded soldier like that; so they took counsel with each other how to get rid of him and his companions. Then said the King to her, "I have thought of a way; don't be afraid, they shall not come back again." And he said to them, "You shall now make merry together, and eat and drink," and he conducted them to a room which had a floor of iron, and the doors also were of iron, and the windows were guarded with iron bars. There was a table in the room covered with delicious food, and the King said to them, "Go in, and enjoy yourselves." And when they were inside, he ordered the doors to be shut and bolted. Then he sent for the cook, and commanded him to make a fire under the room until the iron became red-hot. This the cook did, and the six who were sitting at table began to feel quite warm, and they thought the heat was caused by the food; but as it became still greater, and they wanted to get out, and found that the doors and windows were bolted, they became aware that the King must have an evil intention, and wanted to suffocate them. "He shall not succeed, however," said the one with the cap. "I will cause a frost to come, before which the fire shall be ashamed, and creep away." Then he put his cap on straight, and immediately there came such a frost that all heat disappeared, and the food on the dishes began to freeze. When an hour or two had passed by, and the King believed that they had perished in the heat, he had the doors opened to behold them himself. But when the doors were opened, all six were standing there, alive and well, and said that they should very much like to get out to warm themselves, for the very food was fast frozen to the dishes with the cold. Then, full of anger, the King went down to the cook, scolded him, and asked why he had not done what he had been ordered to do. But the cook replied, "There is heat enough there, just look yourself." Then the King saw that a fierce fire was burning under the iron room, and perceived that there was no getting the better of the six in this way.

Again the King considered how to get rid of his unpleasant guests, and caused their chief to be brought and said, "If thou wilt take gold and renounce my daughter, thou shalt have as much as thou wilt."

"Oh, yes, Lord King," he answered, "give me as much as my servant can carry, and I will not ask for your daughter."

On this the King was satisfied, and the other continued, "In fourteen days, I will come and fetch it." Thereupon he summoned together all the tailors in the whole kingdom, and they were to sit for fourteen days and sew a sack. And when it was ready, the strong one who could tear up trees had to take it on his back, and go with it to the King. Then said the King, "Who can that strong fellow be who is carrying a bundle of linen on his back that is as big as a house?" and he was alarmed and said, "What a lot of gold he can carry away!" Then he commanded a ton of gold to be brought; it took sixteen of his strongest men to carry it, but the strong one snatched it up in one hand, put it in his sack, and said, "Why don't you bring more at the same time? that hardly covers the bottom!" Then, little by little, the King caused all his treasure to be brought thither, and the strong one pushed it into the sack, and still the sack was not half full with it." "Bring more," cried he, "these few crumbs don't fill it." Then seven thousand carts with gold had to be gathered together in the whole kingdom, and the strong one thrust them and the oxen harnessed to them into his sack. "I will examine it no longer," said he, "but will just take what comes, so long as the sack is but full." When all that was inside, there was still room for a great deal more; Then he said, "I will just make an end of the thing; people do sometimes tie up a sack even when it is not full." So he took it on his back, and went away with his comrades. When the King now saw how one single man was carrying away the entire wealth of the country, he became enraged, and bade his horsemen mount and pursue the six, and ordered them to take the sack away from the strong one. Two regiments speedily overtook the six, and called out, "You are prisoners, put down the sack with the gold, or you will all be cut to pieces!" "What say you?" cried the blower, "that we are prisoners! Rather than that should happen, all of you shall dance about in the air." And he closed one nostril, and with the other blew on the two regiments. Then they were driven away from each other, and carried into the blue sky over all the mountains one here, the other there. One sergeant cried for mercy; he had nine wounds, and was a brave fellow who did not deserve ill treatment. The blower stopped a little so that he came down without injury, and then the blower said to him, "Now go home to thy King, and tell him he had better send some more horsemen, and I will blow them all into the air." When the King was informed of this he said, "Let the rascals go. They have the best of it." Then the six conveyed the riches home, divided it amongst them, and lived in content until their death.

The Goose-Girl

The king of a great land died, and left his queen to take care of their only child. This child was a daughter, who was very beautiful; and her mother loved her dearly, and was very kind to her. And there was a good fairy too, who was fond of the princess, and helped her mother to watch over her. When she grew up, she was betrothed to a prince who lived a great way off; and as the time drew near for her to be married, she got ready to set off on her journey to his country. Then the queen her mother, packed up a great many costly things; jewels, and gold, and silver; trinkets, fine dresses, and in short everything that became a royal bride. And she gave her a waiting-maid to ride with her, and give her into the bridegroom's hands; and each had a horse for the journey. Now the princess's horse was the fairy's gift, and it was called Falada, and could speak.

When the time came for them to set out, the fairy went into her bed-chamber, and took a little knife, and cut off a lock of her hair, and gave it to the princess, and said, 'Take care of it, dear child; for it is a charm that may be of use to you on the road.' Then they all took a sorrowful leave of the princess; and she put the lock of hair into her bosom, got upon her horse, and set off on her journey to her bridegroom's kingdom.

One day, as they were riding along by a brook, the princess began to feel very thirsty: and she said to her maid, 'Pray get down, and fetch me some water in my golden cup out of yonder brook, for I want to drink.'

'Nay,' said the maid, 'if you are thirsty, get off yourself, and stoop down by the water and drink; I shall not be your waiting-maid any longer.' Then she was so thirsty that she got down, and knelt over the little brook, and drank; for she was frightened, and dared not bring out her golden cup; and she wept and said, 'Alas! what will become of me?' And the lock answered her, and said:

'Alas! alas! if thy mother knew it,

  Sadly, sadly, would she rue it.'

But the princess was very gentle and meek, so she said nothing to her maid's ill behaviour, but got upon her horse again.

Then all rode farther on their journey, till the day grew so warm, and the sun so scorching, that the bride began to feel very thirsty again; and at last, when they came to a river, she forgot her maid's rude speech, and said, 'Pray get down, and fetch me some water to drink in my golden cup.' But the maid answered her, and even spoke more haughtily than before: 'Drink if you will, but I shall not be your waiting-maid.' Then the princess was so thirsty that she got off her horse, and lay down, and held her head over the running stream, and cried and said, 'What will become of me?' And the lock of hair answered her again:

'Alas! alas! if thy mother knew it,

  Sadly, sadly, would she rue it.'

And as she leaned down to drink, the lock of hair fell from her bosom, and floated away with the water. Now she was so frightened that she did not see it; but her maid saw it, and was very glad, for she knew the charm; and she saw that the poor bride would be in her power, now that she had lost the hair. So when the bride had done drinking, and would have got upon Falada again, the maid said, 'I shall ride upon Falada, and you may have my horse instead'; so she was forced to give up her horse, and soon afterwards to take off her royal clothes and put on her maid's shabby ones.

At last, as they drew near the end of their journey, this treacherous servant threatened to kill her mistress if she ever told anyone what had happened. But Falada saw it all, and marked it well.

Then the waiting-maid got upon Falada, and the real bride rode upon the other horse, and they went on in this way till at last they came to the royal court. There was great joy at their coming, and the prince flew to meet them, and lifted the maid from her horse, thinking she was the one who was to be his wife; and she was led upstairs to the royal chamber; but the true princess was told to stay in the court below.

Now the old king happened just then to have nothing else to do; so he amused himself by sitting at his kitchen window, looking at what was going on; and he saw her in the courtyard. As she looked very pretty, and too delicate for a waiting-maid, he went up into the royal chamber to ask the bride who it was she had brought with her, that was thus left standing in the court below. 'I brought her with me for the sake of her company on the road,' said she; 'pray give the girl some work to do, that she may not be idle.' The old king could not for some time think of any work for her to do; but at last he said, 'I have a lad who takes care of my geese; she may go and help him.' Now the name of this lad, that the real bride was to help in watching the king's geese, was Curdken.

But the false bride said to the prince, 'Dear husband, pray do me one piece of kindness.' 'That I will,' said the prince. 'Then tell one of your slaughterers to cut off the head of the horse I rode upon, for it was very unruly, and plagued me sadly on the road'; but the truth was, she was very much afraid lest Falada should some day or other speak, and tell all she had done to the princess. She carried her point, and the faithful Falada was killed; but when the true princess heard of it, she wept, and begged the man to nail up Falada's head against a large dark gate of the city, through which she had to pass every morning and evening, that there she might still see him sometimes. Then the slaughterer said he would do as she wished; and cut off the head, and nailed it up under the dark gate.

Early the next morning, as she and Curdken went out through the gate, she said sorrowfully:

'Falada, Falada, there thou hangest!'

and the head answered:

'Bride, bride, there thou gangest!

Alas! alas! if thy mother knew it,

Sadly, sadly, would she rue it.'

Then they went out of the city, and drove the geese on. And when she came to the meadow, she sat down upon a bank there, and let down her waving locks of hair, which were all of pure silver; and when Curdken saw it glitter in the sun, he ran up, and would have pulled some of the locks out, but she cried:

'Blow, breezes, blow!

Let
Curdken's hat go!

Blow, breezes, blow!

Let him after it go!

O'er hills, dales, and rocks,

Away be it
whirl'd

Till the silvery locks

Are all
comb'd and curl'd!

Then there came a wind, so strong that it blew off Curdken's hat; and away it flew over the hills: and he was forced to turn and run after it; till, by the time he came back, she had done combing and curling her hair, and had put it up again safe. Then he was very angry and sulky, and would not speak to her at all; but they watched the geese until it grew dark in the evening, and then drove them homewards.

The next morning, as they were going through the dark gate, the poor girl looked up at Falada's head, and cried:

'Falada, Falada, there thou hangest!'

and the head answered:

'Bride, bride, there thou gangest!

Alas! alas! if thy mother knew it,

Sadly, sadly, would she rue it.'

Then she drove on the geese, and sat down again in the meadow, and began to comb out her hair as before; and Curdken ran up to her, and wanted to take hold of it; but she cried out quickly:

'Blow, breezes, blow!

Let
Curdken's hat go!

Blow, breezes, blow!

Let him after it go!

O'er hills, dales, and rocks,

Away be it
whirl'd

Till the silvery locks

Are all
comb'd and curl'd!

Then the wind came and blew away his hat; and off it flew a great way, over the hills and far away, so that he had to run after it; and when he came back she had bound up her hair again, and all was safe. So they watched the geese till it grew dark.

In the evening, after they came home, Curdken went to the old king, and said, 'I cannot have that strange girl to help me to keep the geese any longer.' 'Why?' said the king. 'Because, instead of doing any good, she does nothing but tease me all day long.' Then the king made him tell him what had happened. And Curdken said, 'When we go in the morning through the dark gate with our flock of geese, she cries and talks with the head of a horse that hangs upon the wall, and says:

'Falada, Falada, there thou hangest!'

and the head answers:

'Bride, bride, there thou gangest!

Alas! alas! if thy mother knew it,

Sadly, sadly, would she rue it.'

And Curdken went on telling the king what had happened upon the meadow where the geese fed; how his hat was blown away; and how he was forced to run after it, and to leave his flock of geese to themselves. But the old king told the boy to go out again the next day: and when morning came, he placed himself behind the dark gate, and heard how she spoke to Falada, and how Falada answered. Then he went into the field, and hid himself in a bush by the meadow's side; and he soon saw with his own eyes how they drove the flock of geese; and how, after a little time, she let down her hair that glittered in the sun. And then he heard her say:

'Blow, breezes, blow!

Let
Curdken's hat go!

Blow, breezes, blow!

Let him after it go!

O'er hills, dales, and rocks,

Away be it
whirl'd

Till the silvery locks

Are all
comb'd and curl'd!

And soon came a gale of wind, and carried away Curdken's hat, and away went Curdken after it, while the girl went on combing and curling her hair. All this the old king saw: so he went home without being seen; and when the little goose-girl came back in the evening he called her aside, and asked her why she did so: but she burst into tears, and said, 'That I must not tell you or any man, or I shall lose my life.'

But the old king begged so hard, that she had no peace till she had told him all the tale, from beginning to end, word for word. And it was very lucky for her that she did so, for when she had done the king ordered royal clothes to be put upon her, and gazed on her with wonder, she was so beautiful. Then he called his son and told him that he had only a false bride; for that she was merely a waiting-maid, while the true bride stood by.

And the young king rejoiced when he saw her beauty, and heard how meek and patient she had been; and without saying anything to the false bride, the king ordered a great feast to be got ready for all his court. The bridegroom sat at the top, with the false princess on one side, and the true one on the other; but nobody knew her again, for her beauty was quite dazzling to their eyes; and she did not seem at all like the little goose-girl, now that she had her brilliant dress on.

When they had eaten and drank, and were very merry, the old king said he would tell them a tale. So he began, and told all the story of the princess, as if it was one that he had once heard; and he asked the true waiting-maid what she thought ought to be done to anyone who would behave thus. 'Nothing better,' said this false bride, 'than that she should be thrown into a cask stuck round with sharp nails, and that two white horses should be put to it, and should drag it from street to street till she was dead.' 'Thou art she!' said the old king; 'and as thou has judged thyself, so shall it be done to thee.' And the young king was then married to his true wife, and they reigned over the kingdom in peace and happiness all their lives; and the good fairy came to see them, and restored the faithful Falada to life again.

The Singing, Springing Lark

THERE was once on a time a man who was about to set out on a long journey, and on parting he asked his three daughters what he should bring back with him for them. Whereupon the eldest wished for pearls, the second wished for diamonds, but the third said, "Dear father, I should like a singing, soaring lark." The father said, "Yes, if I can get it, you shall have it," kissed all three, and set out. Now when the time had come for him to be on his way home again, he had brought pearls and diamonds for the two eldest, but he had sought everywhere in vain for a singing, soaring lark for the youngest, and he was very unhappy about it, for she was his favorite child. Then his road lay through a forest, and in the midst of it was a splendid castle, and near the castle stood a tree, but quite on the top of the tree, he saw a singing, soaring lark. "Aha, you come just at the right moment!" he said, quite delighted, and called to his servant to climb up and catch the little creature. But as he approached the tree, a lion leapt from beneath it, shook himself, and roared till the leaves on the trees trembled. "He who tries to steal my singing, soaring lark," he cried, "will I devour." Then the man said, "I did not know that the bird belonged to thee. I will make amends for the wrong I have done and ransom myself with a large sum of money, only spare my life." The lion said, "Nothing can save thee, unless thou wilt promise to give me for mine own what first meets thee on thy return home; and if thou wilt do that, I will grant thee thy life, and thou shalt have the bird for thy daughter, into the bargain." But the man hesitated and said, "That might be my youngest daughter, she loves me best, and always runs to meet me on my return home." The servant, however, was terrified and said, "Why should your daughter be the very one to meet you, it might as easily be a cat, or dog?" Then the man allowed himself to be over-persuaded, took the singing, soaring lark, and promised to give the lion whatsoever should first meet him on his return home.

When he reached home and entered his house, the first who met him was no other than his youngest and dearest daughter, who came running up, kissed and embraced him, and when she saw that he had brought with him a singing, soaring lark, she was beside herself with joy. The father, however, could not rejoice, but began to weep, and said, "My dearest child, I have bought the little bird dear. In return for it, I have been obliged to promise thee to a savage lion, and when he has thee he will tear thee in pieces and devour thee," and he told her all, just as it had happened, and begged her not to go there, come what might. But she consoled him and said, "Dearest father, indeed your promise must be fulfilled. I will go thither and soften the lion, so that I may return to thee safely." Next morning she had the road pointed out to her, took leave, and went fearlessly out into the forest. The lion, however, was an enchanted prince and was by day a lion, and all his people were lions with him, but in the night they resumed their natural human shapes. On her arrival she was kindly received and led into the castle. When night came, the lion turned into a handsome man, and their wedding was celebrated with great magnificence. They lived happily together, remained awake at night, and slept in the daytime. One day he came and said, "To-morrow there is a feast in thy father's house, because your eldest sister is to be married, and if thou art inclined to go there, my lions shall conduct thee." She said, "Yes, I should very much like to see my father again," and went thither, accompanied by the lions. There was great joy when she arrived, for they had all believed that she had been torn in pieces by the lion, and had long ceased to live. But she told them what a handsome husband she had, and how well off she was, remained with them while the wedding-feast lasted, and then went back again to the forest. When the second daughter was about to be married, and she was again invited to the wedding, she said to the lion, "This time I will not be alone, thou must come with me." The lion, however, said that it was too dangerous for him, for if when there a ray from a burning candle fell on him, he would be changed into a dove, and for seven years long would have to fly about with the doves. She said, "Ah, but do come with me, I will take great care of thee, and guard thee from all light." So they went away together, and took with them their little child as well. She had a chamber built there, so strong and thick that no ray could pierce through it; in this he was to shut himself up when the candles were lit for the wedding-feast. But the door was made of green wood which warped and left a little crack which no one noticed. The wedding was celebrated with magnificence, but when the procession with all its candles and torches came back from church, and passed by this apartment, a ray about the bredth of a hair fell on the King's son, and when this ray touched him, he was transformed in an instant, and when she came in and looked for him, she did not see him, but a white dove was sitting there. The dove said to her, "For seven years must I fly about the world, but at every seventh step that you take I will let fall a drop of red blood and a white feather, and these will show thee the way, and if thou followest the trace thou canst release me." Thereupon the dove flew out at the door, and she followed him, and at every seventh step a red drop of blood and a little white feather fell down and showed her the way.

So she went continually further and further in the wide world, never looking about her or resting, and the seven years were almost past; then she rejoiced and thought that they would soon be delivered, and yet they were so far from it! Once when they were thus moving onwards, no little feather and no drop of red blood fell, and when she raised her eyes the dove had disappeared. And as she thought to herself, "In this no man can help thee," she climbed up to the sun, and said to him, "Thou shinest into every crevice, and over every peak, hast thou not seen a white dove flying?" "No," said the sun, "I have seen none, but I present thee with a casket, open it when thou art in sorest need." Then she thanked the sun, and went on until evening came and the moon appeared; she then asked her, "Thou shinest the whole night through, and on every field and forest, hast thou not seen a white dove flying?" "No," said the moon, "I have seen no dove, but here I give thee an egg, break it when thou art in great need." She thanked the moon, and went on until the night wind came up and blew on her, then she said to it, "Thou blowest over every tree and under every leaf, hast thou not seen a white dove flying?" "No," said the night wind, "I have seen none, but I will ask the three other winds, perhaps they have seen it." The east wind and the west wind came, and had seen nothing, but the south wind said, "I have seen the white dove, it has flown to the Red

Sea, where it has become a lion again, for the seven years are over, and the lion is there fighting with a dragon; the dragon, however, is an enchanted princess." The night wind then said to her, "I will advise thee; go to the Red Sea, on the right bank are some tall reeds, count them, break off the eleventh, and strike the dragon with it, then the lion will be able to subdue it, and both then will regain their human form. After that, look round and thou wilt see the griffin which is by the Red Sea; swing thyself, with thy beloved, on to his back, and the bird will carry you over the sea to your own home. Here is a nut for thee, when thou are above the center of the sea, let the nut fall, it will immediately shoot up, and a tall nut-tree will grow out of the water on which the griffin may rest; for if he cannot rest, he will not be strong enough to carry you across, and if thou forgettest to throw down the nut, he will let you fall into the sea."

Then she went thither, and found everything as the night wind had said. She counted the reeds by the sea, and cut off the eleventh, struck the dragon therewith, whereupon the lion overcame it, and immediately both of them regained their human shapes. But when the princess, who had before been the dragon, was delivered from enchantment, she took the youth by the arm, seated herself on the griffin, and carried him off with her. There stood the poor maiden who had wandered so far and was again forsaken. She sat down and cried, but at last she took courage and said, "Still I will go as far as the wind blows and as long as the cock crows, until I find him," and she went forth by long, long roads, until at last she came to the castle where both of them were living together; there she heard that soon a feast was to be held, in which they would celebrate their wedding, but she said, "God still helps me," and opened the casket that the sun had given her. A dress lay therein as brilliant as the sun itself. So she took it out and put it on, and went up into the castle, and everyone, even the bride herself, looked at her with astonishment. The dress pleased the bride so well that she thought it might do for her wedding-dress, and asked if it was for sale? "Not for money or land," answered she, "but for flesh and blood." The bride asked her what she meant by that, so she said, "Let me sleep a night in the chamber where the bridegroom sleeps." The bride would not, yet wanted very much to have the dress; at last she consented, but the page was to give the prince a sleeping-draught. When it was night, therefore, and the youth was already asleep, she was led into the chamber; she seated herself on the bed and said, "I have followed after thee for seven years. I have been to the sun and the moon, and the four winds, and have enquired for thee, and have helped thee against the dragon; wilt thou, then quite forget me?" But the prince slept so soundly that it only seemed to him as if the wind were whistling outside in the fir-trees. When therefore day broke, she was led out again, and had to give up the golden dress. And as that even had been of no avail, she was sad, went out into a meadow, sat down there, and wept. While she was sitting there, she thought of the egg which the moon had given her; she opened it, and there came out a clucking hen with twelve chickens all of gold, and they ran about chirping, and crept again under the old hen's wings; nothing more beautiful was ever seen in the world! Then she arose, and drove them through the meadow before her, until the bride looked out of the window.

The little chickens pleased her so much that she immediately came down and asked if they were for sale. "Not for money or land, but for flesh and blood; let me sleep another night in the chamber where the bridegroom sleeps." The bride said, "Yes," intending to cheat her as on the former evening.

But when the prince went to bed he asked the page what the murmuring and rustling in the night had been? On this the page told all; that he had been forced to give him a sleeping-draught, because a poor girl had slept secretly in the chamber, and that he was to give him another that night. The prince said, "Pour out the draught by the bed-side."

At night, she was again led in, and when she began to relate how ill all had fared with her, he immediately recognized his beloved wife by her voice, sprang up and cried, "Now I really am released! I have been as it were in a dream, for the strange princess has bewitched me so that I have been compelled to forget thee, but God has delivered me from the spell at the right time." Then they both left the castle secretly in the night, for they feared the father of the princess, who was a sorcerer, and they seated themselves on the griffin which bore them across the Red Sea, and when they were in the midst of it, she let fall the nut. Immediately a tall nut-tree grew up, whereon the bird rested, and then carried them home, where they found their child, who had grown tall and beautiful, and they lived thenceforth happily until their death.

Doctor Knowall

There was once upon a time a poor peasant called Crabb, who drove with two oxen a load of wood to the town, and sold it to a doctor for two talers. When the money was being counted out to him, it so happened that the doctor was sitting at table, and when the peasant saw how well he ate and drank, his heart desired what he saw, and would willingly have been a doctor too. So he remained standing a while, and at length inquired if he too could not be a doctor. 'Oh, yes,' said the doctor, 'that is soon managed.' 'What must I do?' asked the peasant. 'In the first place buy yourself an A B C book of the kind which has a cock on the frontispiece; in the second, turn your cart and your two oxen into money, and get yourself some clothes, and whatsoever else pertains to medicine; thirdly, have a sign painted for yourself with the words: "I am Doctor Knowall," and have that nailed up above your house-door.' The peasant did everything that he had been told to do. When he had doctored people awhile, but not long, a rich and great lord had some money stolen. Then he was told about Doctor Knowall who lived in such and such a village, and must know what had become of the money. So the lord had the horses harnessed to his carriage, drove out to the village, and asked Crabb if he were Doctor Knowall. Yes, he was, he said. Then he was to go with him and bring back the stolen money. 'Oh, yes, but Grete, my wife, must go too.' The lord was willing, and let both of them have a seat in the carriage, and they all drove away together. When they came to the nobleman's castle, the table was spread, and Crabb was told to sit down and eat. 'Yes, but my wife, Grete, too,' said he, and he seated himself with her at the table. And when the first servant came with a dish of delicate fare, the peasant nudged his wife, and said: 'Grete, that was the first,' meaning that was the servant who brought the first dish.

The servant, however, thought he intended by that to say: 'That is the first thief,' and as he actually was so, he was terrified, and said to his comrade outside: 'The doctor knows all: we shall fare ill, he said I was the first.' The second did not want to go in at all, but was forced. So when he went in with his dish, the peasant nudged his wife, and said: 'Grete, that is the second.' This servant was equally alarmed, and he got out as fast as he could. The third fared no better, for the peasant again said: 'Grete, that is the third.' The fourth had to carry in a dish that was covered, and the lord told the doctor that he was to show his skill, and guess what was beneath the cover. Actually, there were crabs. The doctor looked at the dish, had no idea what to say, and cried: 'Ah, poor Crabb.' When the lord heard that, he cried: 'There! he knows it; he must also know who has the money!'

On this the servants looked terribly uneasy, and made a sign to the doctor that they wished him to step outside for a moment. When therefore he went out, all four of them confessed to him that they had stolen the money, and said that they would willingly restore it and give him a heavy sum into the bargain, if he would not denounce them, for if he did they would be hanged. They led him to the spot where the money was concealed. With this the doctor was satisfied, and returned to the hall, sat down to the table, and said: 'My lord, now will I search in my book where the gold is hidden.' The fifth servant, however, crept into the stove to hear if the doctor knew still more. But the doctor sat still and opened his A B C book, turned the pages backwards and forwards, and looked for the cock. As he could not find it immediately he said: 'I know you are there, so you had better come out!' Then the fellow in the stove thought that the doctor meant him, and full of terror, sprang out, crying: 'That man knows everything!' Then Doctor Knowall showed the lord where the money was, but did not say who had stolen it, and received from both sides much money in reward, and became a renowned man.

THE BLUE LIGHT

There was once upon a time a soldier who for many years had served the king faithfully, but when the war came to an end could serve no longer because of the many wounds which he had received. The king said to him: 'You may return to your home, I need you no longer, and you will not receive any more money, for he only receives wages who renders me service for them.' Then the soldier did not know how to earn a living, went away greatly troubled, and walked the whole day, until in the evening he entered a forest. When darkness came on, he saw a light, which he went up to, and came to a house wherein lived a witch. 'Do give me one night's lodging, and a little to eat and drink,' said he to her, 'or I shall starve.' 'Oho!' she answered, 'who gives anything to a run-away soldier? Yet will I be compassionate, and take you in, if you will do what I wish.' 'What do you wish?' said the soldier. 'That you should dig all round my garden for me, tomorrow.' The soldier consented, and next day laboured with all his strength, but could not finish it by the evening. 'I see well enough,' said the witch, 'that you can do no more today, but I will keep you yet another night, in payment for which you must tomorrow chop me a load of wood, and chop it small.' The soldier spent the whole day in doing it, and in the evening the witch proposed that he should stay one night more. 'Tomorrow, you shall only do me a very trifling piece of work. Behind my house, there is an old dry well, into which my light has fallen, it burns blue, and never goes out, and you shall bring it up again.' Next day the old woman took him to the well, and let him down in a basket. He found the blue light, and made her a signal to draw him up again. She did draw him up, but when he came near the edge, she stretched down her hand and wanted to take the blue light away from him. 'No,' said he, perceiving her evil intention, 'I will not give you the light until I am standing with both feet upon the ground.' The witch fell into a passion, let him fall again into the well, and went away.

The poor soldier fell without injury on the moist ground, and the blue light went on burning, but of what use was that to him? He saw very well that he could not escape death. He sat for a while very sorrowfully, then suddenly he felt in his pocket and found his tobacco pipe, which was still half full. 'This shall be my last pleasure,' thought he, pulled it out, lit it at the blue light and began to smoke. When the smoke had circled about the cavern, suddenly a little black dwarf stood before him, and said: 'Lord, what are your commands?' 'What my commands are?' replied the soldier, quite astonished. 'I must do everything you bid me,' said the little man. 'Good,' said the soldier; 'then in the first place help me out of this well.' The little man took him by the hand, and led him through an underground passage, but he did not forget to take the blue light with him. On the way the dwarf showed him the treasures which the witch had collected and hidden there, and the soldier took as much gold as he could carry. When he was above, he said to the little man: 'Now go and bind the old witch, and carry her before the judge.' In a short time she came by like the wind, riding on a wild tom-cat and screaming frightfully. Nor was it long before the little man reappeared. 'It is all done,' said he, 'and the witch is already hanging on the gallows. What further commands has my lord?' inquired the dwarf.

'At this moment, none,' answered the soldier; 'you can return home, only be at hand immediately, if I summon you.' 'Nothing more is needed than that you should light your pipe at the blue light, and I will appear before you at once.' Thereupon he vanished from his sight.

The soldier returned to the town from which he came. He went to the best inn, ordered himself handsome clothes, and then bade the landlord furnish him a room as handsome as possible. When it was ready and the soldier had taken possession of it, he summoned the little black manikin and said: 'I have served the king faithfully, but he has dismissed me, and left me to hunger, and now I want to take my revenge.' 'What am I to do?' asked the little man. 'Late at night, when the king's daughter is in bed, bring her here in her sleep, she shall do servant's work for me.' The manikin said: 'That is an easy thing for me to do, but a very dangerous thing for you, for if it is discovered, you will fare ill.' When twelve o'clock had struck, the door sprang open, and the manikin carried in the princess. 'Aha! are you there?' cried the soldier, 'get to your work at once! Fetch the broom and sweep the chamber.' When she had done this, he ordered her to come to his chair, and then he stretched out his feet and said: 'Pull off my boots,' and then he threw them in her face, and made her pick them up again, and clean and brighten them. She, however, did everything he bade her, without opposition, silently and with half-shut eyes. When the first cock crowed, the manikin carried her back to the royal palace, and laid her in her bed.

Next morning when the princess arose she went to her father, and told him that she had had a very strange dream. 'I was carried through the streets with the rapidity of lightning,' said she, 'and taken into a soldier's room, and I had to wait upon him like a servant, sweep his room, clean his boots, and do all kinds of menial work. It was only a dream, and yet I am just as tired as if I really had done everything.' 'The dream may have been true,' said the king. 'I will give you a piece of advice. Fill your pocket full of peas, and make a small hole in the pocket, and then if you are carried away again, they will fall out and leave a track in the streets.' But unseen by the king, the manikin was standing beside him when he said that, and heard all. At night when the sleeping princess was again carried through the streets, some peas certainly did fall out of her pocket, but they made no track, for the crafty manikin had just before scattered peas in every street there was. And again the princess was compelled to do servant's work until cock-crow.

Next morning the king sent his people out to seek the track, but it was all in vain, for in every street poor children were sitting, picking up peas, and saying: 'It must have rained peas, last night.' 'We must think of something else,' said the king; 'keep your shoes on when you go to bed, and before you come back from the place where you are taken, hide one of them there, I will soon contrive to find it.' The black manikin heard this plot, and at night when the soldier again ordered him to bring the princess, revealed it to him, and told him that he knew of no expedient to counteract this stratagem, and that if the shoe were found in the soldier's house it would go badly with him. 'Do what I bid you,' replied the soldier, and again this third night the princess was obliged to work like a servant, but before she went away, she hid her shoe under the bed.

Next morning the king had the entire town searched for his daughter's shoe. It was found at the soldier's, and the soldier himself, who at the entreaty of the dwarf had gone outside the gate, was soon brought back, and thrown into prison. In his flight he had forgotten the most valuable things he had, the blue light and the gold, and had only one ducat in his pocket. And now loaded with chains, he was standing at the window of his dungeon, when he chanced to see one of his comrades passing by. The soldier tapped at the pane of glass, and when this man came up, said to him: 'Be so kind as to fetch me the small bundle I have left lying in the inn, and I will give you a ducat for doing it.' His comrade ran thither and brought him what he wanted. As soon as the soldier was alone again, he lighted his pipe and summoned the black manikin. 'Have no fear,' said the latter to his master. 'Go wheresoever they take you, and let them do what they will, only take the blue light with you.' Next day the soldier was tried, and though he had done nothing wicked, the judge condemned him to death. When he was led forth to die, he begged a last favour of the king. 'What is it?' asked the king. 'That I may smoke one more pipe on my way.' 'You may smoke three,' answered the king, 'but do not imagine that I will spare your life.' Then the soldier pulled out his pipe and lighted it at the blue light, and as soon as a few wreaths of smoke had ascended, the manikin was there with a small cudgel in his hand, and said: 'What does my lord command?' 'Strike down to earth that false judge there, and his constable, and spare not the king who has treated me so ill.' Then the manikin fell on them like lightning, darting this way and that way, and whosoever was so much as touched by his cudgel fell to earth, and did not venture to stir again. The king was terrified; he threw himself on the soldier's mercy, and merely to be allowed to live at all, gave him his kingdom for his own, and his daughter to wife.

The Spindle, The Shuttle, And The Needle

THERE was once a girl whose father and mother died while she was still a little child. All alone, in a small house at the end of the village, dwelt her godmother, who supported herself by spinning, weaving, and sewing. The old woman took the forlorn child to live with her, kept her to her work, and educated her in all that is good. When the girl was fifteen years old, the old woman became ill, called the child to her bedside, and said, "Dear daughter, I feel my end drawing near. I leave thee the little house, which will protect thee from wind and weather, and my spindle, shuttle, and needle, with which thou canst earn thy bread." Then she laid her hands on the girl's head, blessed her, and said, "Only preserve the love of God in thy heart, and all will go well with thee." Thereupon she closed her eyes, and when she was laid in the earth, the maiden followed the coffin, weeping bitterly, and paid her the last mark of respect. And now the maiden lived quite alone in the little house, and was industrious, and span, wove, and sewed, and the blessing of the good old woman was on all that she did. It seemed as if the flax in the room increased of its own accord, and whenever she wove a piece of cloth or carpet, or had made a shirt, she at once found a buyer who paid her amply for it, so that she was in want of nothing, and even had something to share with others.

About this time, the son of the King was travelling about the country looking for a bride. He was not to choose a poor one, and did not want to have a rich one. So he said, "She shall be my wife who is the poorest, and at the same time the richest." When he came to the village where the maiden dwelt, he inquired, as he did wherever he went, who was the richest and also the poorest girl in the place? They first named the richest; the poorest, they said, was the girl who lived in the small house quite at the end of the village. The rich girl was sitting in all her splendour before the door of her house, and when the prince approached her, she got up, went to meet him, and made him a low curtsey. He looked at her, said nothing, and rode on. When he came to the house of the poor girl, she was not standing at the door, but sitting in her little room. He stopped his horse, and saw through the window, on which the bright sun was shining, the girl sitting at her spinning-wheel, busily spinning. She looked up, and when she saw that the prince was looking in, she blushed all over her face, let her eyes fall, and went on spinning. I do not know whether, just at that moment, the thread was quite even; but she went on spinning until the King's son had ridden away again. Then she went to the window, opened it, and said, "It is so warm in this room!" but she still looked after him as long as she could distinguish the white feathers in his hat. Then she sat down to work again in her own room and went on with her spinning, and a saying which the old woman had often repeated when she was sitting at her work, came into her mind, and she sang these words to herself, --

"Spindle, my spindle, haste, haste thee away,
And here to my house bring the wooer, I pray."

And what do you think happened? The spindle sprang out of her hand in an instant, and out of the door, and when, in her astonishment, she got up and looked after it, she saw that it was dancing out merrily into the open country, and drawing a shining golden thread after it. Before long, it had entirely vanished from her sight. As she had now no spindle, the girl took the weaver's shuttle in her hand, sat down to her loom, and began to weave.
The spindle, however, danced continually onwards, and just as the thread came to an end, reached the prince. "What do I see?" he cried; "the spindle certainly wants to show me the way!" turned his horse about, and rode back with the golden thread. The girl was, however, sitting at her work singing,

"Shuttle, my shuttle, weave well this day,
And guide the wooer to me, I pray."

Immediately the shuttle sprang out of her hand and out by the door. Before the threshold, however, it began to weave a carpet which was more beautiful than the eyes of man had ever yet beheld. Lilies and roses blossomed on both sides of it, and on a golden ground in the centre green branches ascended, under which bounded hares and rabbits, stags and deer stretched their heads in between them, brightly-coloured birds were sitting in the branches above; they lacked nothing but the gift of song. The shuttle leapt hither and thither, and everything seemed to grow of its own accord.

As the shuttle had run away, the girl sat down to sew. She held the needle in her hand and sang,

"Needle, my needle, sharp-pointed and fine,
Prepare for a wooer this house of mine."

Then the needle leapt out of her fingers, and flew everywhere about the room as quick as lightning. It was just as if invisible spirits were working; they covered tables and benches with green cloth in an instant, and the chairs with velvet, and hung the windows with silken curtains. Hardly had the needle put in the last stitch than the maiden saw through the window the white feathers of the prince, whom the spindle had brought thither by the golden thread. He alighted, stepped over the carpet into the house, and when he entered the room, there stood the maiden in her poor garments, but she shone out from within them like a rose surrounded by leaves. "Thou art the poorest and also the richest," said he to her. "Come with me, thou shalt be my bride." She did not speak, but she gave him her hand. Then he gave her a kiss, led her forth, lifted her on to his horse, and took her to the royal castle, where the wedding was solemnized with great rejoicings. The spindle, shuttle, and needle were preserved in the treasure-chamber, and held in great honour.

The Three Children Of Fortune

A FATHER once called his three sons before him, and he gave to the first a cock, to the second a scythe, and to the third a cat. "I am already aged," said he, "my death is nigh, and I have wished to take thought for you before my end; money I have not, and what I now give you seems of little worth, but all depends on your making a sensible use of it. Only seek out a country where such things are still unknown, and your fortune is made." After the father's death the eldest went away with his cock, but wherever he came the cock was already known; in the towns he saw him from a long distance, sitting upon the steeples and turning round with the wind, and in the villages he heard more than one crowing; no one would show any wonder at the creature, so that it did not look as if he would make his fortune by it.

At last, however, it happened that he came to an island where the people knew nothing about cocks, and did not even understand how to divide their time. They certainly knew when it was morning or evening, but at night, if they did not sleep through it, not one of them knew how to find out the time.

"Look!" said he, "what a proud creature! it has a ruby-red crown upon its head, and wears spurs like a knight; it calls you three times during the night, at fixed hours, and when it calls for the last time, the sun soon rises. But if it crows by broad daylight, then take notice, for there will certainly be a change of weather."

The people were well pleased; for a whole night they did not sleep, and listened with great delight as the cock at two, four, and six o'clock, loudly and clearly proclaimed the time. They asked if the creature were for sale, and how much he wanted for it? "About as much gold as an ass can carry," answered he. "A ridiculously small price for such a precious creature!" they cried unanimously, and willingly gave him what he had asked.

When he came home with his wealth his brothers were astonished, and the second said, "Well, I will go forth and see whether I cannot get rid of my scythe as profitably." But it did not look as if he would, for labourers met him everywhere, and they had scythes upon their shoulders as well as he.

At last, however, he chanced upon an island where the people knew nothing of scythes. When the corn was ripe there, they took cannon out to the fields and shot it down. Now this was rather an uncertain affair; many shot right over it, others hit the ears instead of the stems, and shot them away, whereby much was lost, and besides all this, it made a terrible noise. So the man set to work and mowed it down so quietly and quickly that the people opened their mouths with astonishment. They agreed to give him what he wanted for the scythe, and he received a horse laden with as much gold as it could carry.

And now the third brother wanted to take his cat to the right man. He fared just like the others; so long as he stayed on the mainland there was nothing to be done. Every place had cats, and there were so many of them that new-born kittens were generally drowned in the ponds.

At last he sailed over to an island, and it luckily happened that no cats had ever yet been seen there, and that the mice had got the upper hand so much that they danced upon the tables and benches whether the master were at home or not. The people complained bitterly of the plague; the King himself in his palace did not know how to secure himself against them; mice squeaked in every corner, and gnawed whatever they could lay hold of with their teeth. But now the cat began her chase, and soon cleared a couple of rooms, and the people begged the King to buy the wonderful beast for the country. The King willingly gave what was asked, which was a mule laden with gold, and the third brother came home with the greatest treasure of all.

The cat made herself merry with the mice in the royal palace, and killed so many that they could not be counted. At last she grew warm with the work and thirsty, so she stood still, lifted up her head and cried, "Mew. Mew!" When they heard this strange cry, the King and all his people were frightened, and in their terror ran all at once out of the palace. Then the King took counsel what was best to be done; at last it was determined to send a herald to the cat, and demand that she should leave the palace, or if not, she was to expect that force would be used against her. The councillors said, "Rather will we let ourselves be plagued with the mice, for to that misfortune we are accustomed, than give up our lives to such a monster as this." A noble youth, therefore, was sent to ask the cat "whether she would peaceably quit the castle?" But the cat, whose thirst had become still greater, merely answered, "Mew! Mew!" The youth understood her to say, "Most certainly not! most certainly not!" and took this answer to the King. "Then," said the councillors, "she shall yield to force." Cannon were brought out, and the palace was soon in flames. When the fire reached the room where the cat was sitting, she sprang safely out of the window; but the besiegers did not leave off until the whole palace was shot down to the ground.

Donkey Cabbages

THERE was once a young huntsman who went into the forest to lie in wait. He had a fresh and joyous heart, and as he was going thither, whistling upon a leaf, an ugly old crone came up, who spoke to him and said, "Good-day, dear huntsman, truly you are merry and contented, but I am suffering from hunger and thirst, do give me an alms." The huntsman had compassion on the poor old creature, felt in his pocket, and gave her what he could afford. He was then about to go further, but the old woman stopped him and said, "Listen, dear huntsman, to what I tell you; I will make you a present in return for your kindness. Go on your way now, but in a little while you will come to a tree, whereon nine birds are sitting which have a cloak in their claws, and are plucking at it; take your gun and shoot into the midst of them, they will let the cloak fall down to you, but one of the birds will be hurt, and will drop down dead. Carry away the cloak, it is a wishing-cloak; when you throw it over your shoulders, you only have to wish to be in a certain place, and you will be there in the twinkling of an eye. Take out the heart of the dead bird and swallow it whole, and every morning early, when you get up, you will find a gold piece under your pillow." The huntsman thanked the wise woman, and thought to himself, "Those are fine things that she has promised me, if all does but come true." And verily when he had walked about a hundred paces, he heard in the branches above him such a screaming and twittering that he looked up and saw there a crowd of birds who were tearing a piece of cloth about with their beaks and claws, and tugging and fighting as if each wanted to have it all to himself. "Well," said the huntsman, "this is wonderful, it has really come to pass just as the old wife foretold!" and he took the gun from his shoulder, aimed and fired right into the midst of them, so that the feathers flew about. The birds instantly took to flight with loud outcries, but one dropped down dead, and the cloak fell at the same time. Then the huntsman did as the old woman had directed him, cut open the bird, sought the heart, swallowed it down, and took the cloak home with him.

Next morning, when he awoke, the promise occurred to him, and he wished to see if it also had been fulfilled. When he lifted up the pillow, the gold piece shone in his eyes, and next day he found another, and so it went on, every time he got up. He gathered together a heap of gold, but at last he thought, "Of what use is all my gold to me if I stay at home? I will go forth and see the world."

He then took leave of his parents, buckled on his huntsman's pouch and gun, and went out into the world. It came to pass, that one day he travelled through a dense forest, and when he came to the end of it, in the plain before him stood a fine castle. An old woman was standing with a wonderfully beautiful maiden, looking out of one of the windows. The old woman, however, was a witch and said to the maiden, "There comes one out of the forest, who has a wonderful treasure in his body, we must filch it from him, my dear daughter, it is more suitable for us than for him. He has a bird's heart about him, by means of which a gold piece lies every morning under his pillow." She told her what she was to do to get it, and what part she had to play, and finally threatened her, and said with angry eyes, "And if you do not attend to what I say, it will be the worse for you." Now when the huntsman came nearer he descried the maiden, and said to himself, "I have travelled about for such a long time, I will take a rest for once, and enter that beautiful castle. I have certainly money enough." Nevertheless, the real reason was that he had caught sight of the pretty girl.

He entered the house, and was well received and courteously entertained. Before long he was so much in love with the young witch that he no longer thought of anything else, and only saw things as she saw them, and did what she desired. The old woman then said, "Now we must have the bird's heart, he will never miss it." She prepared a drink, and when it was ready, poured it into a cup and gave it to the maiden, who was to present it to the huntsman. She did so, saying, "Now, my dearest, drink to me." So he took the cup, and when he had swallowed the draught, he brought up the heart of the bird. The girl had to take it away secretly and swallow it herself, for the old woman would have it so. Thenceforward he found no more gold under his pillow, but it lay instead under that of the maiden, from whence the old woman fetched it away every morning; but he was so much in love and so befooled, that he thought of nothing else but of passing his time with the girl.

Then the old witch said, "We have the bird's heart, but we must also take the wishing-cloak away from him." The girl answered, "We will leave him that, he has lost his wealth." The old woman was angry and said, "Such a mantle is a wonderful thing, and is seldom to be found in this world. I must and will have it!" She gave the girl several blows, and said that if she did not obey, it should fare ill with her. So she did the old woman's bidding, placed herself at the window and looked on the distant country, as if she were very sorrowful. The huntsman asked, "Why dost thou stand there so sorrowfully?" "Ah, my beloved," was her answer, "over yonder lies the Garnet Mountain, where the precious stones grow. I long for them so much that when I think of them, I feel quite sad, but who can get them? Only the birds; they fly and can reach them, but a man never." "Hast thou nothing else to complain of?" said the huntsman. "I will soon remove that burden from thy heart." With that he drew her under his mantle, wished himself on the Garnet Mountain, and in the twinkling of an eye they were sitting on it together. Precious stones were glistening on every side so that it was a joy to see them, and together they gathered the finest and costliest of them. Now, the old woman had, through her sorceries, contrived that the eyes of the huntsman should become heavy. He said to the maiden, "We will sit down and rest awhile, I am so tired that I can no longer stand on my feet." Then they sat down, and he laid his head in her lap, and fell asleep. When he was asleep, she unfastened the mantle from his shoulders, and wrapped herself in it, picked up the garnets and stones, and wished herself back at home with them.

But when the huntsman had had his sleep out and awoke, and perceived that his sweetheart had betrayed him, and left him alone on the wild mountain, he said, "Oh, what treachery there is in the world!" and sat down there in care and sorrow, not knowing what to do. But the mountain belonged to some wild and monstrous giants who dwelt thereon and lived their lives there, and he had not sat long before he saw three of them coming towards him, so he lay down as if he were sunk in a deep sleep.

Then the giants came up, and the first kicked him with his foot and said, "What sort of an earth-worm is lying curled up here? The second said, "Step upon him and kill him." But the third said, "That would indeed be worth your while; just let him live, he cannot remain here; and when he climbs higher, toward the summit of of the mountain, the clouds will lay hold of him and bear him away." So saying they passed by. But the huntsman had paid heed to their words, and as soon as they were gone, he rose and climbed up to the summit of the mountain, and when he had sat there a while, a cloud floated towards him, caught him up, carried him away, and travelled about for a long time in the heavens. Then it sank lower, and let itself down on a great cabbage-garden, girt round by walls, so that he came softly to the ground on cabbages and vegetables.

Then the huntsman looked about him and said, "If I had but something to eat! I am so hungry, and my hunger will increase in course of time; but I see here neither apples nor pears, nor any other sort of fruit, everywhere nothing but cabbages," but at length he thought, "At a pinch I can eat some of the leaves, they do not taste particularly good, but they will refresh me." With that he picked himself out a fine head of cabbage, and ate it, but scarcely had he swallowed a couple of mouthfuls than he felt very strange and quite different.

Four legs grew on him, a large head and two thick ears, and he saw with horror that he was changed into an ass. Still as his hunger increased every minute, and as the juicy leaves were suitable to his present nature, he went on eating with great zest. At last he arrived at a different kind of cabbage, but as soon as he had swallowed it, he again felt a change, and reassumed his former human shape.

Then the huntsman lay down and slept off his fatigue. When he awoke next morning, he broke off one head of the bad cabbages and another of the good ones, and thought to himself, "This shall help me to get my own again and punish treachery." Then he took the cabbages with him, climbed over the wall, and went forth to seek for the castle of his sweetheart. After wandering about for a couple of days he was lucky enough to find it again. He dyed his face brown, so that his own mother would not have known him; and begged for shelter: "I am so tired," said he, "that I can go no further." The witch asked, "Who are you, countryman, and what is your business?" "I am a King's messenger, and was sent out to seek the most delicious salad which grows beneath the sun. I have even been so fortunate as to find it, and am carrying it about with me; but the heat of the sun is so intense that the delicate cabbage threatens to wither, and I do not know if I can carry it any further."

When the old woman heard of the exquisite salad, she was greedy, and said, "Dear countryman, let me just taste this wonderful salad." "Why not?" answered he, "I have brought two heads with me, and will give you one of them," and he opened his pouch and handed her the bad cabbage. The witch suspected nothing amiss, and her mouth watered so for this new dish that she herself went into the kitchen and dressed it. When it was prepared she could not wait until it was set on the table, but took a couple of leaves at once, and put them in her mouth, but hardly had she swallowed them than she was deprived of her human shape, and she ran out into the courtyard in the form of an ass. Presently the maid-servant entered the kitchen, saw the salad standing there ready prepared, and was about to carry it up; but on the way, according to habit, she was seized by the desire to taste, and she ate a couple of leaves. Instantly the magic power showed itself, and she likewise became an ass and ran out to the old woman, and the dish of salad fell to the ground. Meantime the messenger sat beside the beautiful girl, and as no one came with the salad and she also was longing for it, she said, "I don't know what has become of the salad." The huntsman thought, "The salad must have already taken effect," and said, "I will go to the kitchen and inquire about it." As he went down he saw the two asses running about in the courtyard; the salad, however, was lying on the ground. "All right," said he, "the two have taken their portion," and he picked up the other leaves, laid them on the dish, and carried them to the maiden. "I bring you the delicate food myself," said he, "in order that you may not have to wait longer." Then she ate of it, and was, like the others, immediately deprived of her human form, and ran out into the courtyard in the shape of an ass.

After the huntsman had washed his face, so that the transformed ones could recognize him, he went down into the courtyard, and said, "Now you shall receive the wages of your treachery," and bound them together, all three with one rope, and drove them along until he came to a mill. He knocked at the window, the miller put out his head, and asked what he wanted. "I have three unmanageable beasts," answered he, "which I don't want to keep any longer. Will you take them in, and give them food and stable room, and manage them as I tell you, and then I will pay you what you ask." The miller said, "Why not? But how am I to manage them?" The huntsman then said that he was to give three beatings and one meal daily to the old donkey, and that was the witch; one beating and three meals to the younger one, which was the servant-girl; and to the youngest, which was the maiden, no beatings and three meals, for he could not bring himself to have the maiden beaten. After that he went back into the castle, and found therein everything he needed.

After a couple of days, the miller came and said he must inform him that the old ass which had received three beatings and only one meal daily was dead; "the two others," he continued, "are certainly not dead, and are fed three times daily, but they are so sad that they cannot last much longer." The huntsman was moved to pity, put away his anger, and told the miller to drive them back again to him. And when they came, he gave them some of the good salad, so that they became human again. The beautiful girl fell on her knees before him, and said, "Ah, my beloved, forgive me for the evil I have done you; my mother drove me to it; it was done against my will, for I love you dearly. Your wishing-cloak hangs in a cupboard, and as for the bird's-heart I will take a vomiting potion." But he thought otherwise, and said, "Keep it; it is all the same, for I will take thee for my true wife." So the wedding was celebrated, and they lived happily together until their death.

Clever Hans

The mother of Hans said: 'Whither away, Hans?' Hans answered: 'To Gretel.' 'Behave well, Hans.' 'Oh, I'll behave well. Goodbye, mother.' 'Goodbye, Hans.' Hans comes to Gretel. 'Good day, Gretel.' 'Good day, Hans. What do you bring that is good?' 'I bring nothing, I want to have something given me.' Gretel presents Hans with a needle, Hans says: 'Goodbye, Gretel.' 'Goodbye, Hans.'

Hans takes the needle, sticks it into a hay-cart, and follows the cart home. 'Good evening, mother.' 'Good evening, Hans. Where have you been?' 'With Gretel.' 'What did you take her?' 'Took nothing; had something given me.' 'What did Gretel give you?' 'Gave me a needle.' 'Where is the needle, Hans?' 'Stuck in the hay-cart.' 'That was ill done, Hans. You should have stuck the needle in your sleeve.' 'Never mind, I'll do better next time.'

'Whither away, Hans?' 'To Gretel, mother.' 'Behave well, Hans.' 'Oh, I'll behave well. Goodbye, mother.' 'Goodbye, Hans.' Hans comes to Gretel. 'Good day, Gretel.' 'Good day, Hans. What do you bring that is good?' 'I bring nothing. I want to have something given to me.' Gretel presents Hans with a knife. 'Goodbye, Gretel.' 'Goodbye, Hans.' Hans takes the knife, sticks it in his sleeve, and goes home. 'Good evening, mother.' 'Good evening, Hans. Where have you been?' 'With Gretel.' What did you take her?' 'Took her nothing, she gave me something.' 'What did Gretel give you?' 'Gave me a knife.' 'Where is the knife, Hans?' 'Stuck in my sleeve.' 'That's ill done,

Hans, you should have put the knife in your pocket.' 'Never mind, will do better next time.'

'Whither away, Hans?' 'To Gretel, mother.' 'Behave well, Hans.' 'Oh, I'll behave well. Goodbye, mother.' 'Goodbye, Hans.' Hans comes to Gretel. 'Good day, Gretel.' 'Good day, Hans. What good thing do you bring?' 'I bring nothing, I want something given me.' Gretel presents Hans with a young goat. 'Goodbye, Gretel.' 'Goodbye, Hans.' Hans takes the goat, ties its legs, and puts it in his pocket. When he gets home it is suffocated. 'Good evening, mother.' 'Good evening, Hans. Where have you been?' 'With Gretel.' 'What did you take her?' 'Took nothing, she gave me something.' 'What did Gretel give you?' 'She gave me a goat.' 'Where is the goat, Hans?' 'Put it in my pocket.' 'That was ill done, Hans, you should have put a rope round the goat's neck.' 'Never mind, will do better next time.'

'Whither away, Hans?' 'To Gretel, mother.' 'Behave well, Hans.' 'Oh, I'll behave well. Goodbye, mother.' 'Goodbye, Hans.' Hans comes to Gretel. 'Good day, Gretel.' 'Good day, Hans. What good thing do you bring?' 'I bring nothing, I want something given me.' Gretel presents Hans with a piece of bacon. 'Goodbye, Gretel.' 'Goodbye, Hans.'

Hans takes the bacon, ties it to a rope, and drags it away behind him. The dogs come and devour the bacon. When he gets home, he has the rope in his hand, and there is no longer anything hanging on to it. 'Good evening, mother.' 'Good evening, Hans. Where have you been?' 'With Gretel.' 'What did you take her?' 'I took her nothing, she gave me something.' 'What did Gretel give you?' 'Gave me a bit of bacon.' 'Where is the bacon, Hans?' 'I tied it to a rope, brought it home, dogs took it.' 'That was ill done, Hans, you should have carried the bacon on your head.' 'Never mind, will do better next time.'

'Whither away, Hans?' 'To Gretel, mother.' 'Behave well, Hans.' 'I'll behave well. Goodbye, mother.' 'Goodbye, Hans.' Hans comes to Gretel. 'Good day, Gretel.' 'Good day, Hans, What good thing do you bring?' 'I bring nothing, but would have something given.' Gretel presents Hans with a calf. 'Goodbye, Gretel.' 'Goodbye, Hans.'

Hans takes the calf, puts it on his head, and the calf kicks his face. 'Good evening, mother.' 'Good evening, Hans. Where have you been?' 'With Gretel.' 'What did you take her?' 'I took nothing, but had something given me.' 'What did Gretel give you?' 'A calf.' 'Where have you the calf, Hans?' 'I set it on my head and it kicked my face.' 'That was ill done, Hans, you should have led the calf, and put it in the stall.' 'Never mind, will do better next time.'

'Whither away, Hans?' 'To Gretel, mother.' 'Behave well, Hans.' 'I'll behave well. Goodbye, mother.' 'Goodbye, Hans.'

Hans comes to Gretel. 'Good day, Gretel.' 'Good day, Hans. What good thing do you bring?' 'I bring nothing, but would have something given.' Gretel says to Hans: 'I will go with you.'

Hans takes Gretel, ties her to a rope, leads her to the rack, and binds her fast. Then Hans goes to his mother. 'Good evening, mother.' 'Good evening, Hans. Where have you been?' 'With Gretel.' 'What did you take her?' 'I took her nothing.' 'What did Gretel give you?' 'She gave me nothing, she came with me.' 'Where have you left Gretel?' 'I led her by the rope, tied her to the rack, and scattered some grass for her.' 'That was ill done, Hans, you should have cast friendly eyes on her.' 'Never mind, will do better.'

Hans went into the stable, cut out all the calves' and sheep's eyes, and threw them in Gretel's face. Then Gretel became angry, tore herself loose and ran away, and was no longer the bride of Hans.

THE IRON STOVE

IN the days when wishing was still of some use, a King's son was bewitched by an old witch, and shut up in an iron stove in a forest. There he passed many years, and no one could deliver him. Then a King's daughter came into the forest, who had lost herself, and could not find her father's kingdom again. After she had wandered about for nine days, she at length came to the iron stove. Then a voice came forth from it, and asked her, "Whence comest thou, and whither goest, thou?" She answered, "I have lost my father's kingdom, and cannot get home again." Then a voice inside the iron stove said, "I will help thee to get home again, and that indeed most swiftly, if thou wilt promise to do what I desire of thee. I am the son of a far greater King than thy father, and I will marry thee."

Then was she afraid, and thought, "Good heavens! What can I do with an iron stove?" But as she much wished to get home to her father, she promised to do as he desired. But he said, "Thou shalt return here, and bring a knife with thee, and scrape a hole in the iron." Then he gave her a companion who walked near her, but did not speak, but in two hours he took her home; there was great joy in the castle when the King's daughter came home, and the old King fell on her neck and kissed her. She, however, was sorely troubled, and said, "Dear father, what I have suffered! I should never have got home again from the great wild forest, if I had not come to an iron stove, but I have been forced to give my word that I will go back to it, set it free, and marry it." Then the old King was so terrified that he all but fainted, for he had but this one daughter. They therefore resolved they would send, in her place, the miller's daughter, who was very beautiful. They took her there, gave her a knife, and said she was to scrape at the iron stove. So she scraped at it for four-and-twenty hours, but could not bring off the least morsel of it. When day dawned, a voice in the stove said, "It seems to me it is day outside." Then she answered, "It seems so to me too; I fancy I hear the noise of my father's mill."

"So thou art a miller's daughter! Then go thy way at once, and let the King's daughter come here." Then she went away at once, and told the old King that the man outside there, would have none of her he wanted the King's daughter. They, however, still had a swine-herd's daughter, who was even prettier than the miller's daughter, and they determined to give her a piece of gold to go to the iron stove instead of the King's daughter. So she was taken thither, and she also had to scrape for four-and-twenty hours. She, however, made nothing of it. When day broke, a voice inside the stove cried, "It seems to me it is day outside!" Then answered she, "So it seems to me also; I fancy I hear my father's horn blowing."

"Then thou art a swine-herd's daughter! Go away at once, and tell the King's daughter to come, and tell her all must be done as promised, and if she does not come, everything in the kingdom shall be ruined and destroyed, and not one stone be left standing on another." When the King's daughter heard that she began to weep, but now there was nothing for it but to keep her promise. So she took leave of her father, put a knife in her pocket, and went forth to the iron stove in the forest. When she got there, she began to scrape, and the iron gave way, and when two hours were over, she had already scraped a small hole. Then she peeped in, and saw a youth so handsome, and so brilliant with gold and with precious jewels, that her very soul was delighted. Now, therefore, she went on scraping, and made the hole so large that he was able to get out. Then said he, "Thou art mine, and I am thine; thou art my bride, and hast released me." He wanted to take her away with him to his kingdom, but she entreated him to let her go once again to her father, and the King's son allowed her to do so, but she was not to say more to her father than three words, and then she was to come back again. So she went home, but she spoke more than three words, and instantly the iron stove disappeared, and was taken far away over glass mountains and piercing swords; but the King's son was set free, and no longer shut up in it. After this she bade good-bye to her father, took some money with her, but not much, and went back to the great forest, and looked for the iron stove, but it was nowhere to be found. For nine days she sought it, and then her hunger grew so great that she did not know what to do, for she could no longer live. When it was evening, she seated herself in a small tree, and made up her mind to spend the night there, as she was afraid of wild beasts. When midnight drew near she saw in the distance a small light, and thought, "Ah, there I should be saved!" She got down from the tree, and went towards the light, but on the way she prayed.

Then she came to a little old house, and much grass had grown all about it, and a small heap of wood lay in front of it. She thought, "Ah, whither have I come," and peeped in through the window, but she saw nothing inside but toads, big and little, except a table well covered with wine and roast meat, and the plates and glasses were of silver. Then she took courage, and knocked at the door. The fat toad cried,

"Little green waiting-maid,
Waiting-maid with the limping leg,
Little dog of the limping leg,
Hop hither and thither,
And quickly see who is without:"

and a small toad came walking by and opened the door to her. When she entered, they all bade her welcome, and she was forced to sit down. They asked, "Where hast thou come from, and whither art thou going?" Then she related all that had befallen her, and how because she had transgressed the order which had been given her not to say more than three words, the stove, and the King's son also, had disappeared, and now she was about to seek him over hill and dale until she found him. Then the old fat one said,

"Little green waiting-maid,
Waiting-maid with the limping leg,
Little dog of the limping leg,
Hop hither and thither,
And bring me the great box."

Then the little one went and brought the box. After this they gave her meat and drink, and took her to a well-made bed, which felt like silk and velvet, and she laid herself therein, in God's name, and slept. When morning came she arose, and the old toad gave her three needles out of the great box which she was to take with her; they would be needed by her, for she had to cross a high glass mountain, and go over three piercing swords and a great lake. If she did all this she would get her lover back again. Then she gave her three things, which she was to take the greatest care of, namely, three large needles, a plough-wheel, and three nuts. With these she travelled onwards, and when she came to the glass mountain which was so slippery, she stuck the three needles first behind her feet and then before them, and so got over it, and when she was over it, she hid them in a place which she marked carefully. After this she came to the three piercing swords, and then she seated herself on her plough-wheel, and rolled over them. At last she arrived in front of a great lake, and when she had crossed it, she came to a large and beautiful castle. She went and asked for a place; she was a poor girl, she said, and would like to be hired. She knew, however, that the King's son whom she had released from the iron stove in the great forest was in the castle. Then she was taken as a scullery-maid at low wages. But, already the King's son had another maiden by his side whom he wanted to marry, for he thought that she had long been dead.

In the evening, when she had washed up and was done, she felt in her pocket and found the three nuts which the old toad had given her. She cracked one with her teeth, and was going to eat the kernel when lo and behold there was a stately royal garment in it! But when the bride heard of this she came and asked for the dress, and wanted to buy it, and said, "It is not a dress for a servant-girl." But she said no, she would not sell it, but if the bride would grant her one thing she should have it, and that was, leave to sleep one night in her bridegroom's chamber. The bride gave her permission because the dress was so pretty, and she had never had one like it. When it was evening she said to her bridegroom, "That silly girl will sleep in thy room." "If thou art willing so am I," said he. She, however, gave him a glass of wine in which she had poured a sleeping-draught. So the bridegroom and the scullery-maid went to sleep in the room, and he slept so soundly that she could not waken him.

She wept the whole night and cried, "I set thee free when thou wert in an iron stove in the wild forest, I sought thee, and walked over a glass mountain, and three sharp swords, and a great lake before I found thee, and yet thou wilt not hear me!"

The servants sat by the chamber-door, and heard how she thus wept the whole night through, and in the morning they told it to their lord. And the next evening when she had washed up, she opened the second nut, and a far more beautiful dress was within it, and when the bride beheld it, she wished to buy that also. But the girl would not take money, and begged that she might once again sleep in the bridegroom's chamber. The bride, however, gave him a sleeping-drink, and he slept so soundly that he could hear nothing. But the scullery-maid wept the whole night long, and cried, "I set thee free when thou wert in an iron stove in the wild forest, I sought thee, and walked over a glass mountain, and over three sharp swords and a great lake before I found thee, and yet thou wilt not hear me!" The servants sat by the chamber-door and heard her weeping the whole night through, and in the morning informed their lord of it. And on the third evening, when she had washed up, she opened the third nut, and within it was a still more beautiful dress which was stiff with pure gold. When the bride saw that she wanted to have it, but the maiden only gave it up on condition that she might for the third time sleep in the bridegroom's apartment. The

King's son was, however, on his guard, and threw the sleeping-draught away. Now, therefore, when she began to weep and to cry, "Dearest love, I set thee free when thou wert in the iron stove in the terrible wild forest," the King's son leapt up and said, "Thou art the true one, thou art mine, and I am thine." Thereupon, while it was still night, he got into a carriage with her, and they took away the false bride's clothes so that she could not get up. When they came to the great lake, they sailed across it, and when they reached the three sharp-cutting swords they seated themselves on the plough-wheel, and when they got to the glass mountain they thrust the three needles in it, and so at length they got to the little old house; but when they went inside that, it was a great castle, and the toads were all disenchanted, and were King's children, and full of happiness. Then the wedding was celebrated, and the King's son and the princess remained in the castle, which was much larger than the castles of their fathers. As, however, the old King grieved at being left alone, they fetched him away, and brought him to live with them, and they had two kingdoms, and lived in happy wedlock.

A mouse did run,
This story is done.

SWEET PORRIDGE

THERE was a poor but good little girl who lived alone with her mother, and they no longer had anything to eat. So the child went into the forest, and there an aged woman met her who was aware of her sorrow, and presented her with a little pot, which when she said,

"Cook, little pot, cook," would cook good, sweet porridge, and when she said, "Stop, little pot," it ceased to cook.

The girl took the pot home to her mother, and now they were freed from their poverty and hunger, and ate sweet porridge as often as they chose.

Once on a time when the girl had gone out, her mother said, "Cook, little pot, cook." And it did cook and she ate till she was satisfied, and then she wanted the pot to stop cooking, but did not know the word. So it went on cooking and the porridge rose over the edge, and still it cooked on until the kitchen and whole house were full, and then the next house, and then the whole street, just as if it wanted to satisfy the hunger of the whole world, and there was the greatest distress, but no one knew how to stop it. At last when only one single house remained, the child came home and just said, "Stop, little pot," and it stopped and gave up cooking, and whosoever wished to return to the town had to eat his way back.

Snow-White And Rose-Red

There was once a poor widow who lived in a lonely cottage. In front of the cottage was a garden wherein stood two rose-trees, one of which bore white and the other red roses. She had two children who were like the two rose-trees, and one was called Snow-white, and the other Rose-red. They were as good and happy, as busy and cheerful as ever two children in the world were, only Snow-white was more quiet and gentle than Rose-red. Rose-red liked better to run about in the meadows and fields seeking flowers and catching butterflies; but Snow-white sat at home with her mother, and helped her with her housework, or read to her when there was nothing to do.

The two children were so fond of one another that they always held each other by the hand when they went out together, and when Snow-white said: 'We will not leave each other,' Rose-red answered: 'Never so long as we live,' and their mother would add: 'What one has she must share with the other.'

They often ran about the forest alone and gathered red berries, and no beasts did them any harm, but came close to them trustfully. The little hare would eat a cabbage-leaf out of their hands, the roe grazed by their side, the stag leapt merrily by them, and the birds sat still upon the boughs, and sang whatever they knew.

No mishap overtook them; if they had stayed too late in the forest, and night came on, they laid themselves down near one another upon the moss, and slept until morning came, and their mother knew this and did not worry on their account.

Once when they had spent the night in the wood and the dawn had roused them, they saw a beautiful child in a shining white dress sitting near their bed. He got up and looked quite kindly at them, but said nothing and went into the forest. And when they looked round they found that they had been sleeping quite close to a precipice, and would certainly have fallen into it in the darkness if they had gone only a few paces further. And their mother told them that it must have been the angel who watches over good children.

Snow-white and Rose-red kept their mother's little cottage so neat that it was a pleasure to look inside it. In the summer Rose-red took care of the house, and every morning laid a wreath of flowers by her mother's bed before she awoke, in which was a rose from each tree. In the winter Snow-white lit the fire and hung the kettle on the hob. The kettle was of brass and shone like gold, so brightly was it polished. In the evening, when the snowflakes fell, the mother said: 'Go, Snow-white, and bolt the door,' and then they sat round the hearth, and the mother took her spectacles and read aloud out of a large book, and the two girls listened as they sat and spun. And close by them lay a lamb upon the floor, and behind them upon a perch sat a white dove with its head hidden beneath its wings.

One evening, as they were thus sitting comfortably together, someone knocked at the door as if he wished to be let in. The mother said: 'Quick, Rose-red, open the door, it must be a traveller who is seeking shelter.' Rose-red went and pushed back the bolt, thinking that it was a poor man, but it was not; it was a bear that stretched his broad, black head within the door.

Rose-red screamed and sprang back, the lamb bleated, the dove fluttered, and Snow-white hid herself behind her mother's bed. But the bear began to speak and said: 'Do not be afraid, I will do you no harm! I am half-frozen, and only want to warm myself a little beside you.'

'Poor bear,' said the mother, 'lie down by the fire, only take care that you do not burn your coat.' Then she cried: 'Snow-white, Rose-red, come out, the bear will do you no harm, he means well.' So they both came out, and by-and-by the lamb and dove came nearer, and were not afraid of him. The bear said: 'Here, children, knock the snow out of my coat a little'; so they brought the broom and swept the bear's hide clean; and he stretched himself by the fire and growled contentedly and comfortably. It was not long before they grew quite at home, and played tricks with their clumsy guest. They tugged his hair with their hands, put their feet upon his back and rolled him about, or they took a hazel-switch and beat him, and when he growled they laughed. But the bear took it all in good part, only when they were too rough he called out: 'Leave me alive, children,

Snow-white, Rose-red,

Will you beat your wooer dead?'

When it was bed-time, and the others went to bed, the mother said to the bear: 'You can lie there by the hearth, and then you will be safe from the cold and the bad weather.' As soon as day dawned the two children let him out, and he trotted across the snow into the forest.

Henceforth the bear came every evening at the same time, laid himself down by the hearth, and let the children amuse themselves with him as much as they liked; and they got so used to him that the doors were never fastened until their black friend had arrived.

When spring had come and all outside was green, the bear said one morning to Snow-white: 'Now I must go away, and cannot come back for the whole summer.' 'Where are you going, then, dear bear?' asked Snow-white. 'I must go into the forest and guard my treasures from the wicked dwarfs. In the winter, when the earth is frozen hard, they are obliged to stay below and cannot work their way through; but now, when the sun has thawed and warmed the earth, they break through it, and come out to pry and steal; and what once gets into their hands, and in their caves, does not easily see daylight again.'

Snow-white was quite sorry at his departure, and as she unbolted the door for him, and the bear was hurrying out, he caught against the bolt and a piece of his hairy coat was torn off, and it seemed to Snow-white as if she had seen gold shining through it, but she was not sure about it. The bear ran away quickly, and was soon out of sight behind the trees.

A short time afterwards the mother sent her children into the forest to get firewood. There they found a big tree which lay felled on the ground, and close by the trunk something was jumping backwards and forwards in the grass, but they could not make out what it was. When they came nearer they saw a dwarf with an old withered face and a snow-white beard a yard long. The end of the beard was caught in a crevice of the tree, and the little fellow was jumping about like a dog tied to a rope, and did not know what to do.

He glared at the girls with his fiery red eyes and cried: 'Why do you stand there? Can you not come here and help me?' 'What are you up to, little man?' asked Rose-red. 'You stupid, prying goose!' answered the dwarf: 'I was going to split the tree to get a little wood for cooking. The little bit of food that we people get is immediately burnt up with heavy logs; we do not swallow so much as you coarse, greedy folk. I had just driven the wedge safely in, and everything was going as I wished; but the cursed wedge was too smooth and suddenly sprang out, and the tree closed so quickly that I could not pull out my beautiful white beard; so now it is tight and I cannot get away, and the silly, sleek, milk-faced things laugh! Ugh! how odious you are!'

The children tried very hard, but they could not pull the beard out, it was caught too fast. 'I will run and fetch someone,' said Rose-red. 'You senseless goose!' snarled the dwarf; 'why should you fetch someone? You are already two too many for me; can you not think of something better?' 'Don't be impatient,' said Snow-white, 'I will help you,' and she pulled her scissors out of her pocket, and cut off the end of the beard.

As soon as the dwarf felt himself free he laid hold of a bag which lay amongst the roots of the tree, and which was full of gold, and lifted it up, grumbling to himself: 'Uncouth people, to cut off a piece of my fine beard. Bad luck to you!' and then he swung the bag upon his back, and went off without even once looking at the children.

Some time afterwards Snow-white and Rose-red went to catch a dish of fish. As they came near the brook they saw something like a large grasshopper jumping towards the water, as if it were going to leap in. They ran to it and found it was the dwarf. 'Where are you going?' said Rose-red; 'you surely don't want to go into the water?' 'I am not such a fool!' cried the dwarf; 'don't you see that the accursed fish wants to pull me in?' The little man had been sitting there fishing, and unluckily the wind had tangled up his beard with the fishing-line; a moment later a big fish made a bite and the feeble creature had not strength to pull it out; the fish kept the upper hand and pulled the dwarf towards him. He held on to all the reeds and rushes, but it was of little good, for he was forced to follow the movements of the fish, and was in urgent danger of being dragged into the water.

The girls came just in time; they held him fast and tried to free his beard from the line, but all in vain, beard and line were entangled fast together. There was nothing to do but to bring out the scissors and cut the beard, whereby a small part of it was lost. When the dwarf saw that he screamed out: 'Is that civil, you toadstool, to disfigure a man's face? Was it not enough to clip off the end of my beard? Now you have cut off the best part of it. I cannot let myself be seen by my people. I wish you had been made to run the soles off your shoes!' Then he took out a sack of pearls which lay in the rushes, and without another word he dragged it away and disappeared behind a stone.

It happened that soon afterwards the mother sent the two children to the town to buy needles and thread, and laces and ribbons. The road led them across a heath upon which huge pieces of rock lay strewn about. There they noticed a large bird hovering in the air, flying slowly round and round above them; it sank lower and lower, and at last settled near a rock not far away. Immediately they heard a loud, piteous cry. They ran up and saw with horror that the eagle had seized their old acquaintance the dwarf, and was going to carry him off.

The children, full of pity, at once took tight hold of the little man, and pulled against the eagle so long that at last he let his booty go. As soon as the dwarf had recovered from his first fright he cried with his shrill voice: 'Could you not have done it more carefully! You dragged at my brown coat so that it is all torn and full of holes, you clumsy creatures!' Then he took up a sack full of precious stones, and slipped away again under the rock into his hole. The girls, who by this time were used to his ingratitude, went on their way and did their business in town.

As they crossed the heath again on their way home they surprised the dwarf, who had emptied out his bag of precious stones in a clean spot, and had not thought that anyone would come there so late. The evening sun shone upon the brilliant stones; they glittered and sparkled with all colours so beautifully that the children stood still and stared at them. 'Why do you stand gaping there?' cried the dwarf, and his ashen-grey face became copper-red with rage. He was still cursing when a loud growling was heard, and a black bear came trotting towards them out of the forest. The dwarf sprang up in a fright, but he could not reach his cave, for the bear was already close. Then in the dread of his heart he cried: 'Dear Mr Bear, spare me, I will give you all my treasures; look, the beautiful jewels lying there! Grant me my life; what do you want with such a slender little fellow as I? you would not feel me between your teeth. Come, take these two wicked girls, they are tender morsels for you, fat as young quails; for mercy's sake eat them!' The bear took no heed of his words, but gave the wicked creature a single blow with his paw, and he did not move again.

The girls had run away, but the bear called to them: 'Snow-white and Rose-red, do not be afraid; wait, I will come with you.' Then they recognized his voice and waited, and when he came up to them suddenly his bearskin fell off, and he stood there a handsome man, clothed all in gold. 'I am a king's son,' he said, 'and I was bewitched by that wicked dwarf, who had stolen my treasures; I have had to run about the forest as a savage bear until I was freed by his death. Now he has got his well-deserved punishment.

Snow-white was married to him, and Rose-red to his brother, and they divided between them the great treasure which the dwarf had gathered together in his cave. The old mother lived peacefully and happily with her children for many years. She took the two rose-trees with her, and they stood before her window, and every year bore the most beautiful roses, white and red.

One-Eye, Two-Eyes, And Three-Eyes

THERE was once a woman who had three daughters, the eldest of whom was called One-eye, because she had only one eye in the middle of her forehead, and the second, Two-eyes, because she had two eyes like other folks, and the youngest, Three-eyes, because she had three eyes; and her third eye was also in the centre of her forehead. However, as Two-eyes saw just as other human beings did, her sisters and her mother could not endure her. They said to her, "Thou, with thy two eyes, art no better than the common people; thou dost not belong to us!" They pushed her about, and threw old clothes to her, and gave her nothing to eat but what they left, and did everything that they could to make her unhappy. It came to pass that Two-eyes had to go out into the fields and tend the goat, but she was still quite hungry, because her sisters had given her so little to eat. So she sat down on a ridge and began to weep, and so bitterly that two streams ran down from her eyes. And once when she looked up in her grief, a woman was standing beside her, who said, "Why art thou weeping, little Two-eyes?" Two-Eyes answered, "Have I not reason to weep, when I have two eyes like other people, and my sisters and mother hate me for it, and push me from one corner to another, throw old clothes at me, and give me nothing to eat but the scraps they leave? To-day they have given me so little that I am still quite hungry." Then the wise woman said, "Wipe away thy tears, Two-eyes, and I will tell thee something to stop thee ever suffering from hunger again; just say to thy goat,

"Bleat, my little goat, bleat,
Cover the table with something to eat,"

and then a clean well-spread little table will stand before thee, with the most delicious food upon it of which thou mayst eat as much as thou art inclined for, and when thou hast had enough, and hast no more need of the little table, just say,

"Bleat, bleat, my little goat, I pray,
And take the table quite away,"

and then it will vanish again from thy sight." Hereupon the wise woman departed. But Two-eyes thought, "I must instantly make a trial, and see if what she said is true, for I am far too hungry," and she said,

"Bleat, my little goat, bleat,
Cover the table with something to eat,"

and scarcely had she spoken the words than a little table, covered with a white cloth, was standing there, and on it was a plate with a knife and fork, and a silver spoon; and the most delicious food was there also, warm and smoking as if it had just come out of the kitchen. Then Two-eyes said the shortest prayer she knew, "Lord God, be with us always, Amen," and helped herself to some food, and enjoyed it. And when she was satisfied, she said, as the wise woman had taught her,

"Bleat, bleat, my little goat, I pray,
And take the table quite away,"

and immediately the little table and everything on it was gone again. "That is a delightful way of keeping house!" thought Two-eyes, and was quite glad and happy.

In the evening, when she went home with her goat, she found a small earthenware dish with some food, which her sisters had set ready for her, but she did not touch it. Next day she again went out with her goat, and left the few bits of broken bread which had been handed to her, lying untouched. The first and second time that she did this, her sisters did not remark it at all, but as it happened every time, they did observe it, and said, "There is something wrong about Two-eyes, she always leaves her food untasted, and she used to eat up everything that was given her; she must have discovered other ways of getting food." In order that they might learn the truth, they resolved to send One-eye with Two-eyes when she went to drive her goat to the pasture, to observe what Two-eyes did when she was there, and whether any one brought her anything to eat and drink. So when Two-eyes set out the next time, One-eye went to her and said, "I will go with you to the pasture, and see that the goat is well taken care of, and driven where there is food." But Two-eyes knew what was in One-eye's mind, and drove the goat into high grass and said, "Come, One-eye, we will sit down, and I will sing something to you." One-eye sat down and was tired with the unaccustomed walk and the heat of the sun, and Two-eyes sang constantly,

"One eye, wakest thou?
One eye, sleepest thou?"

until One-eye shut her one eye, and fell asleep, and as soon as Two-eyes saw that One-eye was fast asleep, and could discover nothing, she said,

"Bleat, my little goat, bleat,
Cover the table with something to eat,"

and seated herself at her table, and ate and drank until she was satisfied, and then she again cried,

"Bleat, bleat, my little goat, I pray,
And take the table quite away,"

and in an instant all was gone. Two-eyes now awakened One-eye, and said, "One-eye, you want to take care of the goat, and go to sleep while you are doing it, and in the meantime the goat might run all over the world. Come, let us go home again." So they went home, and again Two-eyes let her little dish stand untouched, and One-eye could not tell her mother why she would not eat it, and to excuse herself said, "I fell asleep when I was out."

Next day the mother said to Three-eyes, "This time thou shalt go and observe if Two-eyes eats anything when she is out, and if any one fetches her food and drink, for she must eat and drink in secret." So Three-eyes went to Two-eyes, and said, "I will go with you and see if the goat is taken proper care of, and driven where there is food." But Two-eyes knew what was in Three-eyes' mind, and drove the goat into high grass and said, "We will sit down, and I will sing something to you, Three-eyes." Three-eyes sat down and was tired with the walk and with the heat of the sun, and Two-eyes began the same song as before, and sang,

"Three eyes, are you waking?"

but then, instead of singing,

"Three eyes, are you sleeping?"

as she ought to have done, she thoughtlessly sang,

"Two eyes, are you sleeping?"

and sang all the time,

"Three eyes, are you waking?
Two eyes, are you sleeping?"

Then two of the eyes which Three-eyes had, shut and fell asleep, but the third, as it had not been named in the song, did not sleep. It is true that Three-eyes shut it, but only in her cunning, to pretend it was asleep too, but it blinked, and could see everything very well. And when Two-eyes thought that Three-eyes was fast asleep, she used her little charm,

"Bleat, my little goat, bleat,
Cover the table with something to eat,"

and ate and drank as much as her heart desired, and then ordered the table to go away again,

"Bleat, bleat, my little goat, I pray,
And take the table quite away,"

and Three-eyes had seen everything. Then Two-eyes came to her, waked her and said, "Have you been asleep, Three-eyes? You are a good care-taker! Come, we will go home." And when they got home, Two-eyes again did not eat, and Three-eyes said to the mother, "Now, I know why that high-minded thing there does not eat. When she is out, she says to the goat,

"Bleat, my little goat, bleat,
Cover the table with something to eat,"

and then a little table appears before her covered with the best of food, much better than any we have here, and when she has eaten all she wants, she says,

"Bleat, bleat, my little goat, I pray,
And take the table quite away,"

and all disappears. I watched everything closely. She put two of my eyes to sleep by using a certain form of words, but luckily the one in my forehead kept awake." Then the envious mother cried, "Dost thou want to fare better than we do? The desire shall pass away," and she fetched a butcher's knife, and thrust it into the heart of the goat, which fell down dead.

When Two-eyes saw that, she went out full of trouble, seated herself on the ridge of grass at the edge of the field, and wept bitter tears. Suddenly the wise woman once more stood by her side, and said, "Two-eyes, why art thou weeping?" "Have I not reason to weep?" she answered. "The goat which covered the table for me every day when I spoke your charm, has been killed by my mother, and now I shall again have to bear hunger and want." The wise woman said, "Two-eyes, I will give thee a piece of good advice; ask thy sisters to give thee the entrails of the slaughtered goat, and bury them in the ground in front of the house, and thy fortune will be made." Then she vanished, and Two-eyes went home and said to her sisters, "Dear sisters, do give me some part of my goat; I don't wish for what is good, but give me the entrails." Then they laughed and said, "If that's all you want, you can have it." So Two-eyes took the entrails and buried them quietly in the evening, in front of the house-door, as the wise woman had counselled her to do.

Next morning, when they all awoke, and went to the house-door, there stood a strangely magnificent tree with leaves of silver, and fruit of gold hanging among them, so that in all the wide world there was nothing more beautiful or precious. They did not know how the tree could have come there during the night, but Two-eyes saw that it had grown up out of the entrails of the goat, for it was standing on the exact spot where she had buried them. Then the mother said to One-eye, "Climb up, my child, and gather some of the fruit of the tree for us." One-eye climbed up, but when she was about to get hold of one of the golden apples, the branch escaped from her hands, and that happened each time, so that she could not pluck a single apple, let her do what she might. Then said the mother, "Three-eyes, do you climb up; you with your three eyes can look about you better than One-eye." One-eye slipped down, and Three-eyes climbed up. Three-eyes was not more skilful, and might search as she liked, but the golden apples always escaped her. At length the mother grew impatient, and climbed up herself, but could get hold of the fruit no better than One-eye and Three-eyes, for she always clutched empty air. Then said Two-eyes, "I will just go up, perhaps I may succeed better." The sisters cried, "You indeed, with your two eyes, what can you do?" But Two-eyes climbed up, and the golden apples did get out of her way, but came into her hand of their own accord, so that she could pluck them one after the other, and brought a whole apronful down with her.

The mother took them away from her, and instead of treating poor Two-eyes any better for this, she and One-eye and Three-eyes were only envious, because Two-eyes alone had been able to get the fruit, and they treated her still more cruelly.

It so befell that once when they were all standing together by the tree, a young knight came up. "Quick, Two-eyes," cried the two sisters, "creep under this, and don't disgrace us!" and with all speed they turned an empty barrel which was standing close by the tree over poor Two-eyes, and they pushed the golden apples which she had been gathering, under it too. When the knight came nearer he was a handsome lord, who stopped and admired the magnificent gold and silver tree, and said to the two sisters, "To whom does this fine tree belong? Any one who would bestow one branch of it on me might in return for it ask whatsoever he desired." Then One-eye and Three-eyes replied that the tree belonged to them, and that they would give him a branch. They both took great trouble, but they were not able to do it, for the branches and fruit both moved away from them every time. Then said the knight, "It is very strange that the tree should belong to you, and that you should still not be able to break a piece off." They again asserted that the tree was their property. Whilst they were saying so, Two-eyes rolled out a couple of golden apples from under the barrel to the feet of the knight, for she was vexed with One-eye and Three-eyes, for not speaking the truth. When the knight saw the apples he was astonished, and asked where they came from. One-eye and Three-eyes answered that they had another sister, who was not allowed to show herself, for she had only two eyes like any common person. The knight, however, desired to see her, and cried, "Two-eyes, come forth." Then Two-eyes, quite comforted, came from beneath the barrel, and the knight was surprised at her great beauty, and said, "Thou, Two-eyes, canst certainly break off a branch from the tree for me." "Yes," replied Two-eyes, "that I certainly shall be able to do, for the tree belongs to me." And she climbed up, and with the greatest ease broke off a branch with beautiful silver leaves and golden fruit, and gave it to the knight. Then said the knight, "Two-eyes, what shall I give thee for it?" "Alas!" answered Two-eyes, "I suffer from hunger and thirst, grief and want, from early morning till late night; if you would take me with you, and deliver me from these things, I should be happy." So the knight lifted Two-eyes on to his horse, and took her home with him to his father's castle, and there he gave her beautiful clothes, and meat and drink to her heart's content, and as he loved her so much he married her, and the wedding was solemnized with great rejoicing. When Two-eyes was thus carried away by the handsome knight, her two sisters grudged her good fortune in downright earnest. The wonderful tree, however, still remains with us," thought they, "and even if we can gather no fruit from it, still every one will stand still and look at it, and come to us and admire it. Who knows what good things may be in store for us?" But next morning, the tree had vanished, and all their hopes were at an end. And when Two-eyes looked out of the window of her own little room, to her great delight it was standing in front of it, and so it had followed her.

Two-eyes lived a long time in happiness. Once two poor women came to her in her castle, and begged for alms. She looked in their faces, and recognized her sisters, One-eye, and Three-eyes, who had fallen into such poverty that they had to wander about and beg their bread from door to door. Two-eyes, however, made them welcome, and was kind to them, and took care of them, so that they both with all their hearts repented the evil that they had done their sister in their youth.

THE GOOSE-GIRL AT THE WELL

THERE was once upon a time a very old woman, who lived with he flock of geese in a waste place among the mountains, and there had a little house. The waste was surrounded by a large forest, and every morning the old woman took her crutch and hobbled into it. There, however, the dame was quite active, more so than any one would have thought, considering her age, and collected grass for her geese, picked all the wild fruit she could reach, and carried everything home on her back. Any one would have thought that the heavy load would have weighed her to the ground, but she always brought it safely home. If any one met her, she greeted him quite courteously. "Good day, dear countryman, it is a fine day. Ah! you wonder that I should drag grass about, but every one must take his burthen on his back." Nevertheless, people did not like to meet her if they could help it, and took by preference a round-about way, and when a father with his boys passed her, he whispered to them, "Beware of the old woman. She has claws beneath her gloves; she is a witch." One morning, a handsome young man was going through the forest. The sun shone bright, the birds sang, a cool breeze crept through the leaves, and he was full of joy and gladness. He had as yet met no one, when he suddenly perceived the old witch kneeling on the ground cutting grass with a sickle. She had already thrust a whole load into her cloth, and near it stood two baskets, which were filled with wild apples and pears. "But, good little mother," said he, "how canst thou carry all that away?" "I must carry it, dear sir," answered she, "rich folk's children have no need to do such things, but with the peasant folk the saying goes, don't look behind you, you will only see how crooked your back is!"

"Will you help me?" she said, as he remained standing by her. "You have still a straight back and young legs, it would be a trifle to you. Besides, my house is not so very far from here, it stands there on the heath behind the hill. How soon you would bound up thither." The young man took compassion on the old woman. "My father is certainly no peasant," replied he, "but a rich count; nevertheless, that you may see that it is not only peasants who can carry things, I will take your bundle." If you will try it," said she, "I shall be very glad. You will certainly have to walk for an hour, but what will that signify to you; only you must carry the apples and pears as well?" It now seemed to the young man just a little serious, when he heard of an hour's walk, but the old woman would not let him off, packed the bundle on his back, and hung the two baskets on his arm. "See, it is quite light," said she. "No, it is not light," answered the count, and pulled a rueful face. "Verily, the bundle weighs as heavily as if it were full of cobble stones, and the apples and pears are as heavy as lead! I can scarcely breathe." He had a mind to put everything down again, but the old woman would not allow it. "Just look," said she mockingly, "the young gentleman will not carry what I, an old woman, have so often dragged along. You are ready with fine words, but when it comes to be earnest, you want to take to your heels. Why are you standing loitering there?" she continued. "Step out. No one will take the bundle off again." As long as he walked on level ground, it was still bearable, but when they came to the hill and had to climb, and the stones rolled down under his feet as if they were alive, it was beyond his strength. The drops of perspiration stood on his forehead, and ran, hot and cold, down his back. "Dame," said he, "I can go no farther. I want to rest a little." "Not here," answered the old woman, "when we have arrived at our journey's end, you can rest; but now you must go forward. Who knows what good it may do you?" "Old woman, thou art becoming shameless!" said the count, and tried to throw off the bundle, but he laboured in vain; it stuck as fast to his back as if it grew there. He turned and twisted, but he could not get rid of it. The old woman laughed at this, and sprang about quite delighted on her crutch. "Don't get angry, dear sir," said she, "you are growing as red in the face as a turkey-cock! Carry your bundle patiently. I will give you a good present when we get home."

What could he do. He was obliged to submit to his fate, and crawl along patiently behind the old woman. She seemed to grow more and more nimble, and his burden still heavier. All at once she made a spring, jumped on to the bundle and seated herself on the top of it; and however withered she might be, she was yet heavier than the stoutest country lass. The youth's knees trembled, but when he did not go on, the old woman hit him about the legs with a switch and with stinging-nettles. Groaning continually, he climbed the mountain, and at length reached the old woman's house, when he was just about to drop. When the geese perceived the old woman, they flapped their wings, stretched out their necks, ran to meet her, cackling all the while. Behind the flock walked, stick in hand, an old wench, strong and big, but ugly as night. "Good mother," said she to the old woman, "has anything happened to you, you have stayed away so long?" "By no means, my dear daughter," answered she, I have met with nothing bad, but, on the contrary, with this kind gentleman, who has carried my burthen for me; only think, he even took me on his back when I was tired. The way, too, has not seemed long to us; we have been merry, and have been cracking jokes with each other all the time." At last the old woman slid down, took the bundle off the young man's back, and the baskets from his arm, looked at him quite kindly, and said, "Now seat yourself on the bench before the door, and rest. You have fairly earned your wages, and they shall not be wanting." Then she said to the goose-girl, "Go into the house, my dear daughter, it is not becoming for thee to be alone with a young gentleman; one must not pour oil on to the fire, he might fall in love with thee." The count knew not whether to laugh or to cry. "Such a sweetheart as that," thought he, "could not touch my heart, even if she were thirty years younger." In the meantime the old woman stroked and fondled her geese as if they were children, and then went into the house with her daughter. The youth lay down on the bench, under a wild apple-tree. The air was warm and mild; on all sides stretched a green meadow, which was set with cowslips, wild thyme, and a thousand other flowers; through the midst of it rippled a clear brook on which the sun sparkled, and the white geese went walking backwards and forwards, or paddled in the water. "It is quite delightful here," said he, "but I am so tired that I cannot keep my eyes open; I will sleep a little. If only a gust of wind does not come and blow my legs off my body, for they are as rotten as tinder."

When he had slept a little while, the old woman came and shook him till he awoke. "Sit up," said she, "thou canst not stay here; I have certainly treated thee hardly, still it has not cost thee thy life. Of money and land thou hast no need, here is something else for thee." Thereupon she thrust a little book into his hand, which was cut out of a single emerald. "Take great care of it," said she, "it will bring thee good fortune." The count sprang up, and as he felt that he was quite fresh, and had recovered his vigor, he thanked the old woman for her present, and set off without even once looking back at the beautiful daughter. When he was already some way off, he still heard in the distance the noisy cry of the geese.

For three days the count had to wander in the wilderness before he could find his way out. He then reached a large town, and as no one knew him, he was led into the royal palace, where the King and Queen were sitting on their throne. The count fell on one knee, drew the emerald book out of his pocket, and laid it at the Queen's feet. She bade him rise and hand her the little book. Hardly, however, had she opened it, and looked therein, than she fell as if dead to the ground. The count was seized by the King's servants, and was being led to prison, when the Queen opened her eyes, and ordered them to release him, and every one was to go out, as she wished to speak with him in private.

When the Queen was alone, she began to weep bitterly, and said, "Of what use to me are the splendours and honours with which I am surrounded; every morning I awake in pain and sorrow. I had three daughters, the youngest of whom was so beautiful that the whole world looked on her as a wonder. She was as white as snow, as rosy as apple-blossom, and her hair as radiant as sun-beams. When she cried, not tears fell from her eyes, but pearls and jewels only. When she was fifteen years old, the King summoned all three sisters to come before his throne. You should have seen how all the people gazed when the youngest entered, it was just as if the sun were rising! Then the King spoke, "My daughters, I know not when my last day may arrive; I will to-day decide what each shall receive at my death. You all love me, but the one of you who loves me best, shall fare the best." Each of them said she loved him best. "Can you not express to me," said the King, "how much you do love me, and thus I shall see what you mean?" The eldest spoke. "I love my father as dearly as the sweetest sugar." The second, "I love my father as dearly as my prettiest dress." But the youngest was silent. Then the father said, "And thou, my dearest child, how much dost thou love me?" "I do not know, and can compare my love with nothing." But her father insisted that she should name something. So she said at last, "The best food does not please me without salt, therefore I love my father like salt." When the King heard that, he fell into a passion, and said, "If thou lovest me like salt, thy love shall also be repaid thee with salt." Then he divided the kingdom between the two elder, but caused a sack of salt to be bound on the back of the youngest, and two servants had to lead her forth into the wild forest. We all begged and prayed for her, said the Queen, "but the King's anger was not to be appeased. How she cried when she had to leave us! The whole road was strewn with the pearls which flowed from her eyes. The King soon afterwards repented of his great severity, and had the whole forest searched for the poor child, but no one could find her. When I think that the wild beasts have devoured her, I know not how to contain myself for sorrow; many a time I console myself with the hope that she is still alive, and may have hidden herself in a cave, or has found shelter with compassionate people. But picture to yourself, when I opened your little emerald book, a pearl lay therein, of exactly the same kind as those which used to fall from my daughter's eyes; and then you can also imagine how the sight of it stirred my heart. You must tell me how you came by that pearl." The count told her that he had received it from the old woman in the forest, who had appeared very strange to him, and must be a witch, but he had neither seen nor hear anything of the Queen's child. The King and the Queen resolved to seek out the old woman. They thought that there where the pearl had been, they would obtain news of their daughter.

The old woman was sitting in that lonely place at her spinning-wheel, spinning. It was already dusk, and a log which was burning on the hearth gave a scanty light. All at once there was a noise outside, the geese were coming home from the pasture, and uttering their hoarse cries. Soon afterwards the daughter also entered. But the old woman scarcely thanked her, and only shook her head a little. The daughter sat down beside her, took her spinning-wheel, and twisted the threads as nimbly as a young girl. Thus they both sat for two hours, and exchanged never a word.

At last something rustled at the window, and two fiery eyes peered in. It was an old night-owl, which cried, "Uhu!" three times. The old woman looked up just a little, then she said, "Now, my little daughter, it is time for thee to go out and do thy work." She rose and went out, and where did she go? Over the meadows ever onward into the valley. At last she came to a well, with three old oak-trees standing beside it; meanwhile the moon had risen large and round over the mountain, and it was so light that one could have found a needle. She removed a skin which covered her face, then bent down to the well, and began to wash herself. When she had finished, she dipped the skin also in the water, and then laid it on the meadow, so that it should bleach in the moonlight, and dry again. But how the maiden was changed! Such a change as that was never seen before! When the gray mask fell off, her golden hair broke forth like sunbeams, and spread about like a mantle over her whole form. Her eyes shone out as brightly as the stars in heaven, and her cheeks bloomed a soft red like apple-blossom.

But the fair maiden was sad. She sat down and wept bitterly. One tear after another forced itself out of her eyes, and rolled through her long hair to the ground. There she sat, and would have remained sitting a long time, if there had not been a rustling and cracking in the boughs of the neighbouring tree. She sprang up like a roe which has been overtaken by the shot of the hunter. Just then the moon was obscured by a dark cloud, and in an instant the maiden had put on the old skin and vanished, like a light blown out by the wind.

She ran back home, trembling like an aspen-leaf. The old woman was standing on the threshold, and the girl was about to relate what had befallen her, but the old woman laughed kindly, and said, "I already know all." She led her into the room and lighted a new log. She did not, however, sit down to her spinning again, but fetched a broom and began to sweep and scour, "All must be clean and sweet," she said to the girl. "But, mother," said the maiden, "why do you begin work at so late an hour?

What do you expect?" "Dost thou know then what time it is?" asked the old woman. "Not yet midnight," answered the maiden, "but already past eleven o'clock." "Dost thou not remember," continued the old woman, "that it is three years to-day since thou camest to me? Thy time is up, we can no longer remain together." The girl was terrified, and said, "Alas! dear mother, will you cast me off? Where shall I go? I have no friends, and no home to which I can go. I have always done as you bade me, and you have always been satisfied with me; do not send me away." The old woman would not tell the maiden what lay before her. "My stay here is over," she said to her, "but when I depart, house and parlour must be clean: therefore do not hinder me in my work. Have no care for thyself, thou shalt find a roof to shelter thee, and the wages which I will give thee shall also content thee." "But tell me what is about to happen," the maiden continued to entreat. "I tell thee again, do not hinder me in my work. Do not say a word more, go to thy chamber, take the skin off thy face, and put on the silken gown which thou hadst on when thou camest to me, and then wait in thy chamber until I call thee."

But I must once more tell of the King and Queen, who had journeyed forth with the count in order to seek out the old woman in the wilderness. The count had strayed away from them in the wood by night, and had to walk onwards alone. Next day it seemed to him that he was on the right track. He still went forward, until darkness came on, then he climbed a tree, intending to pass the night there, for he feared that he might lose his way. When the moon illumined the surrounding country he perceived a figure coming down the mountain. She had no stick in her hand, but yet he could see that it was the goose-girl, whom he had seen before in the house of the old woman. "Oho," cried he, "there she comes, and if I once get hold of one of the witches, the other shall not escape me!" But how astonished he was, when she went to the well, took off the skin and washed herself, when her golden hair fell down all about her, and she was more beautiful than any one whom he had ever seen in the whole world. He hardly dared to breathe, but stretched his head as far forward through the leaves as he dared, and stared at her. Either he bent over too far, or whatever the cause might be, the bough suddenly cracked, and that very moment the maiden slipped into the skin, sprang away like a roe, and as the moon was suddenly covered, disappeared from his eyes. Hardly had she disappeared, before the count descended from the tree, and hastened after her with nimble steps. He had not been gone long before he saw, in the twilight, two figures coming over the meadow. It was the King and Queen, who had perceived from a distance the light shining in the old woman's little house, and were going to it. The count told them what wonderful things he had seen by the well, and they did not doubt that it had been their lost daughter. They walked onwards full of joy, and soon came to the little house. The geese were sitting all round it, and had thrust their heads under their wings and were sleeping, and not one of them moved. The King and Queen looked in at the window, the old woman was sitting there quite quietly spinning, nodding her head and never looking round. The room was perfectly clean, as if the little mist men, who carry no dust on their feet, lived there. Their daughter, however, they did not see. They gazed at all this for a long time, at last they took heart, and knocked softly at the window. The old woman appeared to have been expecting them; she rose, and called out quite kindly, "Come in,--I know you already." When they had entered the room, the old woman said, "You might have spared yourself the long walk, if you had not three years ago unjustly driven away your child, who is so good and lovable. No harm has come to her; for three years she has had to tend the geese; with them she has learnt no evil, but has preserved her purity of heart. You, however, have been sufficiently punished by the misery in which you have lived." Then she went to the chamber and called, "Come out, my little daughter." Thereupon the door opened, and the princess stepped out in her silken garments, with her golden hair and her shining eyes, and it was as if an angel from heaven had entered.

She went up to her father and mother, fell on their necks and kissed them; there was no help for it, they all had to weep for joy. The young count stood near them, and when she perceived him she became as red in the face as a moss-rose, she herself did not know why. The King said, "My dear child, I have given away my kingdom, what shall I give thee?" "She needs nothing," said the old woman. "I give her the tears that she has wept on your account; they are precious pearls, finer than those that are found in the sea, and worth more than your whole kingdom, and I give her my little house as payment for her services." When the old woman had said that, she disappeared from their sight. The walls rattled a little, and when the King and Queen looked round, the little house had changed into a splendid palace, a royal table had been spread, and the servants were running hither and thither.

The story goes still further, but my grandmother, who related it to me, had partly lost her memory, and had forgotten the rest. I shall always believe that the beautiful princess married the count, and that they remained together in the palace, and lived there in all happiness so long as God willed it.

Whether the snow-white geese, which were kept near the little hut, were verily young maidens (no one need take offence,) whom the old woman had taken under her protection, and whether they now received their human form again, and stayed as handmaids to the young Queen, I do not exactly know, but I suspect it.

This much is certain, that the old woman was no witch, as people thought, but a wise woman, who meant well. Very likely it was she who, at the princess's birth, gave her the gift of weeping pearls instead of tears. That does not happen now-a-days, or else the poor would soon become rich.

The Shoes That Were Danced To Pieces

THERE was once upon a time a King who had twelve daughters, each one more beautiful than the other. They all slept together in one chamber, in which their beds stood side by side, and every night when they were in them the King locked the door, and bolted it. But in the morning when he unlocked the door, he saw that their shoes were worn out with dancing, and no one could find out how that had come to pass. Then the King caused it to be proclaimed that whosoever could discover where they danced at night, should choose one of them for his wife and be King after his death, but that whosoever came forward and had not discovered it within three days and nights, should have forfeited his life. It was not long before a King's son presented himself, and offered to undertake the enterprise. He was well received, and in the evening was led into a room adjoining the princesses' sleeping-chamber. His bed was placed there, and he was to observe where they went and danced, and in order that they might do nothing secretly or go away to some other place, the door of their room was left open.

But the eyelids of the prince grew heavy as lead, and he fell asleep, and when he awoke in the morning, all twelve had been to the dance, for their shoes were standing there with holes in the soles. On the second and third nights it fell out just the same, and then his head was struck off without mercy. Many others came after this and undertook the enterprise, but all forfeited their lives. Now it came to pass that a poor soldier, who had a wound, and could serve no longer, found himself on the road to the town where the King lived. There he met an old woman, who asked him where he was going. "I hardly know myself," answered he, and added in jest, "I had half a mind to discover where the princesses danced their shoes into holes, and thus become King." "That is not so difficult," said the old woman, "you must not drink the wine which will be brought to you at night, and must pretend to be sound asleep." With that she gave him a little cloak, and said, "If you put on that, you will be invisible, and then you can steal after the twelve." When the soldier had received this good advice, he went into the thing in earnest, took heart, went to the King, and announced himself as a suitor. He was as well received as the others, and royal garments were put upon him. He was conducted that evening at bed-time into the ante-chamber, and as he was about to go to bed, the eldest came and brought him a cup of wine, but he had tied a sponge under his chin, and let the wine run down into it, without drinking a drop. Then he lay down and when he had lain a while, he began to snore, as if in the deepest sleep. The twelve princesses heard that, and laughed, and the eldest said, "He, too, might as well have saved his life." With that they got up, opened wardrobes, presses, cupboards, and brought out pretty dresses; dressed themselves before the mirrors, sprang about, and rejoiced at the prospect of the dance. Only the youngest said, "I know not how it is; you are very happy, but I feel very strange; some misfortune is certainly about to befall us." "Thou art a goose, who art always frightened," said the eldest. "Hast thou forgotten how many Kings' sons have already come here in vain? I had hardly any need to give the soldier a sleeping-draught, in any case the clown would not have awakened." When they were all ready they looked carefully at the soldier, but he had closed his eyes and did not move or stir, so they felt themselves quite secure. The eldest then went to her bed and tapped it; it immediately sank into the earth, and one after the other they descended through the opening, the eldest going first. The soldier, who had watched everything, tarried no longer, put on his little cloak, and went down last with the youngest. Half-way down the steps, he just trod a little on her dress; she was terrified at that, and cried out, "What is that? who is pulling my dress?" "Don't be so silly!" said the eldest, "you have caught it on a nail." Then they went all the way down, and when they were at the bottom, they were standing in a wonderfully pretty avenue of trees, all the leaves of which were of silver, and shone and glistened. The soldier thought, "I must carry a token away with me," and broke off a twig from one of them, on which the tree cracked with a loud report. The youngest cried out again. "Something is wrong, did you hear the crack?" But the eldest said, "It is a gun fired for joy, because we have got rid of our prince so quickly." After that they came into an avenue where all the leaves were of gold, and lastly into a third where they were of bright diamonds; he broke off a twig from each, which made such a crack each time that the youngest started back in terror, but the eldest still maintained that they were salutes. They went on and came to a great lake whereon stood twelve little boats, and in every boat sat a handsome prince, all of whom were waiting for the twelve, and each took one of them with him, but the soldier seated himself by the youngest. Then her prince said, "I can't tell why the boat is so much heavier to-day; I shall have to row with all my strength, if

I am to get it across." "What should cause that," said the youngest, "but the warm weather? I feel very warm too." On the opposite side of the lake stood a splendid, brightly-lit castle, from whence resounded the joyous music of trumpets and kettle-drums. They rowed over there, entered, and each prince danced with the girl he loved, but the soldier danced with them unseen, and when one of them had a cup of wine in her hand he drank it up, so that the cup was empty when she carried it to her mouth; the youngest was alarmed at this, but the eldest always made her be silent. They danced there till three o'clock in the morning when all the shoes were danced into holes, and they were forced to leave off; the princes rowed them back again over the lake, and this time the soldier seated himself by the eldest. On the shore they took leave of their princes, and promised to return the following night. When they reached the stairs the soldier ran on in front and lay down in his bed, and when the twelve had come up slowly and wearily, he was already snoring so loudly that they could all hear him, and they said, "So far as he is concerned, we are safe." They took off their beautiful dresses, laid them away, put the worn-out shoes under the bed, and lay down. Next morning the soldier was resolved not to speak, but to watch the wonderful goings on, and again went with them. Then everything was done just as it had been done the first time, and each time they danced until their shoes were worn to pieces. But the third time he took a cup away with him as a token. When the hour had arrived for him to give his answer, he took the three twigs and the cup, and went to the King, but the twelve stood behind the door, and listened for what he was going to say. When the King put the question, "Where have my twelve daughters danced their shoes to pieces in the night?" he answered,

"In an underground castle with twelve princes," and related how it had come to pass, and brought out the tokens. The King then summoned his daughters, and asked them if the soldier had told the truth, and when they saw that they were betrayed, and that falsehood would be of no avail, they were obliged to confess all. Thereupon the King asked which of them he would have to wife? He answered, "I am no longer young, so give me the eldest." Then the wedding was celebrated on the self-same day, and the kingdom was promised him after the King's death. But the princes were bewitched for as many days as they had danced nights with the twelve.

The Nixie Of The Mill-Pond

THERE was once upon a time a miller who lived with his wife in great contentment. They had money and land, and their prosperity increased year by year more and more. But ill-luck comes like a thief in the night, as their wealth had increased so did it again decrease, year by year, and at last the miller could hardly call the mill in which he lived, his own. He was in great distress, and when he lay down after his day's work, found no rest, but tossed about in his bed, full of care. One morning he rose before daybreak and went out into the open air, thinking that perhaps there his heart might become lighter. As he was stepping over the mill-dam the first sunbeam was just breaking forth, and he heard a rippling sound in the pond. He turned round and perceived a beautiful woman, rising slowly out of the water. Her long hair, which she was holding off her shoulders with her soft hands, fell down on both sides, and covered her white body. He soon saw that she was the Nix of the Mill-pond, and in his fright did not know whether he should run away or stay where he was. But the nix made her sweet voice heard, called him by his name, and asked him why he was so sad? The miller was at first struck dumb, but when he heard her speak so kindly, he took heart, and told her how he had formerly lived in wealth and happiness, but that now he was so poor that he did not know what to do. "Be easy," answered the nix, "I will make thee richer and happier than thou hast ever been before, only thou must promise to give me the young thing which has just been born in thy house." "What else can that be," thought the miller, "but a young puppy or kitten?" and he promised her what she desired. The nix descended into the water again, and he hurried back to his mill, consoled and in good spirits. He had not yet reached it, when the maid-servant came out of the house, and cried to him to rejoice, for his wife had given birth to a little boy. The miller stood as if struck by lightning; he saw very well that the cunning nix had been aware of it, and had cheated him. Hanging his head, he went up to his wife's bedside and when she said, "Why dost thou not rejoice over the fine boy?" he told her what had befallen him, and what kind of a promise he had given to the nix. "Of what use to me are riches and prosperity?" he added, "if I am to lose my child; but what can I do?" Even the relations, who had come thither to wish them joy, did not know what to say. In the meantime prosperity again returned to the miller's house. All that he undertook succeeded, it was as if presses and coffers filled themselves of their own accord, and as if money multiplied nightly in the cupboards. It was not long before his wealth was greater than it had ever been before. But he could not rejoice over it untroubled, for the bargain which he had made with the nix tormented his soul. Whenever he passed the mill-pond, he feared she might ascend and remind him of his debt. He never let the boy himself go near the water. "Beware," he said to him, "if thou dost but touch the water, a hand will rise, seize thee, and draw thee down." But as year after year went by and the nix did not show herself again, the miller began to feel at ease. The boy grew up to be a youth and was apprenticed to a huntsman. When he had learnt everything, and had become an excellent huntsman, the lord of the village took him into his service. In the village lived a beautiful and true-hearted maiden, who pleased the huntsman, and when his master perceived that, he gave him a little house, the two were married, lived peacefully and happily, and loved each other with all their hearts.

One day the huntsman was chasing a roe; and when the animal turned aside from the forest into the open country, he pursued it and at last shot it. He did not notice that he was now in the neighbourhood of the dangerous mill-pond, and went, after he had disembowelled the stag, to the water, in order to wash his blood-stained hands. Scarcely, however, had he dipped them in than the nix ascended, smilingly wound her dripping arms around him, and drew him quickly down under the waves, which closed over him. When it was evening, and the huntsman did not return home, his wife became alarmed. She went out to seek him, and as he had often told her that he had to be on his guard against the snares of the nix, and dared not venture into the neighbourhood of the mill-pond, she already suspected what had happened. She hastened to the water, and when she found his hunting-pouch lying on the shore, she could no longer have any doubt of the misfortune. Lamenting her sorrow, and wringing her hands, she called on her beloved by name, but in vain. She hurried across to the other side of the pond, and called him anew; she reviled the nix with harsh words, but no answer followed. The surface of the water remained calm, only the crescent moon stared steadily back at her.

The poor woman did not leave the pond. With hasty steps, she paced round and round it, without resting a moment, sometimes in silence, sometimes uttering a loud cry, sometimes softly sobbing. At last her strength came to an end, she sank down to the ground and fell into a heavy sleep. Presently a dream took possession of her. She was anxiously climbing upwards between great masses of rock; thorns and briars caught her feet, the rain beat in her face, and the wind tossed her long hair about. When she had reached the summit, quite a different sight presented itself to her; the sky was blue, the air soft, the ground sloped gently downwards, and on a green meadow, gay with flowers of every colour, stood a pretty cottage. She went up to it and opened the door; there sat an old woman with white hair, who beckoned to her kindly. At that very moment, the poor woman awoke, day had already dawned, and she at once resolved to act in accordance with her dream. She laboriously climbed the mountain; everything was exactly as she had seen it in the night. The old woman received her kindly, and pointed out a chair on which she might sit. "Thou must have met with a misfortune," she said, "since thou hast sought out my lonely cottage." With tears, the woman related what had befallen her. "Be comforted," said the old woman, "I will help thee. Here is a golden comb for thee. Tarry till the full moon has risen, then go to the mill-pond, seat thyself on the shore, and comb thy long black hair with this comb. When thou hast done, lay it down on the bank, and thou wilt see what will happen."

The woman returned home, but the time till the full moon came, passed slowly. At last the shining disc appeared in the heavens, then she went out to the mill-pond, sat down and combed her long black hair with the golden comb, and when she had finished, she laid it down at the water's edge. It was not long before there was a movement in the depths, a wave rose, rolled to the shore, and bore the comb away with it. In not more than the time necessary for the comb to sink to the bottom, the surface of the water parted, and the head of the huntsman arose.

He did not speak, but looked at his wife with sorrowful glances. At the same instant, a second wave came rushing up, and covered the man's head. All had vanished, the mill-pond lay peaceful as before, and nothing but the face of the full moon shone on it. Full of sorrow, the woman went back, but again the dream showed her the cottage of the old woman. Next morning she again set out and complained of her woes to the wise woman. The old woman gave her a golden flute, and said, "Tarry till the full moon comes again, then take this flute; play a beautiful air on it, and when thou hast finished, lay it on the sand; then thou wilt see what will happen." The wife did as the old woman told her. No sooner was the flute lying on the sand than there was a stirring in the depths, and a wave rushed up and bore the flute away with it. Immediately afterwards the water parted, and not only the head of the man, but half of his body also arose. He stretched out his arms longingly towards her, but a second wave came up, covered him, and drew him down again. "Alas, what does it profit me?" said the unhappy woman, "that I should see my beloved, only to lose him again!" Despair filled her heart anew, but the dream led her a third time to the house of the old woman. She set out, and the wise woman gave her a golden spinning-wheel, consoled her and said, "All is not yet fulfilled, tarry until the time of the full moon, then take the spinning-wheel, seat thyself on the shore, and spin the spool full, and when thou hast done that, place the spinning-wheel near the water, and thou wilt see what will happen." The woman obeyed all she said exactly; as soon as the full moon showed itself, she carried the golden spinning-wheel to the shore, and span industriously until the flax came to an end, and the spool was quite filled with the threads. No sooner was the wheel standing on the shore than there was a more violent movement than before in the depths of the pond, and a mighty wave rushed up, and bore the wheel away with it. Immediately the head and the whole body of the man rose into the air, in a water-spout. He quickly sprang to the shore, caught his wife by the hand and fled. But they had scarcely gone a very little distance, when the whole pond rose with a frightful roar, and streamed out over the open country. The fugitives already saw death before their eyes, when the woman in her terror implored the help of the old woman, and in an instant they were transformed, she into a toad, he into a frog. The flood which had overtaken them could not destroy them, but it tore them apart and carried them far away.

When the water had dispersed and they both touched dry land again, they regained their human form, but neither knew where the other was; they found themselves among strange people, who did not know their native land.

High mountains and deep valleys lay between them. In order to keep themselves alive, they were both obliged to tend sheep. For many long years they drove their flocks through field and forest and were full of sorrow and longing. When spring had once more broken forth on the earth, they both went out one day with their flocks, and as chance would have it, they drew near each other. They met in a valley, but did not recognize each other; yet they rejoiced that they were no longer so lonely.

Henceforth they each day drove their flocks to the same place; they did not speak much, but they felt comforted. One evening when the full moon was shining in the sky, and the sheep were already at rest, the shepherd pulled the flute out of his pocket, and played on it a beautiful but sorrowful air. When he had finished he saw that the shepherdess was weeping bitterly. "Why art thou weeping?" he asked. "Alas," answered she, "thus shone the full moon when I played this air on the flute for the last time, and the head of my beloved rose out of the water." He looked at her, and it seemed as if a veil fell from his eyes, and he recognized his dear wife, and when she looked at him, and the moon shone in his face she knew him also. They embraced and kissed each other, and no one need ask if they were happy.

The Hut In The Forest

A POOR wood-cutter lived with his wife and three daughters in a little hut on the edge of a lonely forest. One morning as he was about to go to his work, he said to his wife, "Let my dinner be brought into the forest to me by my eldest daughter, or I shall never get my work done, and in order that she may not miss her way," he added, "I will take a bag of millet with me and strew the seeds on the path." When, therefore, the sun was just above the center of the forest, the girl set out on her way with a bowl of soup, but the field-sparrows, and wood-sparrows, larks and finches, blackbirds and siskins had picked up the millet long before, and the girl could not find the track. Then trusting to chance, she went on and on, until the sun sank and night began to fall. The trees rustled in the darkness, the owls hooted, and she began to be afraid. Then in the distance she perceived a light which glimmered between the trees. "There ought to be some people living there, who can take me in for the night," thought she, and went up to the light. It was not long before she came to a house the windows of which were all lighted up. She knocked, and a rough voice from inside cried, "Come in." The girl stepped into the dark entrance, and knocked at the door of the room. "Just come in," cried the voice, and when she opened the door, an old gray-haired man was sitting at the table, supporting his face with both hands, and his white beard fell down over the table almost as far as the ground. By the stove lay three animals, a hen, a cock, and a brindled cow. The girl told her story to the old man, and begged for shelter for the night. The man said,

"Pretty little hen,
Pretty little cock,
And pretty brindled cow,
What say ye to that?"

"Duks," answered the animals, and that must have meant, "We are willing," for the old man said, "Here you shall have shelter and food, go to the fire, and cook us our supper." The girl found in the kitchen abundance of everything, and cooked a good supper, but had no thought of the animals. She carried the full dishes to the table, seated herself by the gray-haired man, ate and satisfied her hunger. When she had had enough, she said, "But now I am tired, where is there a bed in which I can lie down, and sleep?" The animals replied,

"Thou hast eaten with him,
Thou hast drunk with him,
Thou hast had no thought for us,
So find out for thyself where thou canst pass the night."

Then said the old man, "Just go upstairs, and thou wilt find a room with two beds, shake them up, and put white linen on them, and then I, too, will come and lie down to sleep." The girl went up, and when she had shaken the beds and put clean sheets on, she lay down in one of them without waiting any longer for the old man. After some time, however, the gray-haired man came, took his candle, looked at the girl and shook his head. When he saw that she had fallen into a sound sleep, he opened a trap-door, and let her down into the cellar.

Late at night the wood-cutter came home, and reproached his wife for leaving him to hunger all day. "It is not my fault," she replied, "the girl went out with your dinner, and must have lost herself, but she is sure to come back to-morrow." The wood-cutter, however, arose before dawn to go into the forest, and requested that the second daughter should take him his dinner that day. "I will take a bag with lentils," said he; "the seeds are larger than millet, the girl will see them better, and can't lose her way." At dinner-time, therefore, the girl took out the food, but the lentils had disappeared. The birds of the forest had picked them up as they had done the day before, and had left none. The girl wandered about in the forest until night, and then she too reached the house of the old man, was told to go in, and begged for food and a bed. The man with the white beard again asked the animals,

"Pretty little hen,
Pretty little cock,
And pretty brindled cow,
What say ye to that?"

The animals again replied "Duks," and everything happened just as it had happened the day before. The girl cooked a good meal, ate and drank with the old man, and did not concern herself about the animals, and when she inquired about her bed they answered,

"Thou hast eaten with him, Thou hast drunk with him,
Thou hast had no thought for us,
To find out for thyself where thou canst pass the night."

When she was asleep the old man came, looked at her, shook his head, and let her down into the cellar.

On the third morning the wood-cutter said to his wife, "Send our youngest child out with my dinner to-day, she has always been good and obedient, and will stay in the right path, and not run about after every wild humble-bee, as her sisters did." The mother did not want to do it, and said, "Am I to lose my dearest child, as well?"

"Have no fear,' he replied, "the girl will not go astray; she is too prudent and sensible; besides I will take some peas with me, and strew them about. They are still larger than lentils, and will show her the way." But when the girl went out with her basket on her arm, the wood-pigeons had already got all the peas in their crops, and she did not know which way she was to turn. She was full of sorrow and never ceased to think how hungry her father would be, and how her good mother would grieve, if she did not go home. At length when it grew dark, she saw the light and came to the house in the forest. She begged quite prettily to be allowed to spend the night there, and the man with the white beard once more asked his animals,

"Pretty little hen,
Pretty little cock,
And beautiful brindled cow,
What say ye to that?"

"Duks," said they. Then the girl went to the stove where the animals were lying, and petted the cock and hen, and stroked their smooth feathers with her hand, and caressed the brindled cow between her horns, and when, in obedience to the old man's orders, she had made ready some good soup, and the bowl was placed upon the table, she said, "Am I to eat as much as I want, and the good animals to have nothing? Outside is food in plenty, I will look after them first." So she went and brought some barley and stewed it for the cock and hen, and a whole armful of sweet- smelling hay for the cow. "I hope you will like it, dear animals," said she, "and you shall have a refreshing draught in case you are thirsty." Then she fetched in a bucketful of water, and the cock and hen jumped on to the edge of it and dipped their beaks in, and then held up their heads as the birds do when they drink, and the brindled cow also took a hearty draught. When the animals were fed, the girl seated herself at the table by the old man, and ate what he had left. It was not long before the cock and the hen began to thrust their heads beneath their wings, and the eyes of the cow likewise began to blink. Then said the girl, "Ought we not to go to bed?"

"Pretty little hen,
Pretty little cock,
And pretty brindled cow,
What say ye to that?"

The animals answered "Duks,"

"Thou hast eaten with us,
Thou hast drunk with us,
Thou hast had kind thought for all of us,
We wish thee good-night."

Then the maiden went upstairs, shook the feather-beds, and laid clean sheets on them, and when she had done it the old man came and lay down on one of the beds, and his white beard reached down to his feet. The girl lay down on the other, said her prayers, and fell asleep.

She slept quietly till midnight, and then there was such a noise in the house that she awoke. There was a sound of cracking and splitting in every corner, and the doors sprang open, and beat against the walls. The beams groaned as if they were being torn out of their joints, it seemed as if the staircase were falling down, and at length there was a crash as if the entire roof had fallen in. As, however, all grew quiet once more, and the girl was not hurt, she stayed quietly lying where she was, and fell asleep again. But when she woke up in the morning with the brilliancy of the sunshine, what did her eyes behold? She was lying in a vast hall, and everything around her shone with royal splendor; on the walls, golden flowers grew up on a ground of green silk, the bed was of ivory, and the canopy of red velvet, and on a chair close by, was a pair of shoes embroidered with pearls. The girl believed that she was in a dream, but three richly clad attendants came in, and asked what orders she would like to give? "If you will go," she replied, "I will get up at once and make ready some soup for the old man, and then I will feed the pretty little hen, and the cock, and the beautiful brindled cow." She thought the old man was up already, and looked round at his bed; he, however, was not lying in it, but a stranger. And while she was looking at him, and becoming aware that he was young and handsome, he awoke, sat up in bed, and said, "I am a King's son, and was bewitched by a wicked witch, and made to live in this forest, as an old gray-haired man; no one was allowed to be with me but my three attendants in the form of a cock, a hen, and a brindled cow. The spell was not to be broken until a girl came to us whose heart was so good that she showed herself full of love, not only towards mankind, but towards animals - and that thou hast done, and by thee at midnight we were set free, and the old hut in the forest was changed back again into my royal palace." And when they had arisen, the King's son ordered the three attendants to set out and fetch the father and mother of the girl to the marriage feast. "But where are my two sisters?" inquired the maiden. "I have locked them in the cellar, and to-morrow they shall be led into the forest, and shall live as servants to a charcoal-burner, until they have grown kinder, and do not leave poor animals to suffer hunger."

Maid Maleen

THERE was once a King who had a son who asked in marriage the daughter of a mighty King; she was called Maid Maleen, and was very beautiful. As her father wished to give her to another, the prince was rejected; but as they both loved each other with all their hearts, they would not give each other up, and Maid Maleen said to her father, "I can and will take no other for my husband." Then the King flew into a passion, and ordered a dark tower to be built, into which no ray of sunlight or moonlight should enter. When it was finished, he said, "Therein shalt thou be imprisoned for seven years, and then I will come and see if thy perverse spirit is broken." Meat and drink for the seven years were carried into the tower, and then she and her waiting-woman were led into it and walled up, and thus cut off from the sky and from the earth. There they sat in the darkness, and knew not when day or night began. The King's son often went round and round the tower, and called their names, but no sound from without pierced through the thick walls. What else could they do but lament and complain? Meanwhile the time passed, and by the diminution of the food and drink they knew that the seven years were coming to an end. They thought the moment of their deliverance was come; but no stroke of the hammer was heard, no stone fell out of the wall, and it seemed to Maid Maleen that her father had forgotten her. As they only had food for a short time longer, and saw a miserable death awaiting them, Maid Maleen said, "We must try our last chance, and see if we can break through the wall." She took the bread-knife, and picked and bored at the mortar of a stone, and when she was tired, the waiting-maid took her turn. With great labour they succeeded in getting out one stone, and then a second, and a third, and when three days were over the first ray of light fell on their darkness, and at last the opening was so large that they could look out. The sky was blue, and a fresh breeze played on their faces; but how melancholy everything looked all around! Her father's castle lay in ruins, the town and the villages were, so far as could be seen, destroyed by fire, the fields far and wide laid to waste, and no human being was visible. When the opening in the wall was large enough for them to slip through, the waiting-maid sprang down first, and then Maid Maleen followed. But where were they to go? The enemy had ravaged the whole kingdom, driven away the King, and slain all the inhabitants. They wandered forth to seek another country, but nowhere did they find a shelter, or a human being to give them a mouthful of bread, and their need was so great that they were forced to appease their hunger with nettles. When, after long journeying, they came into another country, they tried to get work everywhere; but wherever they knocked they were turned away, and no one would have pity on them. At last they arrived in a large city and went to the royal palace. There also they were ordered to go away, but at last the cook said that they might stay in the kitchen and be scullions.

The son of the King in whose kingdom they were, was, however, the very man who had been betrothed to Maid Maleen. His father had chosen another bride for him, whose face was as ugly as her heart was wicked. The wedding was fixed, and the maiden had already arrived; but because of her great ugliness, however, she shut herself in her room, and allowed no one to see her, and Maid Maleen had to take her her meals from the kitchen. When the day came for the bride and the bridegroom to go to church, she was ashamed of her ugliness, and afraid that if she showed herself in the streets, she would be mocked and laughed at by the people. Then said she to Maid Maleen, "A great piece of luck has befallen thee. I have sprained my foot, and cannot well walk through the streets; thou shalt put on my wedding-clothes and take my place; a greater honour than that thou canst not have!" Maid Maleen, however, refused it, and said, "I wish for no honour which is not suitable for me." It was in vain, too, that the bride offered her gold. At last she said angrily, "If thou dost not obey me, it shall cost thee thy life. I have but to speak the word, and thy head will lie at thy feet." Then she was forced to obey, and put on the bride's magnificent clothes and all her jewels. When she entered the royal hall, every one was amazed at her great beauty, and the King said to his son, "This is the bride whom I have chosen for thee, and whom thou must lead to church." The bridegroom was astonished, and thought, "She is like my Maid Maleen, and I should believe that it was she herself, but she has long been shut up in the tower, or dead."

He took her by the hand and led her to church. On the way was a nettle-plant, and she said,

"Oh, nettle-plant,
Little nettle-plant,
What dost thou here alone?
I have known the time
When I ate thee unboiled,
When I ate thee unroasted."

"What art thou saying?" asked the King's son. "Nothing," she replied, "I was only thinking of Maid Maleen." He was surprised that she knew about her, but kept silence. When they came to the foot-plank into the churchyard, she said,

"Foot-bridge, do not break,
I am not the true bride."

"What art thou saying there?" asked the King's son. "Nothing," she replied, "I was only thinking of Maid Maleen." "Dost thou know Maid Maleen?" "No," she answered, "how should I know her; I have only heard of her." When they came to the church-door, she said once more,

"Church-door, break not,
I am not the true bride."

"What art thou saying there?" asked he. "Ah," she answered, "I was only thinking of Maid Maleen." Then he took out a precious chain, put it round her neck, and fastened the clasp. Thereupon they entered the church, and the priest joined their hands together before the altar, and married them. He led her home, but she did not speak a single word the whole way. When they got back to the royal palace, she hurried into the bride's chamber, put off the magnificent clothes and the jewels, dressed herself in her gray gown, and kept nothing but the jewel on her neck, which she had received from the bridegroom.

When the night came, and the bride was to be led into the prince's apartment, she let her veil fall over her face, that he might not observe the deception. As soon as every one had gone away, he said to her, "What didst thou say to the nettle-plant which was growing by the wayside?"

"To which nettle-plant?" asked she; "I don't talk to nettle-plants." "If thou didst not do it, then thou art not the true bride," said he. So she bethought herself, and said,

"I must go out unto my maid,
Who keeps my thoughts for me."

She went out and sought Maid Maleen. "Girl, what hast thou been saying to the nettle?" "I said nothing but,

"Oh, nettle-plant,
Little nettle-plant,
What dost thou here alone?
I have known the time
When I ate thee unboiled,
When I ate thee unroasted."

The bride ran back into the chamber, and said, "I know now what I said to the nettle," and she repeated the words which she had just heard. "But what didst thou say to the foot-bridge when we went over it?" asked the King's son. "To the foot-bridge?" she answered. "I don't talk to foot-bridges." "Then thou art not the true bride."

She again said,

"I must go out unto my maid,
Who keeps my thoughts for me,"

And ran out and found Maid Maleen, "Girl, what didst thou say to the foot-bridge?"

"I said nothing but,

"Foot-bridge, do not break,
I am not the true bride."

"That costs thee thy life!" cried the bride, but she hurried into the room, and said, "I know now what I said to the foot-bridge," and she repeated the words. "But what didst thou say to the church-door?" "To the church-door?" she replied; "I don't talk to church-doors." "Then thou art not the true bride."

She went out and found Maid Maleen, and said, "Girl, what didst thou say to the church-door?"

"I said nothing but,

"Church-door, break not,
I am not the true bride."

"That will break thy neck for thee!" cried the bride, and flew into a terrible passion, but she hastened back into the room, and said, "I know now what I said to the church-door," and she repeated the words. "But where hast thou the jewel which I gave thee at the church-door?" "What jewel?" she answered; "thou didst not give me any jewel." "I myself put it round thy neck, and I myself fastened it; if thou dost not know that, thou art not the true bride." He drew the veil from her face, and when he saw her immeasurable ugliness, he sprang back terrified, and said, "How comest thou here? Who art thou?" "I am thy betrothed bride, but because I feared lest the people should mock me when they saw me out of doors, I commanded the scullery-maid to dress herself in my clothes, and to go to church instead of me." "Where is the girl?" said he; "I want to see her, go and bring her here." She went out and told the servants that the scullery-maid was an impostor, and that they must take her out into the court-yard and strike off her head. The servants laid hold of Maid Maleen and wanted to drag her out, but she screamed so loudly for help, that the King's son heard her voice, hurried out of his chamber and ordered them to set the maiden free instantly. Lights were brought, and then he saw on her neck the gold chain which he had given her at the church-door. "Thou art the true bride, said he, "who went with me to the church; come with me now to my room." When they were both alone, he said, "On the way to church thou didst name Maid Maleen, who was my betrothed bride; if I could believe it possible, I should think she was standing before me thou art like her in every respect." She answered, "I am Maid Maleen, who for thy sake was imprisoned seven years in the darkness, who suffered hunger and thirst, and has lived so long in want and poverty. To-day, however, the sun is shining on me once more. I was married to thee in the church, and I am thy lawful wife." Then they kissed each other, and were happy all the days of their lives. The false bride was rewarded for what she had done by having her head cut off.

The tower in which Maid Maleen had been imprisoned remained standing for a long time, and when the children passed by it they sang,

"Kling, klang, gloria.
Who sits within this tower?
A King's daughter, she sits within,
A sight of her I cannot win,
The wall it will not break,
The stone cannot be pierced.

Little Hans, with your coat so gay,
Follow me, follow me, fast as you may."

THE END

www.ingramcontent.com/pod-product-compliance
Lightning Source LLC
Chambersburg PA
CBHW072026020726
47501CB00006B/1972
9781950326280